PRAISE FOR JAMES A MOORE

"James A Moore is the new prince of grimdark fantasy. His work is full of dark philosophy and savage violence, desperate warriors and capricious gods. This is fantasy for people who like to wander nighttime forests and scream at the moon. Exhilarating as hell."

– *Christopher Golden, New York times bestselling author of* Snowblind

"Fast-paced fantasy that you simply can't put down. Great action adventure."

– Morpheus Tales

"Gripping, horrific, and unique, James Moore continues to be a winner, whatever genre he's writing in. Well worth your time."

– *Seanan McGuire, New York Times bestselling author of the* InCryptid *and* Toby Daye *series*

"Moore has laid the groundwork for a trilogy that promises to be loaded with terrifically grim fantasy storytelling. I might even call it epic. There is a lot of swift, merciless violence in this book, mingled with an undercurrent of very welcome, if very dark, humor. All of it together takes me back to what made me giddy about epic fantasy way back when. I'd say I'm happy to be back, but I'm not sure that's quite the right word for a book packed with this much violent incident. Let's say instead that I'm bloody satisfied."

– *Rich Rosell for the* B&N Sci-Fi & F

BY THE SAME AUTHOR

The Tides of War series
The Last Sacrifice • Fallen Gods • Gates of the Dead

The Seven Forges series
Seven Forges • The Blasted Lands
City of Wonders • The Silent Army
The Godless

The Blood Red series
Blood Red • Blood Harvest • Blood of the Damned

The Chris Corin Chronicles
Possessions • Rabid Growth • Newbies

The Serenity Falls Trilogy
Writ in Blood • The Pack • Dark Carnival

The Griffin & Price series (with Charles R Rutledge)
Blind Shadows • Congregations of the Dead • A Hell Within

Alien: Sea of Sorrows
The Predator: Hunters & Hunted
The Haunted Forest Tour *(with Jeff Strand)*
Bloodstained Oz *(with Christopher Golden)*
Buffy the Vampire Slayer: Chaos Bleeds
Cherry Hill
Deeper
Fireworks
Harvest Moon
Homestead
Under the Overtree
Vampire: House of Secrets *(with Kevin Andrew Murphy)*
Vendetta
Werewolf: Hellstorm
The Wild Hunt
Slices *(stories)*
This is Halloween *(stories)*

James A Moore

THE WAR BORN

Seven Forges, Book VI

ANGRY ROBOT
An imprint of Watkins Media Ltd

Unit 11, Shepperton House
89-93 Shepperton Road
London N1 3DF
UK

angryrobotbooks.com
twitter.com/angryrobotbooks
The End of An Era

An Angry Robot paperback original, 2023

Cover by Alejandro Colluci and Sneha Alexander
Edited by Paul Simpson and Robin Triggs
Set in Meridien

ISBN 978 1 91520 261 1
Ebook ISBN 978 1 91520 276 5

Printed and bound in the United Kingdom by TJ Books Limited

9 8 7 6 5 4 3 2 1

For Tessa, who completes me, and to all the nice folks who've made it through these books, thank you very kindly!

CHAPTER ONE

The mountain loomed above them all, a freshly grown tower of unearthed stone that bled smoke and molten rock from its top. Nearly a hundred soldiers did their best to recover from watching the volcano birthed on the steppes, most so stunned by the unexpected appearance of several thousand feet of jagged outcroppings and peaks that they could barely manage the luxury of thinking coherently.

Merros Dulver considered himself a good man and a decent leader. He was in charge of the armies of the Fellein Empire because Nachia Krous, the Empress, and Desh Krohan, her First Advisor, agreed with that assessment. That fact did not change how he felt as he looked up at the black rock or the fiery halo it sported near the very highest points.

He had seen other mountains force themselves from the land in the past, but never so close.

The skies above were as black as the freshly risen stone, save where flames licked at the underbellies of the newly formed clouds. Not far away, Darsken Murdro of the Inquisition was also recovering from the unexpected birth.

From above came the sound of horns blowing. Merros knew the type. Somehow the new mountain had come complete with enough soldiers to need horns to call the troops to arms.

"This day is one I'll remember, I expect." He was speaking to himself, but the Inquisitor laughed just the same, shaking his head and looking at Merros as if he'd just made the funniest possible jest.

Maybe he had. You simply had to appreciate it in the moment.

From far above them the horns echoed, and the heavy tread of infantrymen made itself known even over the rumble of the nascent volcano.

Which god was this, Merros wondered? Which of the Seven Forges had moved itself to a new location? He had seen all of the mountains over time, had seen them first where they were originally located and then where they had moved themselves when the gods willed it, but this vast stone structure did not look at all familiar.

The sound of the rumbling from the mountain changed and Merros closed his eyes, listening as carefully as he could. Spend enough time in an army and certain noises become familiar. The tread of a thousand soldiers sounds different than the marching of a thousand horses, for example. What he was hearing was definitely not infantry.

"We have cavalry above us," he muttered. "How in the name of all the gods is that possible?"

"Not gods, Merros Dulver." The voice was that of the sorcerer that had been sent with him as a messenger of the empire. Try though he might, he still could not remember her name. Desh Krohan had insisted that one of his wizards accompany them on their quest, the better to offer quick reports to the First Advisor and the Empress. The woman speaking to him was heavyset and older than him, with gray hair shot with streaks of brown. She had wisely stayed out of his way for most of the trip but availed herself to him when he needed to communicate. Now she spoke plainly, but with a different voice. She was passing on a message from Desh Krohan.

"This is the work of the Wellish Overlords. I can sense them. They have awakened, as I feared they would."

"Well, can you put them back to sleep?"

The woman shook her head. "No. You need to rally your troops and get away from there before it is too late."

"It's already too late! I have soldiers coming down the mountainside. I can't see them yet, but I can hear them!"

Next to him Darsken nodded and moved closer, looking up at the mountain, frowning as he tried to spot any sign of the horses and men they could already hear. The horns sounded again, a long solemn note that promised pain in the near future.

The horses showed themselves as if coming from a hidden passage – and perhaps they were. Sorcery was upon them, and Merros knew from experience that where magic was concerned, almost anything was possible.

They did not charge down the mountain. They could not, there were no clearly discernable passages or pathways. The riders were at the mercy of their mounts, who were in turn at the mercy of the terrain. They might have longed for easy combat but that was not what they received. Instead the horses moved carefully, placing hooves where they could in order to avoid sliding down the slope and falling to their deaths.

Merros gestured to one of the foot soldiers standing nearby. "Sound the alarm! Call the troops to order." The man stared at him gape-mouthed for a moment and then remembered the horn he was carrying. A moment later, despite the dazed expression on his face, he managed to blow into the horn and a clear note rang out. The reaction was exactly what Merros would have hoped for on any occasion. Soldiers who, like him, had been staring at the mountain, shook off their shock and prepared to meet their enemy or retreat as Merros decided.

From above, the cavalry continued to descend and, yes, now he heard foot soldiers moving behind them. Though the angle made them nearly impossible to see, he expected a very large number of them. One of his reasons for coming to the Wellish Steppes had been to solve the mystery of where so many mercenaries might have gone. He'd followed the latest trails of freelance soldiers into the area and remained baffled when they disappeared ahead of him. He understood now where all of the mercenaries had been hiding. Alright, not how they had hidden on a mountain that had only just showed up, but that was the nature of sorcery, and it continued to annoy him constantly.

"They will reach us soon." Darsken was staring at the slowly descending soldiers. "Do you have archers?"

"I have no proof that they mean to attack."

"They are sounding war horns, are they not?"

"Good point."

Merros walked over to where the troops were gathering as best they could under the circumstances. Most of his men had been on horses. Those horses had decided to vacate the area as soon as the mountain started forcing itself from the ground. Getting them back was not likely to happen any time soon.

"Who has spears? Who has bows? If you've got ranged weapons, form on my left!" Not nearly as many as he would have liked were answering favorably. As most of his equipment had left with his horse, he understood why.

The horns above him blew again, and before he could call on his men to sound off, another, different horn responded.

They came out of the Blasted Lands, or what he assumed were the Blasted Lands. In the past the endless storms of the Blasted Lands had separated the Sa'ba Taalor, the grey-skinned warriors who followed the gods of the Seven Forges, from Fellein. There were mystical properties to those storms, as Merros knew after spending half a year moving through them, but they had gone away when the war with the people of the forges had ended.

They had come back not long ago, storms that did not move but instead surrounded each of the seven volcanoes and locked them away from easy sight. From where he stood, the mountain hid away the closest of the storms, but he knew it existed because Desh Krohan's wizards had found out about them and reported on their reappearance.

Yet more sorcery. Yet more madness. He clenched his jaw unconsciously at the very notion.

The Sa'ba Taalor came from the direction of the storms, and they came in great numbers. Merros felt his stomach twist at the very notion of their arrival. The last time he'd seen large numbers of the gray skins they'd been in the process of killing his soldiers.

Even from a distance he recognized the leader of the group. The man at the head of the charge was Tarag Paedori, the King in Iron, the very same man who had led the assault on Fellein five years earlier. But for the interference of another of his people, Drask Silver Hand, he would likely have ruled all Fellein.

There looked to be several hundred of his people following him.

The man did not even seem to notice Merros. Instead, he rode toward the newly formed mountain, and looked up toward the pinnacle.

Merros decided to be seen. If there was going to be war between their people again, he wanted to know about it before the battle started.

Even as he walked toward the King in Iron, another of the rulers of the Sa'ba Taalor made himself known.

Tarag Paedori was a massive man. He was taller than Merros, broader than Merros, and almost the largest man Merros had ever seen.

He was second to only Tuskandru, the King in Obsidian. It was Tusk who charged in now with another army of his followers, and this time he brought people on horseback with him.

Merros managed to not look panicked. He stared first at Paedori and then at Tuskandru, drinking in the details of the men as they moved closer to each other and looked up the mountain.

Rather than try explaining, Merros moved closer to the two kings, fully aware that they were almost as likely to war with each other as they were to war with him. They were followers of different war gods. Even when they fought against a common enemy, they shared a history of conflicts that ran back decades at the very least.

"Merros Dulver!" came a bellow. Tuskandru looked his way with a broad, eager smile on his scarred face. The man rode toward him on the predatory mount that carried him into almost every combat situation, and reached down to give him a familiar thump on his shoulder. Merros managed not to fall over, but he had a moment of doubt about his ability to keep his feet. "It has been far too long."

"Yes, well, the last time we saw each other we were at war. Tends to make socializing a bit more challenging." He resisted the urge to rub at the sore spot on his shoulder.

"You are still a funny man." Tusk looked up the side of the mountain. "These are your soldiers approaching?"

"No, not in the least."

"Then who do they follow?"

"They're mercenaries. I came here to find out who they follow."

"I think they are enemies of the Sa'ba Taalor. They sound war horns."

"To be fair, they may not even know you're here." Merros looked up the side of the mountain himself, uncertain as to how many soldiers were up there and heading down.

"Where is your horse?" asked Tusk.

"Didn't seem to like the mountain growing from the ground. The nag bucked me."

Tusk laughed and swatted his shoulder again. "So, you ride with me. This time we fight on the same side!" Before Merros could comment, the man was grabbing his arm and lifting him into the air. Merros resisted the urge to fight, realizing that Tusk was making a friendly gesture. A moment later he was seated in front of Tusk on the broad back of the mount.

Before he could truly settle himself – or protest for that matter – Tusk urged the great beast forward and Merros was forced to grab onto the thick mane of the creature to keep his seat.

The ride was nothing at all like being on a horse. Tusk pressed up against him from behind and the muscular mount surged under him, leaping and charging up the mountain's steep slope even as others of the gray skins began their ascent. Tarag Paedori rode next to them, his face hidden behind a scowling visage made of iron. All around them the Sa'ba Taalor moved in a wave toward the descending mercenaries.

Horns sounded from both sides and before the notes had finished rolling across the sheer face of the mountain the two groups gathered in bloody combat.

The mercenaries were unorganized, and if anyone was leading the attack, they were doing a poor job of it. The Sa'ba Taalor on the other hand were synchronized despite their chaotic appearance. Spears dropped into place and lancers charged forward, striking the descending warriors, impaling some and unseating others. The mounts were predators, and the horses were their prey. Great claws lashed out, rending flesh, tearing riders from their saddles, even as the horses began to panic.

In seconds the full brunt of the descending mercenaries hit the Sa'ba Taalor. Their horses may have been spooked but there was nowhere for them to go but down toward the mounts, and the creatures reared back, attacking savagely. Merros would have been thrown for certain, but Tusk held onto him and kept him from falling, laughing as the great beast he rode lunged forward and tore the throat from the closest equine.

A moment later Tusk was dropping from his mount and not so gently pulling Merros after him. It was for the best, as Tusk's mount attacked the next horse and rider, pulling both down savagely and ripping into them with claws and teeth.

By the time Merros had regained his balance, the fighting had become a proper battlefield. Soldiers fought desperately as they collided with the Sa'ba Taalor. Merros had enough time to draw his sword before the first of his enemies descended, letting out a hoarse battle cry and swinging a mace at the general.

Merros' heart raced and he let out a cry of his own, dancing back from the attempt to bash in his skull and hacking halfway through his attacker's arm with his blade. The man was screaming and bleeding yet still he tried to hit Merros. His mace fell from his wounded arm and the screamer looked almost comically surprised when the weapon hit the ground instead of the general.

Merros feinted with his sword and then drove his dagger into the side of the bastard's neck. Beside him Tusk very nearly split a man in half with a weapon that seemed more axe than sword, despite the long blade. He drove his shoulder into another mercenary and sent the man staggering backward, directly into the great sword of Tarag Paedori.

Realizing their peril, the mercenaries tried to break away, some of them running down the side of the mountain, others trying to go back the way they'd come, but it wasn't meant to be. The infantry behind the mounted riders were too thick for them to get past, and the ones descending the mountain found still more of the gray skins waiting for them. There were easily a thousand or more mercenaries, but they were heavily outnumbered by the Sa'ba Taalor, and the mounts added another two hundred killers to their list of obstacles.

Merros fought hard, cutting, striking, forcing back the blades that tried to cut him. Twice weapons slid past his defenses, but the heavy cloak he wore was enough to stop one and took the worst of the damage from the other.

Lucky. He was very lucky.

The mercenaries did not have his luck. The Sa'ba Taalor

were relentless, and their mounts were worse. Long before the fighting was done, several of the paid fighters tried to surrender, but Merros could have told them that would not work in their favor. He had spent time with Tusk, had learned some of the man's traditions, including that he followed a god known as the Wounder, because he was unforgiving. Once engaged in combat, no quarter was ever given.

The end result was bloody and, though a few of the enemy survived, most were slaughtered. Really, it was hardly a surprise. Merros stared at the dead and dying and found little to bother him.

He had spent months training with Andover Lashk, and the man had been trained by the very gods of the Sa'ba Taalor themselves. He knew the chances of surviving a fight with the people of the forges weren't good. That he had survived was something he considered proof of kind gods.

Asher

The Tolfah were not kind, and they were not human. They could easily be confused for human from a distance, and according to some they had been human once upon a time, but those days were long gone. If the legends were true, the Overlords changed all of that when they fought to capture Fellein in the distant past.

In Morwhen the Tolfah lived among the lower valleys, where plague winds often blew and carried with them the stench of death and disaster.

Morwhen was a part of Fellein but, according to most of the people who traveled through the area, just barely. The civilized world was more of an afterthought in Morwhen, where the roads were treacherous, the towns were well-guarded by walls and watchmen, and where the local nobles were more likely to bar the gates than welcome travelers with open arms. It had always been that way, but in the last five years the area had become, if anything, less welcoming.

Morwhen was unkind, and unforgiving of weakness. Only the strong thrived in the area, and it had always been that way, as far back as anyone could remember. There were more than a few sayings about the area, but one of the most complimentary was simply this: the best swords in the empire come from Morwhen.

Morwhen, where the clouds from Paedle obscured the sky and hid the sun away on most days, leaving nights that came early, and rains that fell to earth as mud more often than not, tainted by volcanic ash and bitter to the taste. The volcano had changed everything – though, to be fair, not as much as some people claimed. Before Paedle grew from the ground, the skies were still dark, and the sun peered through only one day in ten. Some once again said the Overlords had left that mark on the land, but there was no proof of that claim.

If half of the stories were true, the Overlords were responsible for damned near every problem and the Sa'ba Taalor were responsible for the rest. The people of Fellein were innocent of all sins, and victims to be pitied.

Asher spit at the very notion. He had known plenty of people from Morwhen and Fellein, and most were far from innocent waifs.

It was true, though, that the Dark Passage had gotten worse after the gray skins and their damned mountain had grown over night. Morwhen had been a better place before the Sa'ba Taalor dropped a volcano in the area and claimed it as their own. True, they did little but stay on their mountain, Paedle, named after one of their war gods, but the people who had lived there before they rearranged the world could only say that their world had been made worse since the mountain showed up.

The skies were bloody and red from the active volcano's glowing heart, and the storms dropped their ashen rain, and the air was colder than it had been. All of that was true. The ashes, however, made crops grow stronger for reasons Asher did not understand, but was glad to take advantage of. As he was a man who raised his crops with an eye toward selling most of them, he was perfectly content to deal with better harvests.

Paedle was a live volcano, and it was active. The passages that had once been well lit and relatively safe were now buried under the clouds of volcanic ash flowing down the western side of the mountain with every breeze, and the roads were now called the Dark Passage, because the ash and clouds hid the sun away at the best of times and brought a perpetual twilight to the area.

And twilight brought with it the Tolfah. The attacks had been far more frequent in the last five years.

The riders along the Dark Passage knew to be careful. It was seldom less than a score of soldiers who accompanied the wagons that dared the roads from Morwhen through the Arkennen Mountains, and often as many as forty or fifty armed soldiers, depending on who rode the highway.

Asher was in charge of the caravan, and he paid his soldiers handsomely. He had to, as these days there were men actively looking for sellswords, and they promised good compensation for the men who were willing to fight, so long as no questions were asked. For that reason Asher had promised preposterous amounts to the men in his employ. It was a market where a man who wanted coin for his sword arm could make good money and they all knew it.

The challenge was deciding which was the safer form of employment, a trip through the Dark Passage or a journey across Fellein to the Wellish Steppes. The steppes were a long way off, but the money for making the journey was a handsome sum, and the promise of combat was a good one.

Somebody was building an army, and they meant business, from all that Asher had heard.

On the other hand, the Dark Passage paid well and was regular work. There was a risk in either job but at least the locals got to go home and see their family sooner than the ones traveling to Wellish and the promise of a war.

That part was inevitable. One did not pay so well for the possibility of war, and there were plenty who were smart enough to understand that.

One such was Daken Hardesty, a man who preferred to stay local. He had a wife and three children, and they were close by. Better to go home to them every fortnight or so than to travel half the continent and fight for someone who was untested. Mostly, Daken was convinced, the ones who were traveling were younger men who were looking to build a fortune. The promised coin was too good to ignore, and there were young men aplenty who felt they could do better as mercenaries than as soldiers for Fellein when the offer of work was sincere.

Asher cleared his throat and looked to the blond mercenary. The man had been a soldier for Fellein for a long time before leaving the army. He would have likely stayed on as a soldier, too, but the war against the gray-skins has changed the minds of a lot of career soldiers. One thing to fight for your life against an occasional brigand and another to fight the Sa'ba Taalor in a full-scale war. Too many long-timers had been slaughtered when the war took place, and those that fought and survived were no longer quite as enthusiastic when it came to being paid a soldier's wages.

Daken looked at him through eyes that were haunted by the past, but he managed a smile just the same. That was one of the things Asher liked about the mercenary. He at least kept a cheerful disposition regardless of the circumstances.

"So far we're doing well enough." Daken's voice was rough. He'd had his throat cut in the war, and though it hadn't killed him it had changed the way he spoke.

"Aye, but I've been told the Tolfah are active again." That was a lie, but Asher felt it in his bones. They were close by, and he wanted his men ready for fast, brutal combat.

"I've four men watching the road. If they show, we'll be ready for them."

They were brave words, but Daken was not as familiar with the Tolfah as he thought he was. He had never encountered the bestial men before and Asher had. The Sa'ba Taalor were deadly – and Asher would rather face the beast men than the gray-skins, it was true – but the Tolfah tended to run in larger numbers, and what they lacked in skill they made up for in savagery. That was why Asher paid as well as he did. He needed the warm bodies to keep his supplies safe.

The Dark Passage was the only way to get half of his goods to the markets. The farming season was done and the Pabba fruit was at least half of his fortune in any given year. They were hardy fruit, and they lasted well, but they were also a rarity. The orchards had given a bountiful harvest and he needed to sell what he had in Goltha and Canhoon. The markets there always paid handsomely for the fruit, but the challenge was getting them there, and that meant either risking taking ships along the coast, or reaching the rivers and riding on barges. The ships meant a risk of Sa'ba Taalor and pirates. The rivers were far safer – and faster too.

"Don't get cocky on me now, Daken," he warned. "I've seen the Tolfah when they were truly hungry, and it's not pretty."

Daken nodded and scowled. "I've heard the tales. The lads know to be ready."

Asher looked around the highway at the low stone walls, the heavy foliage and the skies that were already going bloody as the clouds rolled in. It was safe enough to ride through and the passage was mostly secure, but the Tolfah tended to wait for darkness to attack and Asher just knew the bastards were nearby.

He could practically smell them.

"The Tolfah are close," Asher spat. "I know how that sounds and I know I've said it before, but I trust my guts to tell me true and I think they're closer than they have been in a long time."

Daken looked around the area and nodded. "It's you I work for. I'm not paid to disagree; I'm paid to protect your shipment. I'll trust your guts before I'll trust mine."

That was one of the things he liked best about the man. He listened and followed orders. Daken waved over one of his men, a long, lean fellow with sharp features and a dour expression named Harris. He was also a terror in combat. There were stories of him fighting against the gray-skins and holding his own, and he'd encountered the Tolfah on four separate occasions and lived to tell the tale. Having him along made Asher feel better about the journey.

When Harris rode over, he and Daken spoke quickly then Harris rode away to where the main gathering of mercenaries was, ahead of the wagons. He called to the others, and they listened. Several of the mercenaries looked back toward Asher and nodded. It was enough. They were listening and that was all he could ask of them.

The skies were bloody, the underbellies of the clouds painted a dull red, and in the distance the volcano flared sullenly, offering its glare to the skies. The Sa'ba Taalor were out there, likely on their mountain and watching all that happened. They didn't often move from Paedle, but they were also a consideration. Though it happened rarely, there were tales of the warriors attacking the caravans that came through the area. Especially those that got too close to the mountain. The way was longer if one avoided Paedle. Asher always made sure to go the long way.

Sadly, that precaution did nothing to help with the Tolfah when, as Asher had expected, they came barging in.

They came in a wave, a horde of brutal creatures that gibbered and howled as they pushed between the trees and jumped over the low wall around the road. They were dressed in rags of fur and strips of leather wrapped around limbs and draped over faces in an effort to keep them safe from the meager sunlight. If the stories were true, the Tolfah feared the light of the sun, regardless of how weak it was.

Asher couldn't have said how many there were, but he had never seen such vast numbers before. Truth be told, he'd always expected there weren't that many of the creatures left. He was very, very wrong.

There were hundreds of the bestial subhumans, he realized. His eyes bulged as the Tolfah came over the wall, loping forward, barely standing upright at all, and waving clubs, crude axes, and war hammers in their gnarled fists.

They were brutal things. They had the rough shape of men but were thicker in their bodies, with muscular arms that seemed too long and thick legs that were too short, allowing them to run on all fours like animals. Their faces were broad, and their mouths were too wide and filled with pointed teeth, more like those of wild cats than people. They were hairy in odd patches, and bald in spots where he would have expected hair. They seemed diseased, nearly leprous, and starved.

Yes, starved. The first of the men they attacked screamed as he was pulled from his horse, and then howled in agony as several of the creatures tore pieces of him away to shove into their mouths.

Daken roared a command and took up the bow that was slung on the left side of his saddle. In seconds the warrior was firing arrows into the first wave of the Tolfah. He wasn't alone. More of the mercenaries took up their ranged weapons and did what they could to stop the invaders. Asher liked to think of himself as a competent fighter. The men with him disproved that belief.

They were vastly outnumbered, but they were skilled and desperate. Asher prayed that would be enough. The mercenaries circled around him and his wagons, and he found himself praying to the gods he had nearly forgotten about that they would be enough to keep him alive.

CHAPTER TWO

Jeron

Jeron looked down upon the road to Morwhen and slowly nodded. The savages were plentiful, and they were violent, just as the Overlords had said they'd be. He watched as they did their best to kill all of the defenders around the wagons, attacking with abandon.

Roledru, who stood beside him leaning on his spear, whistled softly between his teeth. "They're a vicious lot."

"No, my friend. They are desperate."

And they *were* desperate. He could see that in their every action. They were starving, they were fighting for their survival. He was hardy surprised. He'd been down below, in the area the Tolfah were now escaping. He'd felt the plague winds as they roared through the lower regions of the mountain passes. Not in reality, no, but in his mind when he was searching for the very creatures he was now looking at.

"So what are they?"

Jeron kept watching as four of the things attacked a man on horseback. One of them grabbed the horse by the head and tried to pull it down toward the ground. He failed and the horse kicked with both front hooves, very likely breaking several of the fool's bones. In any event at the very least it knocked the brute backward as it reared up. The rider fell, screaming, and was pulled away from the bucking animal before he could get trampled.

As the Tolfah savaged the rider, Jeron watched on and suspected the man would have preferred death at the animal's attack. It would have been more merciful. The beast men tore clothing and flesh away from their victim as they fought over who would get the best parts.

He and Roledru had come from the far west, and Jeron still felt the pull of the Overlords though he was on a quest for them. They were powerful beings, and he was drawn to them much like a moth was drawn to a lantern. Their power called and his body listened. It hadn't always been that way. The Overlords had changed him, were still changing him, the better to suit their needs. He should have been offended by the alteration of his body. He was no longer truly human anymore, but the transformation didn't bother him much at all. It was more of something he merely observed as if at a distance.

He saw Roledru wince as he watched another of the soldiers taken down by the Tolfah. Roledru was a good man at heart. Though he worked for Jeron and did things that were not good, he felt sorrow for his actions, and he felt empathy for the people he observed. Jeron had long since given up his empathy. He found it got in the way of progressing.

The perfect example of that was the use of necromancy. It was wrong, morally speaking, and Jeron knew that. But he didn't care. Over the long centuries he had lived, he had grown further and further from his ability to care for the people around him.

Of all the wizards alive in Fellein, he was one of the oldest and most powerful. Desh Krohan was arguably more skilled but these days he was at a distinct disadvantage. He still followed the laws that he had established, banning necromancy as a dark art.

Sorcery was potent stuff, yes, but it required power. There was, as Desh liked to say, a cost for every spell cast. Some of the more powerful spells demanded energies that needed to be stored over months or even years. There were ways around that, of course. Desh Krohan himself had showed Jeron how a raging fire could be extinguished to become the driving power behind certain spells. Of course, that required work and effort, and Jeron had recently been reminded that the best power, the most reliable source of external energies, came from living beings.

Necromancy wasn't outlawed merely because it dealt with the dead. It was outlawed because it *stole* from the dead. Why waste time building a bonfire when you could literally use the lifeforce of a dying person to fuel your greatest sorceries?

Desh Krohan would not allow himself to fuel his power that way.

Jeron had no such qualms.

It was simple math. Jeron was the more powerful because he would steal from living and dead alike to fuel his sorceries.

"Why are we here, Jeron?"

He looked over at Roledru. The man's hair was pulled back in a tight tail, and his face, which had been clean-shaven in the spring, was now covered in a thick, dark beard. He looked like a different man altogether, unless you studied his eyes.

"We are here to gather an army."

"What? Of those things?" Roledru shook his head. Jeron could understand why. They were violent. They were savage, lacked any cohesive leadership and barely knew how to hold the primitive weapons they'd managed to gather.

"They have slept for a very long time."

"Those things?"

"The Tolfah, Roledru. Those *things* are called the Tolfah. It's an old word that means War-Born. No. I mean the Overlords."

"Well, yes, we saw them wake up. There was a volcano and a lot of soldiers running away in a panic."

"They ran away, and we had a chance to get away from the area and hide." There had been more to it than that, but at the end of the event the mercenary army they'd been building left the area.

"True enough."

"The Tolfah are all that is left of one of the greatest armies the world has ever seen. Believe it or not, the ancestors of those creatures almost took over Fellein when it was a young empire."

Roledru stared down at the massed savages and watched as they killed and ate their prey. He did not speak, but his doubt was clear to see.

"You asked what we are doing here, and I will tell you." Jeron moved closer to his companion and then pointed down into the pass, into which the last of the mercenaries had been wise enough to retreat, holding back their enemy with steel and raw courage alone. Each time the Tolfah lunged forward, the three remaining soldiers attacked as a unit and drove them back. They also used those moments to retreat a little further.

"We are here to return the Tolfah to their previous glory."

Roledru looked sideways at him but said nothing.

"You doubt me."

"You are a powerful sorcerer, I'll grant that. I've seen you do incredible things, but you always tell me that magic has a price, and transformation is supposed to be powerful magic."

Jeron smiled and patted his companion on the shoulder. "Good to know you've been listening when I babble on about these things." He looked down at the Tolfah, who were starting to fight among themselves for the scraps.

"Yes. Transformation is one of the hardest sorceries to accomplish, otherwise we'd all be covered in gold and precious gems, and many a fool would have been turned into stone, or just possibly into something worse than the Tolfah."

"But what about the cost? How are you going to accomplish that sort of task?"

Jeron stared down into the valley and considered his words. There were mercenaries marching down a mountain and dying even as he spoke, and he knew that they were actually paying a part of the cost. Each life was more energy for the Overlords, who wasted nothing. "In this case, I am the instrument of the transformation and not the source. The Overlords will pay the price."

"After so many years sleeping?"

"They did so much more than sleep, Roledru."

"Like what?"

"They've rested their bodies and sent their minds out to explore the worlds beyond here." He couldn't keep the jealous tone from his words. "For a thousand years I have aged, and learned a few new tricks, my friend, but the Overlords spent that time learning secrets I may never have a chance to know." He sighed. "If I am fortunate, they may well teach me some of those secrets. That is for them to decide." The Overlords had taught him before, as they had once taught several of the sorcerers in the days long past. That was how necromancy had come to the world. The Overlords learned it first and taught others.

That was the secret he remembered now that Desh Krohan and others had likely forgotten. When the Overlords first showed themselves, they had come as instructors. It was later that they showed themselves as conquerors.

This time, however, he suspected they would not be so willing to share their secrets. But he could still hope.

Jeron looked down on the starving horde and considered what they would soon become.

"In the meantime, I am the vessel through which their powers will flow. And these wretches? They are the ore that must be refined and made into weapons."

"How?"

"How else, Roledru? With blood and fire."

Trigan Garth

Trigan Garth stood with the others at the edge of the Dark Passage. Each held a torch and at least one weapon. They were not here for the Tolfah. He had been warned about them and he had listened to the warning. He was not afraid of the creatures.

He looked down at his hand, which had been familiar to him all of his life and now looked like it belonged to someone else. A quick glance confirmed what he already knew: the same was true of the other Godless. The sorcerer, Jeron, had led all of them down into the darkness where the Overlords rested and, when they came back from that journey, they were changed.

His skin was darker. His eyes still gave off light of their own, but it was a pale yellow in color rather than the silvery glow that had been there for as long as he remembered. He no longer looked like a Sa'ba Taalor. The Overlords had changed him and the rest of the Godless in ways he did not fully understand as yet. In ways that offended his sensibilities. He had been changed without his permission, remade as something different, and he resented it.

He had turned his back on the Daxar Taalor when the gods of his people grew silent at the end of the war with Fellein. He had always known that he would eventually make his way back to the gods, but now that certainty was gone, stolen by whatever the Overlords had done to transform him and the rest of the Godless under their command.

"It is time, Trigan Garth." Jeron's voice spoke in his head, clear as if the wizard stood next to him and spoke in his ear, though he knew the man was miles away.

Without a word Trigan motioned the rest of the Godless forward and they moved together into the town where they'd been told to wait. They did not run or give any sign of hostility. They simply walked past the gate that would be locked when the sun set, and headed for the first houses.

The homes were well built and secure against the darkness. The people were more alert than he expected from the Fellein. By the time he and the rest had reached the first home, the people in the area where aware of them and preparing. Though no alarms sounded, still eyes watched them from all the homes.

The man who came from the first house walked outside carrying a spear in his hand and sporting an axe on his hip.

"We want no trouble." The stranger was tall and older, not a youth. He was seasoned and though he looked at the Godless with a wary eye, he did not seem afraid. When he spoke again, he was just as direct. "Why are you here?"

"The sorcerer Jeron has called us here." Trigan replied just as directly. He was not the sort to lie. When he spoke, it was always with an ear toward the truth.

The man's eyes squinted a bit as he considered the words. "I know no sorcerers."

"Nor does he know you."

"Then why has he sent you here?"

"He needs a sacrifice to his new masters, the Wellish Overlords."

"Leave here, before we are forced to kill you." The words were just as direct as Trigan expected. Just in case the spoken word was not enough of a hint, the man lifted his spear into both hands in a defensive posture. "You will not be given a second warning."

"Nor would I expect one."

From the next house over two men and a woman came forward. All of them carried weapons at the ready.

Trigan waved one hand and the Godless who stood with him raised their weapons., their torches long abandoned. He carried a dagger and a large axe of his own. The axe settled into his right hand as he considered the spear.

"As I said, Jeron demands a sacrifice. You will be the first offering." Without another word he stepped in close to the man with the spear, too close to allow the stranger a chance to easily wield his weapon. The man stepped back hastily and tried to correct that problem, but Trigan was faster and swept his axe in close enough to carve a chunk of flesh from his opponent's shoulder.

The spear fell from a hand that no longer wanted to work properly, and Trigan rammed his weight into the man, knocking him backward. Before he could recover his balance, Trigan brought the axe up and then down on his enemy's head. His skull split like a ripe melon.

By the time the man had fallen lifeless to the ground the Godless were in motion, breaking away from the group and attacking the locals with a savagery that showed how little they had changed. They looked different, true, but they were still Sa'ba Taalor, still killers.

The locals were as prepared as they could be, but they were not prepared enough. The Sa'ba Taalor were raised by the gods of war to become warriors. Whether or not they followed those gods, the lessons they learned remained. The Godless were merciless. Fifteen members of the Sa'ba Taalor race attacked the closest houses and the inhabitants of those homes, with brutal efficiency. The two men and the woman who had been waiting for them died quickly, though they managed to cause a bit of mayhem before they died. One of the men managed to put two arrows into Melax's side before he was killed, and the woman took out Ne'Mara's eye before Ne'Mara crushed her throat with a blow from her mace.

More of the villagers came from their homes, sporting still more weapons and attacking without any more attempts at parlay. Trigan felt himself smile as they spilled forth, ready for war and bloodshed.

His dagger and his axe drank deeply.

In the end it was inevitable that the Fellein fall before the Godless. In the past he had always left the dead to fall where they might, and he'd have been fine with doing that again, but Jeron called for them to take the hearts and heads of the dead with them, and he obeyed because he had no choice. The work was grim, and while he and the rest of the Godless reveled in the brief combat, none of them enjoyed the task of collecting their prizes.

Ne'Mara settled in on the edge of one of the houses and began cleaning her wounded eye as best she could. Trigan did not offer to help. There was still more work to do.

Ne'Mara was from Wheklam. She had spent many years riding the ocean and preferred the water to the land. Still, she was now Godless and followed Trigan and the rest of her new kin instead of working with the followers of the King in Lead.

"This is not the work of warriors, Trigan." Ne'Mara spoke the very problem that bothered him as he looked at the closest house.

"I know. But it is work that must be done, and we'll do it."

"What did they do to us?" She rose from where she'd been sitting, and gestured to the wounded eye while waving a wad of cloth with her free hand. He nodded and came closer. Ne'Mara handed him the cloth and turned her back to him. In a few moments the wound was properly bandaged and bound.

"They remade us." Trigan's jaw clenched as he spoke, and his lips peeled away from his teeth. "They have changed us."

"Into what?" She held out her hands and looked at them pointedly. He understood the problem. She was used to her hands looking a certain way and that was gone. Like him, her entire body had changed. It wasn't merely the color.

It was the way their bodies *felt.* They were different. He couldn't place quite how, but the changes were in the way they moved, in the way they walked and even, he suspected, in the way they thought.

The rest of the Godless did not wait but instead began the work ahead of them, entering the houses and seeking survivors. There. That was a perfect example of the very thing he was thinking about. The Seven Kings and the Seven Gods often asked many things of the Sa'ba Taalor, as was their right as rulers and gods. And though some of the things they asked were brutal, it was nothing beyond what was demanded of warriors in time of war. This? This was something different.

Trigan sighed as the other Godless dragged the children from their homes. The young ones cried and screamed and some even fought but to no avail. Those that struggled the most died all the sooner.

The young were killed just as the warriors had been. Their heads and hearts were gathered together with the rest, their bodies stacked to the side, piled together for burning. Trigan watched on, but did not participate. Instead he worked with Ne'Mara to pull the arrows from Melax's side, cutting the arrows free as they were barbed, and then stitching the wounds as best he could. Melax did not scream, but he hissed a great deal.

By the time that task was finished, the sun had begun the short descent toward the distant mountain, and the sky had grown darker. From this distance the fires from Paedle turned the skies bloody as the darkness crept closer.

The worst of the work was done by the time Jeron joined them. He walked with his servant, Roledru, and led two odd creatures with him. He knew from the discussions they had already had that the creatures were Tolfah, the servants of the Overlords. He had not seen them before, but he had heard of them. Tolfah were supposed to be savages, but the two with him seemed subdued. They stared ahead with little interest in what occurred around them, as if they were drugged or dazed.

"Are they all dead?" the wizard said in his low, raspy voice as he approached, his hood drawn over his head, hiding the continuing changes that he knew the man was undergoing.

"They are dead. The heads and hearts set aside as you demanded."

Jeron looked toward him and nodded slowly. Roledru, the wizard's assistant, looked his way and grew pale.

"We are done here."

"This was not an easy task for you. I know that." It was Roledru who spoke now. "It's not what you were born for, but Jeron says the work is necessary to bring forth the War-Born."

"What are the War-Born?"

It was Jeron who answered. "They are your army, Trigan. You have made the necessary sacrifices to help me bring your army to you." He stepped closer, brushing past the man who served him faithfully. "Watch. See the power of your Overlords."

The man walked slowly over to the collected prizes of his grisly demand and crouched near the bloody hearts. He moved carefully, muttering to himself, chanting words that were whispered rather than shouted, as if they were secrets best not heard by the world at large. His hands touched each bloodied heart and then cast it aside. One after another. He made certain to touch each one and as he did, there was what felt like a gathering of something that could not be seen by Trigan but reminded him of a slowly building storm.

When he was done with the hearts, Jeron moved to the heads of the dead, and lifted each one, touched each face as if memorizing their features, whispering to each as if it might be a lover, though his face remained hidden by the deep hood of his robes.

He was not careful with his prizes. When he finished with his whispers, the heads were tossed aside as if they no longer mattered, and the long fingers of his hands came away bloodied.

"What is he doing?" Ne'Mara watched on, more curious than disturbed by the sorcerer's actions. They had certainly done similar things in their times. The gods had demanded that bodies be cast into the hearts of the volcanoes. They had then brought the dead back as an army before the Fellein had used their wizards to destroy them.

"He is performing sorcery," Roledru confirmed softly, but audibly. "He gathers the spirits of the dead."

"Why?"

"The dead have power, and he knows how to steal that power."

"Why?"

Roledru offered a tiny, tolerant smile. "Because the Overlords want their soldiers back and that takes power, too."

Ne'Mara nodded as if that answered all her questions, and perhaps it did.

Jeron took over an hour to draw whatever power it was he took from the dead. By the time he was finished the sensation of a great storm brewing had increased a thousandfold. The hairs on Trigan's body stood apart from each other as if the air itself were ablaze.

Once done, Jeron approached the two Tolfah he'd brought

with him. By then Trigan had realized that one was male, and one was female. They were beasts, made for fighting and rutting and little else as far as he could see. The strips of hide wrapped around themselves in a haphazard fashion, with little mind toward actual protection from the elements, seeming as if they'd been donned simply following the examples of others before them without any consideration of the reasons for their actions.

"Now, finally, we truly begin." Jeron's hands reached out and wrote on both creatures' faces with the blood staining his hands. The markings were virtually identical on both of the bestial faces; neither Tolfah reacted at all to his touch, their facial expressions not changing in the least. When he was finished, however, both of them convulsed, dropping to the ground and writhing in pain as muscles spasmed and bones changed beneath their flesh.

Roledru watched on, fascinated, as did the Godless. Trigan Garth stood still, mesmerized by the sounds that came from the creatures' bodies, popping noises and wet hisses escaping them as they crawled, trying, it seemed, to escape the sudden and no doubt overwhelming pain that took them. Their skin changed, reddening for a moment as blood seemed to push from deep inside them to the very surface of their flesh, leaving them coated in a patina of crimson droplets. Their eyes bulged and their nostrils flared, and the already feline teeth in their mouths extended and grew wider.

The Tolfah likely would have screamed if they could, but the metamorphosis seemed to steal away their very breaths.

"What are you doing to them, Jeron?" Roledru looked away from the creatures long enough to stare at his master, horrified by what he witnessed.

The wizard did not speak, but instead looked on, his face still hidden deep inside the folds of his hood.

Still the changes continued. The Tolfah writhed, scraping across the ground as if they had forgotten they could stand and move. The expressions on their faces spoke of untold agonies.

What they were becoming was not yet to be revealed. The thick hides on their bodies grew even thicker and pulled away from the meat beneath, hardening like leather until each of the wretched things was hidden within a cocoon. Movements still occurred within those shells, and each of the creatures slowly stopped moving as the outer layers became thick enough to trap them.

"Soon, Trigan Garth, your armies will be ready." Jeron's long fingers caressed the closest hard carapace. "These are the War-Born. They are your new army. Come with me. Learn why you have been chosen and why you have been changed. See your new army, and prepare yourself. It is your task to lead the War-Born into battle and to conquer Fellein for the Overlords."

He looked upon the first of his new army, and for the first time since he had been tricked into giving himself to the Overlords, Trigan Garth smiled. He wanted to see them, what they became.

He would not have to wait terribly long.

Whistler

The soldiers gathered in their tents and did their best to fend off the bitter cold of night on the Wellish Steppes. Those that were on duty stood guard as best they could, wrapped in fur cloaks and coats that seemed as thin as gossamer when it came to storing heat. There were fires aplenty, but the winds were harsh and cut deep at any exposed skin.

In a nearby tent the leaders of the Fellein sat together and considered what to do about the weather, and the massive mountain that had grown from the ground like an unwanted crop of rotten fruit.

Whistler listened as the people inside the tent talked, uncertain who it was that spoke, but knowing the words they uttered were important to someone, somewhere. He really didn't care that much himself, but he'd promised his servitude in exchange for his life when the volcano rose into the air, and he was caught in the wrong place. Or the right place, he supposed, depending on perspective.

The voices that bargained with him had been his companion for a long while now. At first, they were a faint whisper, but as time passed, they became a constant source of distraction until he was forced to go where they led him.

Now? Now those voices were all but gone. He found he almost missed them.

"Well, at least there aren't any invaders coming from the mountaintop." The speaker was trying to sound amused and just failing. He could not see who had spoken but he already knew. This was the one several referred to as "General." There was only one official of that rank in the area, a man named Merros Dulver, who was actually in charge of the empire's armies. He had seen the man before, in Canhoon when he was passing through, and he had even spoken to him – before the Overlords changed Whistler.

His hands moved up to feel his face, though he was barely aware of it. Seemed to have become an obsession, really. Whistler was used to being handsome enough to make the girls smile with him. And that was a thing of the past, he supposed.

"You are vain." The voice spoke only in his head, but he recognized it easily enough as one of the very same voices that had drawn him from his home to the steppes in the first place.

"Nothing wrong with being pretty," he countered.

"If your face is so important, then earn it back. Prove your worth."

Whistler nodded. It was an old argument already, yet it had only been a few days ago that everything in his world went mad. The face beneath his sensitive fingertips felt wrong. It didn't just feel wrong – it was wrong. His lips were thin, and when his mouth was closed, they barely seemed there at all, but still he managed well enough. The steam had boiled his face and head when he was on the hill that became a mountain. By rights he should have been blinded by his eyes boiling away and mute from the tongue being cooked out of his foolish, screaming mouth. Instead, his eyes worked just fine, and he managed well enough to talk, though at the moment all of his conversations were in his head. The voices did not speak so others could hear them, so he merely had to think his responses to them. That was one advantage, he supposed, to hearing voices. He was never truly alone.

Whistler stifled a laugh at that and shook his head to clear the notion away. Still, it lingered like a cobweb he could not shake free.

"I am not listening to these fools for my own entertainment. I'll earn it back then. Just tell me what to do."

That first comment was partially a lie. Whistler found it amusing that he could hide where others did not see him. Currently he was outside the tent proper, in the bitter cold, but not affected by it. Whatever else the Overlords had done when they remade him, he seemed barely to notice the cold around him now, or the heat of the volcano when he'd walked down the side of the mountain as it erupted.

His mouth pulled into a rictus of a grin, and he listened more carefully. The sing-song accent of the man who responded to the general marked him as someone Whistler had met as well, one of the Inquisitors from Louron. He could easily envision the man's dark complexion, his easy smile, and the braided dreadlocks of hair around his head. He liked the man's warmth but, as with anyone from Fellein, he did not trust that warmth to save him if he caught the stranger's attention in the wrong way.

New voices entered into the tent, and Whistler listened on, once again uncertain who was speaking.

CHAPTER THREE

Desh Krohan

Hard to say who was more surprised by Desh's appearance – the general or the Inquisitor.

Either way, Desh was there on a mission. Merros Dulver was needed in Canhoon. "General, your Empress requires your attention at the palace," he explained. "I know it displeases you, but I am your transport."

Merros stared at him, eyes wide with surprise. After the years they'd known each other, the man should have been used to Desh making unexpected arrivals, but no.

In his defense it was seldom that Desh used his sorcery to move him a hundred or more miles from where he had been seconds before. Magic always had a cost, but at the moment Nachia Krous was not to be trifled with.

"What has happened?" Merros asked softly.

"Complications. That's all I can say." It was all he was willing to say. Some issues were simply not the sort he wanted to be involved with, and this was one of them.

Merros stood.

"Apologies," Desh said to the Inquisitor, "but we have to go now." Without another word he touched the general on the shoulder and forced his will upon the world around them. The world faded into a miasma of gray, shifting forms, and he pushed himself and Merros through the rift in space that was as close to the spirit realms as physical forms could get. The Sooth were nearby, their voices calling with taunting promises of madness and secrets best not revealed. As Merros winced, Desh ignored the false assurances of revelation as he pushed through to the Imperial throne room.

One moment the pair were in the cold of the Steppes, the next the air was calmer, warmer, as the hearths of the throne room crackled with great fires. They stood in near-darkness. It was a kindness, really, as Desh knew the general had not prepared himself for their form of transportation. To his credit, Merros Dulver did not vomit. Instead, he stood very, very still and shivered violently. They had arrived in a small alcove behind the tapestry of Emperor Largash that covered the northern wall of the room. The great woven shape hid the small meeting place from view, and for those that knew about it, also hid entrance to an access tunnel that moved through hallways and corridors unseen and unknown to most.

"Collect yourself. We are expected."

Merros nodded and sucked in a deep breath.

A moment later they were entering the great chamber proper, and hearing Ahdra, the priestess of the god Vehndal, try to convince their Empress to make changes.

"All I mean, Majesty, is that the gods wish to offer their help in these troubling times."

"And I appreciate that, Ahdra," the Empress said firmly, "but I have all of the advisors I need, and if the gods wish to speak with me and offer counsel, they will have to do as the Saba Taalor's gods do, and speak with me directly." She paused a moment and then looked to her left. "Is that not what your gods do, Swech?"

Merros Dulver snapped his head around at that name, and looked where the Empress cast her eyes. His surprise could not have been more obvious. Before their two races warred, Desh knew the general and Swech had been lovers. During the time when the two nations were at war, Swech had insinuated herself into Dulver's life a second time, hidden inside the body of another woman. Desh did not know if they had become lovers again, but they had been close. So close that the revelation of what Swech had done left the man devastated emotionally, though he had done his best to hide that fact.

King Swech Durwrae Tothis was one of the seven kings of the Seven Forges. That had not been the case when last she had seen any of the people currently in the room. It was a fairly new development. Desh didn't understand how government worked in the Seven Forges; he only knew that the gods of the Sa'ba Taalor chose new kings when one of their leaders died.

Swech looked directly at the Empress and nodded. She ran one finger across the Great Scar on her left cheek and said, "The Daxar Taalor bless us with the ability to speak to them directly and to hear their voices."

Ahdra looked at the gray-skinned woman and shook her head. "The gods do not speak directly to anyone."

Swech responded, "Your gods do not, perhaps, but mine do."

Nachia cut in. "Then why would I need advice from people they do not speak to?"

"The followers of the gods are your people, Majesty. They have needs."

"We all have needs, Ahdra."

Desh pressed his lips together and made himself stay silent. Nachia was handling the matter herself. She did not need his help.

"Your majesty, you are ignoring a source of wisdom that is offered to you. Is that wise?" The speaker was Lariso, a priest to Kanheer, the god of war. He was a thickset man with numerous scars. His right hand ended in a mass of shriveled flesh and scar tissue.

"Lariso, my answer remains the same. If the gods wish to impart their wisdom to me, they will have to speak to me themselves. I have read the doctrines and heard the tales, and I can interpret those myself."

Lariso opened his mouth to respond again, but Merros Dulver called out, "The Empress has given her answer. Listen to it."

The man looked directly at Merros. "You of all people should understand, General."

"I need only understand that the Empress has declined your offer and you have continued speaking to her as if to a child."

Lariso shut his mouth and his face flushed with embarrassment or with anger, possibly both.

Swech turned to look at Merros Dulver. She said nothing, but her eyes immediately scanned the room and settled on the small boy who was currently looking at a collection of weapons adorning one wall. This, Desh knew, was her son by Merros Dulver, Valam. He was as yet a young child, but already he walked like a Sa'ba Taalor, on the balls of his feet, his arms close to his sides. He was far more interested in the weapons than he was in the adults in the room.

Merros did not know he had a son. This was one of the

reasons he'd been called back to the palace. Nachia, for all her wisdom and patience, had her moments when she wanted to amuse herself and this seemed one of those cases.

Merros Dulver looked pointedly at the collection of religious leaders. The general had as much use for gods as he did for sorcery, which meant he was just fine without them in his life. Desh considered Merros a friend and hoped the feeling was mutual, but the leader of the Imperial Forces seemed perfectly fine without magic in his world, and despite the Silent Army being brought to life by the gods, he seemed inclined to keep them as far away from his life as he could.

To that point he asked, "Is there any other business that you have with the Empress at this time?"

Ahdra shook her head.

"Then, as I have been summoned back to speak with the Empress, I'd ask you to remove yourselves."

Nachia raised an eyebrow. She wasn't upset, near as Desh could decipher from her expression, but neither was she amused by the general's abrupt actions.

Ahdra remained calm. Lariso looked ready to argue his point, but Ovish, the priest to Luhnsh, the god of beggars, nodded his head. "We outstay our welcome." The older man smiled blandly. "Apologies. Perhaps we will talk again soon."

Nachia said, "My general does not mean offense. We find ourselves in a very trying time, and though I still appreciate the kind offer of advice, I fear now is not the time to seek new counsel."

Ahdra looked at Swech and frowned. The two women could not have been further apart from each other, physically, at least. Ahdra was beautiful, and soft in the ways that some women could be. If she had ever worked a hard day of labor in her life it would be a surprise to Desh. Swech, like most of her people, could very easily be identified by the scars on her exposed flesh. Her hands were heavily scarred and callused, and her posture was entirely different from the priestess' demeanor. Even forgetting the fact that the Sa'ba Taalor had gray skin, and usually gray or black hair, there was little that marked the two as having anything at all in common.

Ahdra said nothing but Desh made note of the fact that she was interested in Swech. He didn't know that he'd ever consider Ahdra's attention a good thing.

As the gathered religious leaders left the throne room, Merros walked closer to the Empress and lowered his head. "Apologies if I overstepped, Majesty."

"We've discussed this before, Merros. I am hardly the most polite of people, but we must remember to treat the leaders of the faithful with respect."

The general cast his eyes toward Swech. "I was caught unprepared. I will make it right with them."

"It might be best if you do that now, before the wounded feelings have time to fester." She did not make a request of her words, and Merros listened, moving after the trio of the faithful before they could go far.

Nachia looked at Desh and pouted for exactly one second. He knew why. Her ploy had not worked. Merros had not reacted to Swech's presence.

Swech, on the other hand, followed the general from the room looking at her son and saying, "Stay where you are."

"Well, there goes my fun," Nachia muttered.

"Really, Majesty."

"I'll not be chided. I'm sitting on your dammed throne, and I'll have my fun where I can."

"It's certainly not my throne."

"You built it."

"To protect whomsoever sits in it."

"I'm not the least bit fooled." She shifted her body. "You designed it to be uncomfortable."

"Complacency is hardly a sign of an active mind. I prefer to think I built it to keep you aware."

"I'll have the damned thing burned one of these days."

Before Desh could respond, Merros stormed back into the throne room, his face reddening. "I've arranged to meet with the faithful tomorrow for a discussion."

"Excellent!" Nachia smiled.

"I was unaware that the Sa'ba Taalor are visiting."

"That's one of the reasons I had you called back, Merros."

Swech entered the room and moved on a direct course for Merros. Not far away the rest of the Sa'ba Taalor, who had come with Swech, stood in their own area, not mingling with any of the Fellein. They had no interest in court politics. Perhaps if there were swords involved, they'd have felt differently.

Merros looked at Swech. Without saying a word, he turned on his heel and walked toward the hidden alcove where Desh had brought them into the room. Swech followed.

Desh watched on and Nachia sighed.

"Are you distressed, Majesty?" Desh looked to Nachia with a raised eyebrow.

"Disappointed." She sighed again. "I was looking forward to hearing every last word of that encounter."

Desh said nothing.

Swech

Merros Dulver looked almost the same. He had changed his facial hair again. Currently he sported a short beard and mustache, whereas the last time she'd seen him he had been clean-shaven. She couldn't have said which way she preferred. All she knew was that seeing him now made her pulse race and her knees feel weak. She hated that sensation.

She had missed him.

The last time she had seen him she had been living a lie, wearing the body of a woman named Dretta March. Her goal at that time was the same as always: she lived to obey her gods, to thank them for all they gave her. She listened to their wishes and obeyed. She became Dretta March, living the life the woman would have lived, using her memories and thoughts as a shield against discovery, all the while growing closer to Merros. She saw the man every day and became first a friend and then a lover before her true self was discovered.

To serve her gods she had betrayed the trust she had with Merros Dulver. And if asked to do it again, she surely would, no matter how much she might hate it.

Merros knew that about her. He might not be understanding of her actions, but he knew her devotion to her gods.

Still, he looked at her and said, "Why are you here?"

"The gods have ordered me to serve your Empress. I am here as her servant."

"Why?"

"Because the gods need our people to work together. I am here as an offering. She may do with me what she wants, and I will obey her wishes."

Merros snorted and shook his head, a rueful half smile on his face. "Until the gods tell you otherwise."

"I obey my gods above all else, you know this."

"There is nothing to say, Swech."

"There is. You have a son. His name is Valam." She spoke as calmly as she could. In her time, she had served her gods and killed as they ordered. She had led her people, followed the whims of various kings and as always remined faithful. She would not betray that bond, even for Merros, but she wanted him to know that he had a son.

Merros stared at her, shock written on his features. They had last lain together five years ago.

"What?"

"Valam. He is in the throne room if you want to meet him."

"How could you not tell me?" He closed his eyes. "No, never mind. It's a foolish question."

It was too. He had killed Dretta March, the body Swech had inhabited. Likely he thought her dead, too, at least for a time. The likelihood was that he knew she was a king now, and had known for a long while. The sorcerers of the Fellein could see well beyond the natural limits of the world. They had eyes that could hunt across thousands of miles for secrets. She had no idea how such powerful magic worked, but she understood that it did, in fact, mimic powers she thought only belonged to gods.

"Merros. I could not come to you. I could not send a message, and even if I had, to what point? If I told you there was a child between us, would you have come to Paedle and visited? No."

He nodded.

"So why then let you know if it could only cause you grief?"

"I have a son." He shook his head. "I never suspected."

"He is in the throne room. Would you like to meet him?"

The conflict on his face was obvious. Did he want to meet his son? Of course, he did. But did he want to meet his son by Swech? Perhaps not.

"I will say nothing to him of you unless you want it. That has never been the way of my people."

"What do you mean?"

"You Fellein, you stay with one person, you mate and raise families. My people do not always stay together and when we go our ways, we are done. Children are the responsibility of the mother and the gods. If the gods say two people should be together then they are together. If the gods say nothing, it does not matter. We live to serve the gods. All of us." Sometimes she felt like she was explaining what should be obvious, but their cultures were nothing alike.

Merros looked into her eyes, studied her, even as she returned the favor. "I'd like to meet him."

She nodded. "Come with me."

She was not nervous. They left the antechamber and moved back into the throne room, where Valam was studying a sword that was taller than he was. The weapon was held in place by three hooks, and the boy was eyeing them carefully.

"Valam."

Her son looked at her, curiosity in his eyes. It was rare for her to call out to him by name.

"Valam, this is General Merros Dulver. He commands a great army. He is your father."

The boy looked at Merros and nodded solemnly, not

reacting in any way to his mother's pronouncement. "I am Valam."

Merros stared at his son, clearly unsure what to say, before eventually replying, "You are well met, Valam."

"Will you show me this sword?" the boy asked, like all youngsters of that age focused entirely on what interested him most.

Merros looked at Swech. "He cannot hold the sword himself," she said. "He is too small. He wants you to hold it for him so that he can examine the edge."

"Is that wise?"

"It is how he learns. Valam does not touch another person's weapons without permission."

"I can't see Tusk caring about that sort of thing." Merros chuckled, but as he did so he carefully lifted the sword from its hooks and then knelt near the boy to let him examine the weapon more closely.

"Tusk is not my son, but even he would ask first. It's the only way to ensure not being killed for your curiosity."

Valam's eyes looked at the fine edge of the weapon, and then moved along the hilt and pommel. "Thank you."

"You are most welcome, Valam."

That was all that the man said to the boy, until Valam moved to the other weapons along the wall and once again asked to see one of them more closely.

Through it all, the Empress Nachia watched them without saying a word.

Drask Silver Hand

The winds along the Wellish Steppes blew hard to the south

and stank of sulfur. The new mountain reared across the whole area, spewed volcanic ash and turned the skies a deep slate gray. The snow that drifted down from above was muddied with it, and the whole area was lost in the mountain's shadows.

Drask stared at the mountain and shook his head.

Next to him Tuskandru gestured to the mountain and scowled. "It's an affront to the Daxar Taalor. An attempt to mock our gods for moving from their old homes to new locations."

"Are those your words? Or do you speak for Durhallem?"

Tusk held his hand in front of him and imitated sea waves. "They are my words, and I always speak for Durhallem. He is my master in all things."

"Then why has Durhallem left this mountain here?"

"Because the mountain is a small insult, and he wants to see how I will handle it."

"And what are you going to do about the mountain?"

"I am going to see what my friend Drask can do about it. He claims to have the powers of the gods."

"No. I never said I have the power of the gods. I said that the gods have granted me great power."

Tusk laughed. "You seek to gather the kings and see if you will be accepted back into the Seven Kingdoms. Show that you will not tolerate an insult to the Daxar Taalor. Show that you are grateful for the power they have given you."

Drask looked at his lifelong friend and scowled, feeling the Great Scars along his face pull and expand. "What would you have me do with the mountain, Tusk?"

The King in Obsidian waved a hand in the mountain's direction airily. "Remove it. Make it into something else. You are the one who can make godlike things happen."

"You wish to test me? To see if I am lying?"

Tusk laughed and shook his head. "No. I am the voice of Durhallem. He speaks to me as he does to others, but he speaks to me a great deal more. I know you are not lying. I know what you have been doing for the last five years. I know everything Durhallem thinks I should know, including how powerful you truly are. The Gods know, but you do not. You doubt that you can do this thing the gods ask. So, show the gods that you are grateful for everything they have done for you. See for yourself how mighty you are."

Drask looked at the mountain and considered that request. Five years earlier, for reasons he still did not fully understand, the gods had sent him on a quest. They had told him to do what was explicitly forbidden to the Sa'ba Taalor, and to enter the Mounds, a place of great danger that was off-limits to the people of the forges. He had done as he had always done, and obeyed.

The end result was that he and two of the people from Fellein, Tega and Nolan March, had been bathed in the power of the gods, and changed by it.

They had access to nearly unimaginable power, and much as he wished he could claim he was not changed by it; he knew better. One only had to look at his right hand to see the differences. Through no conscious ability of his own, the silver hand the god Ganem had given to him had changed. The god had replaced his lost hand with a silver imitation that felt, that moved, that worked as well as the original, but had never looked the part. But now, where once a line of scar tissue showed where the metallic hand joined with his flesh, that scar was now smoothed out. The silver had spread up his arm and now looked more like natural flesh than he would have ever imagined possible.

"Durhallem wants me to show how much the mountain offends the gods?"

Tusk stared at him for a long moment, a half-smile on his broad face. "The gods want to know what you will do about the offensive symbol."

The power was there. Tega had explained it to him best. She said that magic was much like the power of the gods. With practice and a source to allow it, magic could reshape the world – but there was always a price. The gods demanded that price to prevent every fool who could manage a spell from altering the world beyond repair.

He scanned the mountain, looked at the sheer size of the thing, at the clouds that hid the pinnacle away, the fire that lit those clouds like embers, and considered the possibilities.

The gods said he could change the mountain. His inner voice of doubt was silenced by that thought. The gods did not lie. If Durhallem told him to remove the insult, he would find a way.

Whatever had happened in the Mounds had changed the three of them. They were not gods, but they had access to the power needed to change the world. If they willed it, and concentrated hard enough, they could work powerful magic without having to pay a powerful price.

He did not completely believe this. There was a price to pay. He knew that simply by looking at his arm. He had been changed. He was still changing, and every time he used the power he had been granted, further changes occurred.

Still, one of the seven kings who spoke for the seven Daxar Taalor wanted him to use that power, and so he would.

The mountain had to be removed. He said nothing but climbed from Brackka's back and walked a distance away.

What does one do with a mountain?

He made no gestures, but both of his hands balled into fists as he considered the options.

The mountain was new. It had only recently broken through the ground and the soil around it was still freshly turned. The steppes were rough terrain where little grew beyond scrub brush and thistles. To honor the gods, he decided to change that.

First, Drask studied the massive edifice thousands of feet high and burning with a heart of magma to rival the Seven Forges. It was, indeed, an affront to the Gods. It would stand no longer. Rather than merely destroy it, however, he chose to transform the rock and minerals into a rich topsoil that he spread across the land as far as could be seen. The ground shook and the air seemed to breathe as he leveled thousands of feet of fresh rock and mutated it to suit his needs.

Drask willed it and watched it happen. The mountain collapsed on itself as surely as ice melts into water, but at a much faster rate. The soil washed across the land in a heavy wave that shoved stunted shrubs and plants aside as easily as flood waters washed away debris.

The world roared. Air pressure pushed a massive wind across the area, scattering debris and staggering people who were unprepared for the transformation. Fellein who watched the mountain collapse screamed and many of them ran. Drask could not blame them. He knew what to expect, was the very source of the transformation, and was still impressed by the change.

Twenty feet away, Tuskandru watched and laughed. Just before the wave could destroy the tents that the Fellein had established near the mountain, Drask willed the protection of those very structures. The wave of soil moved around the area rather than through it.

"Why would you save the pink skins?" Tusk continued laughing and moving, watching everything that happened with wide eyes and a broad smile.

Drask shrugged. "We are not at war."

"Yes, but we could be!"

"Ganem tells me we will be at war again soon enough." Drask smiled. There were seven gods for the seven kingdoms and each and every one of those gods thrived on war, as did their followers.

Tusk laughed again and nodded. It would not be accurate to say that the King in Obsidian was a simple man, but he definitely took pleasure in his simple joys.

"Why have you spread the mountain like paste?"

"Soil. I have fertilized the land."

"Why?"

Drask laughed. "Because I like plants."

"What will you plant here?"

"I do not care. Whatever grows here is enough for me."

The clouds above broke apart slowly, and the skies grew lighter. Drask looked to the north, where he could clearly see Truska-Pren, the volcanic forge of the god of the same name. The mountain existed as the home of the gods and their people. Truska-Pren was the heart of that mountain, the god of the Iron Forge and one of the seven gods Drask had followed all his life. He was, in fact, the very first of the gods that Drask had ever spoken with.

"And do I honor the gods, Tusk?"

"You always have, Drask." The man was standing next to him. While Drask had been lost in thought the King in Obsidian had moved close enough to him to be startling. Drask chided himself for being careless. It was not that he expected trouble from Tusk, it was that he knew better than to let anyone move so close to him without his being aware. He had spent his entire life preparing for war, and that meant being always ready for combat.

"Then I should see if Tarag Paedori agrees with you."

"Tarag may not be as agreeable." Tusk chuckled. "If you had done to me what you did to him, we would not be having a pleasant conversation."

"You follow the Wounder." Durhallem was a god that did not forgive. To slight him or his followers was effectively to demand combat.

"You and Tarag have a long history." Tusk sighed and then slapped him on the shoulder with one hand. "You will work this through."

"We'll see soon enough." Drask climbed back on Brackka and waited while Tusk mounted Brodem. The two were soon on their way; the great beasts they rode charged forward and made a competition of it, and soon the men were too busy holding on to their respective seats to talk.

Darsken Murdro

Mountains should not grow over night or disappear, but Darsken had now seen both occur. What amazed him was that he survived both incidents without injury.

"This world grows too complex, I fear." He spoke only to hear a voice. All around him soldiers were moving about in a panic, which he found perfectly justifiable under the current conditions.

"If the Overlords truly have awakened, I expect it will grow more complex, not less." Tataya spoke softly, which was her way. The woman was not expected, but she was a welcome sight. The Sisters, the three sorceresses who worked most closely with Desh Krohan, were always a welcome sight in his eyes. They were kind and gracious, and tended to draw attention away from him, which was a wonderful thing as an Inquisitor.

"Is this your doing, Tataya?"

"No, I only just heard that the mountain was gone, and Desh sent me to investigate."

"It is gone. I watched it happen."

"No one was injured?"

"No." Darsken shook his head. "Not that I know of."

"I'm surprised to find you here, Darsken."

"I have been speaking with a few of the surviving mercenaries who fought against Merros and his soldiers."

"Some of them survived?" She genuinely looked shocked. "I heard the Sa'ba Taalor were involved in the fighting."

"They were, but several soldiers surrendered rather than face them."

Tataya moved closer and studied his face. "Have they told you anything useful?"

"They have mentioned a wizard. The only name I have is Jeron, but I thought I heard he died in the war."

Tataya frowned and her face grew stormy. "Jeron's tower was destroyed by the King in Iron, but nobody was ever found. As he disappeared it was assumed he'd been killed and burned in the tower. I know several attempts were made to contact him."

"If what I have learned is true, he was the main recruiter of the mercenaries. All I can say for certain is that a sorcerer identifying with that name was the leader of whatever efforts were made here."

"Is there any chance that the people you spoke with were lying?"

"There is always a chance." He smiled. "It is a very slight chance." She looked puzzled. "I tend to seek the truth."

"Oh. No. I didn't mean to imply–"

"I take no offense from an honest question, Lady Tataya."

"I merely meant that it seems strange to me. Jeron has always been loyal. Are you sure it was him – how did this sorcerer look?"

"No one could give me a description. Whoever the wizard, he wears a drawn hood to hide his features."

"Well, that's rather unlike Jeron." She paused. "He tended to think himself quite handsome."

"You did not agree?"

"Let's say he found the idea of us being together more appealing than I did and leave it at that."

"Of course." He sighed and looked around. "I was planning on leaving here and returning to Canhoon. But I might linger if you do. You can probably answer most of my questions about Jeron."

"There's not much more to say. He was the master of the academy for several years and when it comes to mystical abilities, he's… formidable."

"If he is indeed the one who orchestrated all of this, I'd say he's more than that – he's a dangerous man to have as an enemy." That was an understatement. "How much power would it take to level a mountain?"

"I honestly don't know." Tataya shook her head and frowned. "I am a very capable spellcaster, but I don't think I've ever managed that sort of power. There are ways to capture and store power but to raise a mountain or reduce one to powder? If I spent a dozen years working on a spell of that magnitude, I would probably still need to find alternate sources of power to achieve it. That is why I am here, Darsken. This is a level of ability that is terrifying."

"Could Desh Krohan manage a feat like this?"

"Probably, but there would be so many delays, so many setbacks, just from trying to gather the power necessary. If you took all of the energy locked inside a volcano, you might be able to raise a mountain."

"I have never used any magics that powerful." He shook his head. "I helped with resurrecting Goriah, and it was challenging and exhausting. I was drained for weeks. To move a mountain? I can't conceive of that sort of power."

"Magic is a great and powerful thing, but the greater the spell, the more power is required. Whoever managed to destroy that mountain used enough energy to take years. That much power could literally end the caster's life."

"This Jeron, is he a good man?"

Tataya did not answer him, but her expression said no as clearly as words could have.

Trigan Garth

Patience was one of the first lessons a Sa'ba Taalor ever learned. Being impatient or rude with the wrong people tended to result in a severe beating – or worse. For that reason, Trigan had never been the sort to worry about how long he had to wait.

That was a blessing. The War-Born might be a great and powerful army, but they did not seem in any rush to hatch from their cocoons. Trigan used the time while he waited to train with the other Godless.

The sorcerer Jeron was clearly less endowed with patience. He paced endlessly along a small path along the Dark Passage and waited for any sign of life from the hundreds of still forms that had been wrapped in the remains of their own skins after he forced the metamorphosis onto the Tolfah. The creatures had dropped, and their forms were changed where they fell, and they had fallen wherever darkness grew, it seemed. The dark grey cocoons had formed all along the underpass, sliding into shadows and crevices as if the Tolfah had been desperate to avoid any hint of sunlight. There seemed to be hundreds of the things. Hundreds? At least. It could well be that there were thousands of the creatures. He could see cocoons as far as his eyes would focus.

Roledru, Jeron' assistant, remained calmer, and used the time to sharpen his spear's head. For a man who was not a warrior, the man was remarkably calm in his downtime.

"I grow tired of waiting." Jeron grumbled as he paced.

"It's your spell."

"Yes, I know it's my spell. That doesn't mean I can't be impatient."

Roledru looked like he wanted to say something else, but before he could, the first of the cocoons let out a loud cracking noise and almost immediately several others followed suit. It was a sound like a tree branch breaking, and though the area was hardly abandoned, the noise was startling.

Trigan saw the first of the War-Born as it started to emerge from its chrysalis. The limb that came out was not remotely humanoid. It was a light grayish-brown and ended in a deadly barb. The cocoon was shredded quickly enough and what crawled from the remains had six legs under a bulbous form, from which a semi-human torso rose, with two additional limbs that tucked in close to the body. It looked as if someone had fused the top of a human form to the body of a spider. The upper limbs each ended in a chitinous scythe designed to cut and rend with ease. There were several orbs at the front of the thing's head, which he guessed must be eyes. Below those there was a mouth of sorts that looked like it was designed to hold the flesh of whatever the thing decided to eat.

He had been fascinated by spiders when he was younger, watching the way they hunted, the way they fed on their prey, and often times as a child he would capture other insects and cast them into the spider's webs in an effort to see how it was that they killed and fed.

Of course, spiders were much smaller than these things, which must weigh at least as much as grown humans.

Roledru stared at the things, his eyes wide and his face a mask of horror.

Trigon was not horrified, he was fascinated.

Jeron spoke softly. "Yes. They are even better than I'd hoped." He walked to the closest of them and one long-fingered hand slipped from his robes long enough to caress the oddly haired shell of the creature. "Look at them, Trigan. Aren't they magnificent?"

Trigan nodded without saying a word. They were beautiful, in their way, and if they were even half as deadly as they looked, no army would stand before them.

"You created them, you know." Jeron continued speaking just as softly, but he moved closer to Trigan. "The Overlords were looking for hunters and they chose the thing you saw in your mind as the starting point for their newest warriors. They will change them again if need be, but the first form of the War-Born was shaped by you. It is their way of honoring your sacrifice in becoming one of their leaders."

Trigan stepped closer to the first of the creatures, watched as the shell of the body hardened, and the moisture that had spilled from the cocoon dried quickly in the cold winter air.

The creature stood before him, nearly seven feet in height, its long, powerful legs flexing and adjusting subtly as it learned to stand and walk. He looked at the dark orbs of its eyes and saw his face reflected at him, distorted until it looked even less like he should have.

"You have changed, Jeron. You were prepared for your transformation. I was not given an option. Do you understand why that might make me angry?"

"When this is all over, when we have claimed the world for the Overlords, all of this can be undone."

Trigan said nothing, but he licked his lips and slowly nodded. More of the creatures emerged from their cocoons. He watched them silently as they adjusted to their new bodies.

Beside him Vendtril, another of the Godless, shook his head and smiled. "They are living weapons."

"That is good, as I don't think they can hold much with those things at the ends of their arms."

"What will we do with them?"

Jeron answered the question before Trigan could. He said, "You will lead them into battle and command them as your armies. The Overlords have chosen you, one and all, as their generals."

"Where shall we lead them?"

Jeron smiled. "To the Fellein, who must now pay a debt long owed the Overlords."

Goriah

Goriah was tired but there was no time to sleep. The days were starting to blur, and she and the other Sisters did their part to keep Desh Krohan informed of everything going on in the empire.

Their task was made slightly easier by sorcery. They could communicate with the other wizards in different areas, could correlate the information and share it with Desh as needed. Currently she was speaking with a man named Korreia, a ponderously large sorcerer better known for his theatrics than his actual talent as a spellcaster. He was far to the west, and studying the area for signs of trouble.

Of late the Tolfah had become more of an actual problem instead of simply a nuisance and so Korreia had been sent to find out what was happening.

"There had been several assaults lately," the man reported. "Where there might have been one or two serious attacks each month before, it's become almost daily, to the point that most merchants are taking ships the long way around, rather than trying to reach the rivers via the Dark Passage."

"Desh said there have been greater numbers of these Tolfah?"

"I haven't seen any increase myself, of course, but the last few groups that encountered them have claimed several hundred of the things moving together, not a few dozen. I don't think it's a case of exaggeration. I think the claims must be legitimate. There have been too many deaths."

"How many?"

"Well, I wouldn't want to make false claims, Goriah, but there have been at least four caravans where the number of survivors was less than five out of parties in excess of forty. In the past caravans of that size were usually left alone, or could easily drive back the Tolfah. If the numbers are accurate something must have happened to make them more organized."

"So, the savages are learning to rally their troops?"

Korreia sighed mightily. He shook his head hard enough to make his jowls wobble. "That seems to be the other problem. The creatures are little more than animals, savages, really with more in common with a pack of dogs than an army, but they've been acting differently of late. They seem better organized and far more numerous. Do you remember when Jeron used to speak of the Overlords? How it was a common belief that the Tolfah were what was left of the Overlords' armies?"

"Jeron was rather notorious for his stories about the old wars, yes."

"Well, if he's right and they are the remnants, I have to wonder if the stories we've heard about the Overlords waking might have something to do with the increased numbers."

"How do you mean?"

"I mean I did a great deal of reading about the Overlords. They were supposed to have their own systems of sorcery, different from what we learn today, but no less powerful. If they put themselves to sleep, is there any chance they might have done the same with their armies?"

Goriah thought about that. The fact was, there wasn't much known about the Overlords. Most of what was written boiled down to cryptic notes about their abilities and the fact that they weren't human.

"We don't know if they were at all that powerful. The

ability to hide their armies for a thousand years? That would take a great deal of power."

The man nodded. "Maybe you should check with Desh and Corin."

"I've already been discussing the Overlords with Desh. Why Corin?"

"Because he's been around as long as Desh, and he actually fought the Overlords. Him, Jeron and Desh. All three have survived that long."

Corin made Goriah's skin crawl. He was supposedly a good man, but every time she saw him, she wanted to unsee him as quicky as possible. Desh was a good friend, Jeron had been a letch but mostly harmless. Still, there was something about Corin that she did not trust, and it was impossible for her to ignore that. She'd have to mention the idea to Desh and have him handle the situation.

"I'll look into the matter."

"Please do. I'm curious as to what I'm getting myself into out here, and I want to get home sooner rather than later. I miss Dorah's cooking, and I prefer sleeping with my wife to sleeping on the cots they call beds out here."

"I'm sure Dorah misses you too." That was one of the things she had always appreciated about Korreia, he actually had a wife he loved and had never once made an attempt to bed any of the Sisters. That made him an exception. Most of the sorcerers she knew had either attempted seduction or claimed to have been with her, Pella or Tataya. Not that the rumors bothered her much, but they were a nuisance.

"If you should see her, please make sure she remembers me." He smiled. "A woman that lovely, I have to make sure she doesn't forget she's wed to an old man."

"Oh, I think she'd be hard pressed to forget you." Dorah

was a sweet woman with all the courage of a mouse. She'd no sooner cheat on her husband than he would on his wife. Still, she thought it a delight that he worried over the matter.

They arranged to speak the same time the next day, and went their separate ways.

Korreia did not speak with her ever again. He was dead less than four hours later.

Korreia

It is an unfortunate fact of life that the better you get at a job, the more in demand you become. Korreia may not have the title of master sorcerer, but he certainly had the demands of the job, which was why he was half a continent away from his home and handling a delicate matter for Desh Krohan and the Sisters.

Not that he minded. It was good to be needed. Still, the business with the Tolfah was unpleasant. They needed to be eliminated and following his conversation with Goriah, he was riding to the Dark Passage to see for himself how bad the situation was. All of the rumors in the world would never take the place of a firsthand examination. He had spent weeks preparing storage stones to hold energies, should he need to cast any serious spells, and those stones were stored in several pockets on his body.

The Dark Passage was the name the locals now used for what had previously been called the King's Passage. He rode from Darrow, the capitol, for half a day to reach the passage and quickly saw why it lived up to the new name. It might be that Mallifex Krous, the king of Morwhen, could rule his kingdom with a heavy hand but he could not control the clouds that rained ashes down upon the passage constantly. The cobbled roads and multiple bridges had been used by the people of Morwhen for several hundred years, the better to avoid the dangers of the lower valleys, which were rife with plague winds – an unpleasant remainder from the war with the Overlords – and home to the Tolfah.

Those were reasons enough to maintain the passage, but now they had to deal with the volcanic mountain dumping what seemed a nearly endless supply of ashes into the area. As with all of the Seven Forges, the mountain Paedle was an impressive sight. It loomed over everything in the area, but here, especially, it seemed like an ominous presence.

Korreia wasn't foolish – he'd brought a small army with him. There were fifty men on horseback, all of them prepared for an attack. They carried short bows, swords and spears. They were exactly the sort of men who looked like they could handle any situation, and they came highly recommended by General Worlach, who'd picked them himself for their skills. Korreia felt he was as prepared as he could be for the adventure.

Captain Derman, the leader of the horsemen, rode beside him in a crisp uniform. The men acted as if they were escorting royalty, and Korreia was both flattered and impressed by them.

None of them spoke much, but it was a comfortable silence. Up ahead of the captain and Korreia, two horsemen riding side by side started down a steep slope that would lead, apparently, to where the Tolfah were supposed to reside. Korreia moved his hand in the pocket of his tunic until he found the first of his stones.

Sorcery took energy and he wanted to be prepared if things went poorly. Arrows were all good and well, and he certainly wouldn't want to have to stave off a sword, but Korreia had been training for years and knew that, if he had to, he could defend the group from an attack.

Confidence is a lovely thing. Sometimes, however, it leads to folly.

Korreia was absolutely certain that he could handle anything that came to attack them. He had practiced the spells he would use, and he had prepared himself with the necessary sources to cast any incantations.

What he had not prepared himself for was the carnage.

The first of the riders descending the path was almost completely out of view when he screamed. All that the wizard saw was the man suddenly yanked downward. One moment he was a head and shoulders and an instant later he vanished with a scream.

And then the nightmares came into view. A thing came bounding up the dirt pathway ahead of Korreia. The first two riders were now gone from sight and the creature lurched forward. It had too many legs, and the head was wrong. He really had no time to fully absorb the thing's appearance before it was skittering toward the next rider, some sort of blades in each hand that came down and chopped into the soldier, slicing away one arm and cleaving his skull in two.

The poor bastard never even had a chance to scream before he was dead, but his horse made up for it with a screech as it reared up and tried to defend itself. Front hooves rose high in the air and crashed down on the shape before it. All Korreia could see of the attacker was the odd legs on either side of the horse's rearing shape, and then the horse's scream became a bellow of pain that was suddenly silenced as the mare fell backward amid a heavy wave of fountaining blood.

And then the things were swarming, leaping, crawling, skittering up the side of the dirt pass, into the Dark Passage proper. They were not human, not even close to human. They had too many legs. Some walked on six legs and others eight, those legs attached to bloated forms, moving like the crabs he used to capture as a child, multiple limbs clicking and clattering as they hurried into the roadway and attacked everything in their path.

The head of the closest nightmare turned toward Korreia and he clutched harder at the stone in his hand and began to recite the words of power he needed to cast a spell.

One arm scythed sideways and beheaded a horse, even as the creature looked toward Korreia and skittered closer still. Crimson flowed from the mount's severed neck, bathing the rider in blood even as the horse collapsed and the rider fell, pinned under his dead mount.

The spider-thing ignored the rider and fast crawled over the dead horse, scurrying toward Korreia. He finished his incantation and sent a massive tongue of fire toward the thing. The air burned. The creature was caught in a stream of flame that roasted its hard chitinous shell and seared its innards even as it lunged for him.

He looked at the nightmare face, an uneven lump with too many dark eyes and a wide mouth that had mandibles opening and closing on either side of it. It screeched and then recoiled, trying to escape the searing pain of being roasted alive.

And, as it died, the thing fell down and burned. And even as it burned it tried to crawl forward on its too long limbs. His heart was hammering in his chest and his hands shook. Korreia sucked in a gasp of air and stared until sudden motion caught his attention.

Sorcery takes power. He did not have time to grab another of his stones, so Korreia was forced to draw from his own essence to fight the next of the things. It was massive, easily as big as a pony, and it came at him with both of its arms raised up, the blades lifted high as the thing lunged for him, prepared to strike him dead.

Korreia knew many spells for dealing with an enemy, and he reacted instinctively with the spell he thought of as one of the most potent. The power moved from him in a visible wave, and as it touched the thing moving toward him it rotted whatever it connected with. In an instant the spiderlike form decayed. Healthy skin turned black and softened and the blood inside of the creature burst forth as surely as if he had stabbed a full skin of wine.

The thing shrieked as it rotted and collapsed in on itself.

Korreia would have celebrated, but the impact from his spellcasting hit him hard. One moment adrenaline was dancing through his body and the next he was so tired it seemed almost impossible to even consider moving.

To his right, the next of the things took a swipe at Captain Derman, who blocked the first strike with his sword. The second blow was not aimed at the captain, however, but rather at his horse, which was impaled by the thick scything blade of the monster's second arm. The horse staggered to the left and crashed into Korreia's horse. The animal had been incredibly calm through the entire attack, but panicked the moment the other animal fell against it. It reared up and was knocked sideways by the weight of Derman's horse. The captain, caught between the animals, fell toward the ground with a scream of pain as his arm was twisted the wrong way. Bones broke and the captain screamed a second time before he vanished from sight.

Korreia had no time to consider the man further. As his horse reared and bucked, Korreia was thrown through the air, spared from being crushed under his horse by the dumbest of luck.

The ground reared up and punched him in the side of his head, across his stomach and his knee. Now he could see the captain crushed under his horse and a small part of him flinched as the man died but most of his mind was taken by the massive pain from slamming into the cobblestone road.

And then one of the spider things was on him, both of its arms coming down at one time and hacking through his left arm and into his ribs.

The pain was too big, dwarfing even the impact with the road. He could not breathe. He could not think. He could only panic as the creature above him ripped its appendages out of his chest and struck a second time, a third, a fourth.

Then the pain was gone, a distant thought that dwindled away as he died.

Korreia was one of the lucky ones. He was dead before the War-Born began to feast.

CHAPTER FOUR

Andover Iron Hands

The black ship remained in the deeper waters and Andover worked with the others on the small boat to row their way to the shore. Paedle loomed above them, but that no longer mattered. The god was speaking in their heads, speaking to all of them, repeating the same words again and again. THE OVERLORDS HAVE RISEN. REJOICE FOR THE TIMES OF WAR ARE UPON US AGAIN. THE GREAT TIDE WILL WASH THE WORLD IN BLOOD.

There was a small part of Andover that recoiled at the idea, but most of him did indeed rejoice. Andover had spent one year – and several lifetimes – being trained by the gods themselves. He had met each of the Daxar Taalor and been prepared for becoming their champion. He had excelled to the point that he was considered one of the finest warriors among the Sa'ba Taalor. How could he be anything other than excited by the idea of a great conflict?

Paedle called for the sailors of Wheklam's ship to leave the waters and prepare themselves. The War-Born had awakened and they were magnificent. They were, in the words of the god, worthy opponents.

Andover crawled over the side to help pull the boat ashore. Cold water soaked his pants and boots, but he did not care. Once safely on land, he pulled a wrapped bundle of his weapons from the boat and looked toward the mountain. Turnaue, a follower of Wheklam and one of the finest fighters he had ever met, nodded, and then pulled the boat back into the waters. He and three others began rowing back toward the black ship.

Belam, one of Donaie Swarl's closest aides, smiled and nodded as he looked up the steep slope of Paedle. From the waters, Gorwich let out a low rumble and then padded ashore. The mount was dripping water, but otherwise was in fine form.

Andover smiled and moved closer to his friend. The relationship between rider and mount was a simple one. They shared a mental connection and could speak to each other without words. Gorwich still wore his saddle, while Andover carried his collection of weapons.

Several other mounts were working their way to the shore, and there were members of the Sa'ba Taalor joining with their rides and heading for the mountain's far side, where Turath lay buried in the side of the mountain. Turath was much like Paedle, shrouded in mystery. The depths of the city were buried in the side of the mountain, carved over the gods alone knew how many generations.

Andover had spent little time in the vast city, but he headed there now, holding on tightly to Gorwich as the mount charged quickly up the side of the forge. Gorwich grumbled amiably as he went, delighted to be off the ship where he was limited in where he could move and how fast he could travel. The black ships of Wheklam were large but there was no space for exercising and the great predatory beasts weren't fond of being penned into small areas.

The joy of his mount infected Andover and he found himself smiling. That, and the prospect of combat. Not a few sparring contests with the Sa'ba Taalor but actual combat. A fight worth having, where the stakes were life and death.

Darity came up on his left side, riding her mount and smiling brightly. They had met on the black ship, had spoken several times, and he found her interesting. She seemed confused by him, uncertain as to whether he was Fellein or Sa'ba Taalor. That happened a lot, really. And it was something he often considered himself. He was born in Fellein, but he had been changed by his time among the Daxar Taalor and their people. The gods had trained him, had changed him, until he felt more kinship with the people of the forges than with the Fellein. That was something he sometimes had trouble admitting to himself, but it was the truth.

"We go to war, Iron Hands!" Darity called out to him and moved closer to his side. Her hair was braided and kept close to her scalp, and the Great Scar on her right cheek was opened in a dark grin. She looked happy. She looked alive, and that was the thing he liked most about her, about the Sa'ba Taalor. They were as excited by the thought of war as he was.

Would he have felt different if he had a family to worry about? He was uncertain. Possibly yes, but he would never know. He had been without any close family for most of his adult life, and while he supposed he should have felt something like loss at the idea, he was actually pleased to be without the ties that would have bound him to Canhoon or the Fellein Empire.

"War! What a glorious thought!" He laughed out loud at the notion. For five years he had trained select members of the Fellein armies in the ways of combat, trained them to think outside the limits of formal warfare, trained them to understand the Sa'ba Taalor's ways, because he found himself adrift, nearly lost in the society that had once been his home. But now? Now he felt alive again, at the promise of warfare, of close combat and fighting an enemy capable of standing up to him. In single combat he doubted that any member of the Fellein Empire could be a true threat to him. He had been remade, shaped by gods as surely as his hands were forged by Truska-Pren.

He had more in common with the girl who rode next to him, a warrior he had known for only a few weeks, than he did with his own kind. He had been remade in the image the gods of war created for him.

That thought was oddly pleasing.

Up ahead the paths leading to Turath opened up, and he and the Sa'ba Taalor rode all the harder to reach the city, the people who waited there, gathering for war.

He was glad that the Fellein were not the target of the Sa'ba Taalor, but realized with a mild shock that he would have ridden into war against his own people.

Part of him wanted to dwell on that notion, but he brushed it aside. He would contemplate the depths of his feelings another time. For now, there was a war to consider. Seven gods had remade him in their way, and he was pleased with that notion, truly pleased by it for the first time since he had been sent to dwell among the Seven Forges.

King Swech

Paedle called for war, but he did not summon Swech to lead his armies.

Swech considered that as she stood in the throne room of Fellein's Empress. It was where she was supposed to be. It was where Paedle wanted her. Every muscle in her body wanted to shake with repressed fury at the thought, but Swech would not permit that.

Gods do not make mistakes. She believed that. She had believed that her entire life.

Swech was not just a warrior. She was a king. She had been chosen by Paedle as the best possible commander for his followers. That was not a mistake. Could not be a mistake. But, she reminded herself, Paedle was the god of silent combat. She was trained as an assassin and Paedle chose her as one of the best possible examples of his warriors and philosophies.

She reminded herself of that fact several times through the course of another day standing in the throne room and listening to Nachia Krous rule her vast lands. The Empress was very aware of her. She spoke plainly and made her judgments, and she did so with the ruler of one of seven enemy nations in her offices.

Nachia was aware that Swech had killed her cousin and predecessor. They had spoken about the matter. She was here as proof that the Daxar Taalor wanted peace between their people. She had come here solely because the gods wanted her here, and she stayed for the same reason. She and nine of her companions and her son. They were treated well, but every day they stayed in the throne room while the Empress was present and then they were released to their quarters in the southern wing of the palace. Then, when the Fellein did whatever it was they did after the Empress dismissed them, the Sa'ba Taalor trained.

Swech knew they were watched but did nothing about it. She took care of her son, she considered Merros Dulver, and she trained while she waited for the gods to command her. For now she was to serve the Empress and that was exactly what she would do. Even if she wanted to join in the war efforts, that was not for her to decide.

Still, she found ways to keep herself busy. As she had discovered in the past there was a vast network of hidden passages in the castle. She made use of them, moving to look in on the Empress in her chamber, and on Merros Dulver in the rooms he occupied at the castle. He had other properties within the city of Canhoon, but because they were at war, or readying for war, he chose to stay at the castle in a small apartment set aside with his office in the seat of the empire. The castle was vast; there were many rooms that were effectively not used. Those rooms she studied as well as she built her mental map of the entire palace.

She might well continue with such investigations later but for now she stayed in her chamber and practiced throwing punches and kicks as she taught her son the basics of unarmed combat. Valam was learning well, but she corrected the position of his closed fist, making certain that he used the right form for maximum damage to his enemy and also the best way to avoid injuring himself. The body was a glorious weapon, but only effective if used properly.

She was surprised by a knock at the chamber door, as none of her fellow Sa'ba Taalor would bother to do so. They would have called through the closed door.

"Yes?"

"I..." She recognized the voice. "It's Merros Dulver." She felt the nervous flutter that he always brought to her stomach and quelled it.

"You may enter."

Merros opened the door and looked into the room for a moment before he stepped in. His face was impassive, it may as well have been carved from stone, but his eyes betrayed how nervous he was.

It was not Swech who made him uncomfortable, at least not as heavily as Valam, the son he'd never known he had. He looked at the small boy and his eyes shimmered with excitement.

"Hello, Swech. Hello, Valam."

Valam looked at his father with a clinical eye, as if trying to assess his strengths and weaknesses. That was as it should be. They had only met briefly after all. They did not know each other.

"Hello, Father."

Merros had been shocked to know he had a son. Had she told him that on the field of battle she could have struck him down with the mildest of blows as he stared, amazed by the possibility of a son.

This was one of the many differences between their people. In Swech's experience the gods decided who would have children. They had decided it was time for her to carry a child and so she had. She was grateful for the experience, of course, and happy that Merros was the father but before then had never truly considered how important that might be to him. Certainly, she had not sent him a message, or made the child known to him. Their people had been at war, and she had been spying on him when she first discovered she was with child. She had literally been placed in a different body for a time and had been uncertain if she would ever see her old body again or if the gods would allow her child to come into the world. The decision was theirs alone and she was grateful to carry Valam inside her when she was returned to her body but would have understood if they had decided he did not need to live.

She was grateful that Merros was Valam's father, because she had a part of the man she loved to remember him by, but fathers seldom cared for their children in Sa'ba Taalor custom. They might teach a child, they might live with a mate and have children together, but the care of the child was not a consideration.

It simply wasn't their way.

Merros stared at the boy and very nearly trembled.

"How are you this day?"

"Mother is teaching me to use the first weapon of the gods. It is a good lesson to learn."

Merros nodded and smiled. "She is an excellent teacher. Learn your lessons well."

"Did you come here to see your son?" Swech asked. "If you would like, I can leave you alone with him." He was not happy to see her. He was conflicted, and she understood why. The last time they had been together had been a lie. He thought she was someone else, the widow of a man that Swech had killed, a good friend of his who had been in her way when she was trying to escape Fellein after murdering the emperor. They had been together, they had become lovers, and the guilt of sleeping with her had been a sort of torture for Merros.

Swech would never understand the complexities of the emotions the Fellein put themselves through.

"I wanted to see him, yes, but also to see you." The

general's face flushed with red, and he looked at her with that same stony expression.

"What did you wish to say to me, Merros?"

"I'm not really sure, Swech. I don't know how to talk to you."

She tilted her head to the side. "Simply say what you will. They are your words, and I will hear them."

Merros looked down at their son, before continuing in a lower tone, "I'm angry with you."

"I know this. I betrayed you," Swech replied, matching his tone. Although she did not care what the boy heard, it was clear that it was important to the general that this was kept between his parents. "It was what my gods commanded, and as you know, I will always obey my gods."

"So you have said. How can I ever trust you if that is the case?"

"Only you can decide if you will trust me, but I have never lied to you."

"You told me you were Dretta March."

"I had all of her memories and I lived in her body. I *was* Dretta March."

"You were also Swech, but you never told me that."

"You did not ask. If you had, perhaps I would have told you."

"Unless your gods said otherwise."

"Yes. Always the gods are here, with me, Merros. I will never betray them. Not even for you."

"If they told you to kill me?"

"You would be dead."

"If they told you to kill our son?"

"He would die at my hand." Merros stared, his eyes widening. "I have said again and again that the gods rule my life. That does not change. I would never want to hurt you. I would never want to hurt Valam, but the gods command me, and I obey." She felt her eyes sting and forced the notion of tears aside. "I am devoted to my gods, and they have never disappointed that devotion. Not once, not ever."

Merros stared silently and finally nodded. "Be well, Swech." Without another word he looked away from her, stared for three heartbeats at their son and then he left her chambers.

Swech sighed and settled herself on the floor, sitting near her son by Merros. She held up her hands and stared at him. "Hit my palms." His small hands balled into fists, and he struck her open palms with all the strength he could muster. The thick calluses on her hands took the blows easily. "Good. Again." She nodded as he continued his lessons.

Merros Dulver would accept her devotion to the gods, or he would not. She had no control over his actions.

She pushed him from her thoughts as she had so many times before. Not even the gods could know the future. Not all of it. Not all the time. If they did, they could have saved her so much grief.

Once upon a time the gods had claimed that Merros Dulver had an important role to play in their schemes. When Drask Silver Hand first saw the man, he had spoken true words: he had told Merros that he was expected. To this day she did not know why he had been expected.

That was for the gods to know. If they felt that knowledge should be shared with her, they had not yet said so.

All things at the right time.

Drask Silver Hand

The winds of the Blasted Lands roared, spraying sand and grit and ice across the skin of the world. Drask leaned in closer to Brackka and felt the debris of the storm blow across his flesh and the inner eyelids the gods had provided for dealing with the endless storms. Around him several hundred of his people rode toward Paedle, driven by the gods to go to the aid of their kin.

The meeting with Tarag Paedori had gone better than he'd expected. His time among the Fellein might have tinted his perspective. The Fellein and the other peoples he had met across the ocean: the Dunarri; the M'butai, with their odd philosophies and familiar war-like ways; the shape-changing Harrow; and the Somar, all so different from anything he had ever encountered in his homelands or in Fellein. They almost seemed like a distant dream now, but he knew better. They were real and he expected he would see them again when he was done here. For now, however, there was a war to deal with.

Tarag Paedori led a joint force of his own people and the followers of Durhallem. Tuskandru rode to his left and Tarag rode to his right, and they moved through the perpetual storms because, through those endless winds and roaring snow, the Seven Forges were connected. Hundreds of miles became a dozen if one knew how to navigate the Blasted Lands. The Sa'ba Taalor rode through the storms as they always had, enduring the pain of cold, hard winds and ice. It was as the gods demanded and so it was done.

Drask was not a king. He had no desire to be a king. He was merely a follower of all seven gods, and favored among the gods for that reason. Ydramil was the Mirror King, the god of reflection, who sought balance in all things, and Drask, like a few hundred others, sought the same balance. He always had.

The price of forgiveness from Tarag Paedori and Truska-Pren was simple enough. He had to fight with his people against the Overlords and their new War-Born. He did not know what he would be fighting. He did not care. He would gladly join into any combat the gods demanded. He was a warrior first.

Tusk was grinning like a fool, and he held a favored weapon in his right hand, a great blade that seemed a mating of sword and axe. To his other side Stastha rode and grinned just as eagerly. They would soon be at war, killing their enemies and reaping sacrifices for the gods. What could possibly be better?

The forces behind them all rode mounts. Others would come, would find their way through the great storms of the Blasted Lands, but those who had not yet earned the honor of mounts moved at a different pace. They could not hope to keep up with the great beasts. They might well not reach Paedle before the fighting was done.

The War-Born. There were old tales of the creatures, beasts that could change their form, were born and reborn as the Overlords demanded. They were supposed to be horrors in a fight, capable of killing in a thousand different ways.

The thought excited Drask and his brethren. The Fellein might well have been terrified by the thought of the beasts, but the Sa'ba Taalor looked to war as a sign of respect to the gods, an honor.

The Fellein who was adopted by Tarag Paedori, Kallir Lundt of the Iron Face, rode close to the King in Iron. Try though he might to think of the man as a Sa'ba Taalor, he still found himself thinking of him more as a sort of mascot. Still, the Fellein had a sharp mind and a keen sense of his place among the Sa'ba Taalor. Lundt's eyes glowed with the same slivery light as all the Sa'ba Taalor. He was short and lean but rode a mount and carried weapons forged by his own hands. In comparison to most of the people around him he looked like he had only started puberty, but his skin had gone grey, and his hands were scarred and callused as a warrior's should be.

He looked to Drask and nodded silently, as close to a conversation as the two men had managed. In the screaming winds of the storm, it was the best they would manage without bellowing to be heard.

What a strange world they lived in. What a gloriously unusual time they were a part of. Drask found he was smiling now, as they closed in on their destination. He touched the short spear at his side, and then his silver hand drifted over to the heavy sword he so often used when fighting, He remained uncertain which weapon he would use, knowing that his mind would sort out the final choice as soon as he saw his enemy.

The War-Born. In the old tales the gods had shared with him, they were enemies worthy of respect, nightmares that killed and often ate their enemies. How could he not find them fascinating?

He had missed the last war, caught as he was in the designs of the Daxar Taalor. He hoped to earn new scars and kill endless foes in the glory of the gods. He was so very glad that they had called him home. Several of the people he'd met in Fellein would have been horrified by that notion, but they could not understand the concept of enjoying war, of savoring the chaos and the carnage.

The war horns of the King in Iron sounded, barely audible over the screams of the Blasted Lands. Drask's pulse increased, and his hand wrapped around the hilt of his sword.

Beside him Tuskandru leaned forward on his mount, and on his other side Tarag Paedori lowered the visor of his helmet into place, hiding his features behind the likeness of Truska-Pren's iron face.

And a moment later they were out of the raging winds and moving across the land at the edge of Paedle, the land where the enemy was supposed to soon show itself. They moved forward, granting more room to the additional riders, and the horn blowers sounded their presence for all to hear. Almost immediately more horns blasted a reciprocal call from higher up the mountain's slope. The forces waiting on Paedle would be joining them. War was coming and they were as ready as they could be, prepared to fight an enemy they had never seen, regardless of the shape it might take.

The War-Born did not sound horns.

They gave no warning of their presence.

They simply attacked.

Kallir Lundt

The area was very nearly lost in a thick fog. There were shadows of trees nearby, but they were only ghostly images half-obscured by the thick mists. Snow drifted lazily down from above, tainted and gray. Kallir Lundt found himself lost in that fog and simultaneously surrounded by some of the most capable fighters he had met in his entire life. Tarag

Paedori was his friend and mentor, and a terror to watch on the battlefield. Tuskandru was a man that Tarag spoke of with near reverence as a warrior. He had, on several occasions, taken down a Pra-Moresh with one blow.

Now he saw Drask Silver Hand riding on his mount, and couldn't help but stare. The man had bested Tarag Paedori in single combat, had taken down the King in Iron and made it look surprisingly easy. He was also the only man Kallir had ever seen with seven Great Scars, lined up and running in a neat row down his face.

Each god offered a Great Scar to their chosen, those who embodied their beliefs and goals the best. There were only a few people he'd ever seen with more than three of the markings. To have seven was to truly be honored by the gods.

Drask Silver Hand moved differently from others. He had a presence that seemed nearly impossible to define. He was intimidating merely because he had the markings of all the Daxar Taalor. Seven gods favored him, recognized his skills not only as a warrior, but also as someone who understood their ways.

"Can you hear them?" Drask spoke softly, but as he spoke the others quieted down, some obviously listening to his words and others listening for something else.

At first Kallir heard nothing out of the ordinary. The winds blew softly and the few trees that still had foliage sighed in the fog. And then the sounds came, soft clacking noises, like two tree branches bumping each other in the breeze, but there were more of them than should have been possible. Tiny clicks and clacks added up. They grew louder and rose as a wave rises in the ocean.

And then the sound seemed to be everywhere at once, coming from all around them. Shapes danced at the edge of the fog, almost visible and then gone when he tried to spot them properly. Whatever was out there moved in furtive motions and seemed to be the same color as the fog itself.

"They are here!" Drask dropped from his mount's back and held his sword at the ready. The blade was heavy, but he carried it as if it weighed nothing. The others followed suit. The warriors needed to be free to move, to attack without the limitation of riding – and the mounts were more than capable of inflicting damage themselves.

Kallir dismounted, his heart beating faster. He saw nothing.

And then they came from the shroud of mists, great shapes that charged forward, moving in rapid strides even as they attacked. They were not human. They did not ride horses or mounts, but seemed instead to be demons. They had too many legs, bodies that were misshapen. Not as tall as the Sa'ba Taalor, the pale things scuttled forward and raised the great blades of their arms into the air before striking as fast as anything he had ever seen.

Kallir heard himself scream in shock. They were not what he expected. The name War-Born had him thinking of men, of soldiers as well trained as the Sa'ba Taalor. He anticipated a foe of that nature, to have a chance to defend himself from something that made sense – but the War-Born were offensive to his senses.

He had seen spiders before, had watched them with fascination as a child, but had never given them much thought beyond wondering why they had so many limbs. Now these things came for him, moving in ways that defied his senses.

The thing that came his way hacked downward with its arms, and Kallir managed to dance out of the way of those great scythes, avoiding getting cut in two, though it seemed a close thing to him. Now it was closer – too close – Kallir could make out more details. The body of the beast was a bloated mass, two thick segments that swayed over eight long limbs. The legs moved up and down in a sequence that seemed to make no sense to his eyes, and he found himself wanting to stare until he could understand how it moved, the better to predict its next attack. The body rose up in the front, a human torso attached to that bloated form. Where the arms of a man should have been there were instead the two great blades that turned even now to strike at him again. Two natural weapons that seemed as long as his spear. Rather than waiting to see where those blades would strike, Kallir stepped closer, striking with his shield, bashing himself against that obscene body mass, thrusting his spear at the misshapen head of the thing, howling his outrage at the creature as he drove the spearhead into the features.

The tip of the spear slid across the face until it struck one of the oversized eyes, where it dug into the head at last.

The creature let out an obscene shriek and Kallir felt the closest of the sword-like blades clatter down the length of his shield, narrowly missing cutting into his arm as it fell. It might have been injured, but the great thing was not dead and didn't seem much weakened by his attack.

All around him the Sa'ba Taalor were engaging their enemies, fighting forward or in some cases retreating, maneuvering to find better positions to fight. Kallir had no time to consider any of them aside from knowing they were there. The demonic monster was coming for him again, pushing back against his shield, throwing itself toward him with feverish strength that had him sliding across the ground even as he tried to brace himself.

He stabbed forward and into the face of the thing three

more times, the spear scraping against hard, armorlike flesh before puncturing the shell. Its arms rose up and came down, pulling his shield away from his body in one sudden move that left Kallir exposed on his left side. Before he could adjust, one of the organic blades slammed along his breastplate and knocked him backward, scrabbling to keep his balance. Without a doubt, they were stronger than he was, and damned fast.

Rather than risk another direct assault from the thing, Kallir twisted and drove his spear into the chest of the creature, knocking aside the arm that tried to block him and driving the point of his spear deep into the upper belly of the enemy. Once again, the tip skittered across hard armor-like flesh before finding a spot where the armor had a natural fold. Once there his strength was enough to push the tip into the flesh.

There was no chance to celebrate. Even as his spear drove deeper into the beast, one of those insane arms came down, hacking through his breast plate to the meat underneath. Kallir grunted as the serrated edge of the thing sliced into him. It was not a killing blow, but it was painful and messy. His spear struck something vital, yes, but he was deeply wounded in the process.

The spider-thing retreated, screeching, and pulled free of him, leaving a thick trail of Kallir's blood. His own spear seemed to find only clear fluids, which made no sense to him. Was it the beast's blood or something else? He did not know and had no time to consider the mystery before the wounded thing came for him again.

Kallir kicked the thing in the closest leg, driving his heel into the joint of the limb and hearing something crack and splinter under the impact, but the spider-thing had eight legs and the loss of one barely seemed to slow it down. It pushed closer to him and Kallir blocked the next strike with the haft of his spear before turning his body and driving the blade deep into the monster again.

From the corner of his eye, he saw that beside him one of the beasts fell and Tuskandru let out a cry of triumph, his weapon cutting the humanoid torso away from the rest of the creature. It was dead, but the body parts kept spasming even as it collapsed. Tusk stepped in closer and cut one of the arms away from Kallir's enemy even as he continued on to find his own new opponent. Kallir had no idea if the attack was deliberate on Tusk's part or merely an accident as he passed but he was grateful in any event.

The creature teetered as it tried to regain its balance. Kallir drove it backward with his whole body, using the spear as a battering ram of sorts, impaling the hellish thing and shoving it to the ground, his shield already forgotten in the heat of combat.

It went down and Kallir stepped past it, his eyes seeking the next enemy.

They were everywhere, moving over everything, it seemed. One of the Sa'ba Taalor took a double strike to the chest and the scythes of his enemy ran through his body, cutting clear through the man. He did not so much as scream before he fell back, dead.

Kallir took advantage of the moment and rammed the tip of his spear through the neck of the thing with enough force to nearly behead it. He yanked his spear back and spun to the left in time to avoid the next of the beasts as it charged for him.

A woman he did not recognize struck one of the things in the head and caved in its skull even as the beast was moving toward Kallir. He didn't have time to acknowledge her help before the next was on him, hammering down with those double blades that passed for hands, making him dance backward to avoid being cut wide open. The spear jabbed forward but skittered off the natural armor.

To his right, Tarag Paedori hacked through both arms of one of the things that tried to stop his great sword. He slammed his armored form into the monster and sent it backward even as he swept his sword around for another strike. The blade was a terrifying weapon in the giant's hands, and he knew how to use it. He was not as fast as some of the others, but the weapon cleaved his enemies in twain when it landed and the King in Iron knew exactly how to wield his weapon of choice.

Kallir registered more Sa'ba Taalor coming down from the mountainside, riding into the melee with battle cries and horns adding to the sounds of combat. He had to hope that, although the spider-things were everywhere, they didn't outnumber the gray-skins.

Great mounts and their riders descended, the mounts leaping and taking advantage of the height to let them land on the War-Born nightmares, claws rending, teeth biting down even as their riders used spears and lances to further the attacks on the spider-things. The War-Born did not retreat but, when they saw the enemy coming, they chose instead to rear up, lifting half of those oddly bloated bodies into the air and using their forelegs to push back against the descending enemies before striking with their scythe-arms. Some went down in a crash of fury and others struck true, cutting into the sides or bellies of the mounts, wounding in some cases, killing in others.

It was not an easy fight and there was no way to know who might be winning when Kallir was desperate to stay alive himself. They seemed to attack from every direction at once, the legs of the things clattering and clicking as they approached and then crawled over whatever got in their way.

Kallir had trouble catching his breath, keeping his calm as the things continued to press in on him and the surrounding Sa'ba Taalor.

Not far from him, Drask Silver Hand calmly, efficiently, beheaded one of the War-Born. His sword took the thing's head as he slid past, then the weapon arced forward and dug into the chest of the next in line as the man breathed smoothly and struck again.

Tuskandru hopped down on another of the nightmares, his blade carving into the lower part of the humanoid form perched above that bloated spider-like lower body. He ripped the weapon free and struck again in almost the same spot, like a woodsman taking down a tree. He also moved back as the very same creature tried to impale him.

Desta let out a scream as one of the damned things cut along her left arm. Her right hand held a war hammer that pounded through the thing's natural armor and pulped the face of the monster.

Tarag Paedori took longer to strike, but, again, cleanly cut the nightmare he was fighting into two parts.

All this continued around Kallir as he fought his own desperate battles. He rammed his spear into the chest of the beast in front of him, and let out a scream as the staff of his weapon splintered. Enough! He would use his axe; he would kill until all of the damned things were dead and twitching in the dirt.

Four mounts jumped over him, one after the other, leaping high enough to clear even Tarag's great sword before they landed on their enemies, smashing them down with their weight, roaring out battle cries even as their riders did the same. Claws crashed down, teeth slammed around limbs, and weapons drew harsh lines across natural armor.

One of the things struck first, opening a mount from sternum to crotch and was nearly drowned in the viscera that spilled from the wound. The mount let out a small sound and died, collapsing on its enemy, half crushing the thing in its death throes.

Slash, slash, slash. Parry, block, dodge. Kallir ceased any attempts at seeing his surroundings as more of the damnable things came at him in a concentrated attack. There was no time to think, only to react.

His arms were shaking from exertion, but he forced himself to continue, because to do otherwise was a death sentence.

Someone smashed into him from the left and he staggered, confused by the sudden collision. Tarag Paedori moved in close to him, one thick arm reaching past him to grab at something, and then the man was swinging his preposterously large sword, narrowly missing Kallir and hacking into one of the things. The creature shrieked as the sword did its damage; Kallir's axe completed the job.

Another of the Sa'ba Taalor moved past him. At first Kallir thought he was looking at Drask – the man had the same line of Great Scars across his mouth, lined up the same way. Another of the people who followed all seven of the Daxar Taalor.

This one used his hands to pummel one of the War-Born, driving his left fist through the hard carapace of the thing, pounding the creature hard enough to break that natural armor and then grabbing a handful of whatever was inside of it and ripping back, taking meat and entrails with him when he pulled. The creature never even screamed. Before it could, the other hand was driving down, carving a trench through the thing's head.

And then something hit Kallir in the back of his head and he fell, his face slamming into the rocks and soil, a great weight pressing him mercilessly to the ground.

Drask Silver Hand

More war horns, more of the Sa'ba Taalor arriving to fight the War-Born.

Drask welcomed them. There were plenty of the enemy for everyone to fight, and even with his abilities they were a brilliant, beautiful threat. His body ached, his pulse raced, his eyes tried to look everywhere at once, and he was aware in ways that would have baffled most of his people. Whatever the gods had done to him, it let him sense so much more than most did. He could have ended the entire conflict easily, but that was not what the gods wanted. They wanted war. They wanted bloodshed, and so he honored that wish as best he could and fought a mundane battle.

The sword in his left hand cut deep, and his right hand blocked another slicing attack from one of the bladed limbs of the War-Born in front of him. The thing had just landed on Kallir Lundt, slammed him to the ground with ease and one of the creature's arms slashed down at the fallen man even as the other came for Drask himself.

He knocked the blade aside with his silver hand and then stepped in closer to the thing. It focused on him, which was what he wanted. The man on the ground was on his own and looked to be useless for the moment. Perhaps he would recover, perhaps not, but in either event, Drask wanted his enemy's attention.

The fresh wave of Sa'ba Taalor pushed against the constant flow of creatures on the battlefield, driving them back a few paces at a time. Drask grinned and ground his teeth together as the thing fighting against him scuttled in closer and raised both of its blades high into the air.

The sword drove up and into the lower half of the alien face, then into the creature's skull, bringing a quick death before those arms could descend.

Once again, the temptation to use the powers given to him to end the conflict were many, but the gods spoke to him and told him not to. He was born and bred to fight wars, not to end them with a wave of a hand. The gods themselves could have ended the conflict if they desired and he knew that. They wanted blood. They wanted death. They wanted the sacrifices offered with each and every attack, and Drask reveled in that fact.

The gods wanted war and he would give it to them.

And then the interloper showed up and changed everything.

He did not know the man, could not see him under his dark gray robes. The figure seemed to come from nowhere, leaned heavily on a spear he used as a staff, and stared around at the combat as if he had never seen the likes before. He looked in every direction, assessing the situation and then raised the spear high into the air before bringing it down on the hard packed ground, screaming words that Drask could barely hear.

The ground around the newcomer shivered for a moment and then shook harder, hard enough for lines of the earth around him to break into smaller pieces. All around him the Sa'ba Taalor fell. The vibrations were too strong and threw the people of the forges roughly as if they were struck by a sudden tide. As large a man as he was, Drask was cast aside just as easily and fell to the ground even as the spider-things with their squat bodies and multiple legs compensated for the same wave of force.

As one the War-Born turned back the way they had come, scurrying across the shaking ground. Several of the things moved over Drask, surely would have had him at a disadvantage had they been attacking at that moment, and retreated.

Drask scarcely paid them any heed. He stared at the cloaked form instead.

Without another word, the shape under that cloak turned and took three paces in the same direction as the War-Born. Drask rose to his feet, balancing himself carefully, and reached for the shape.

It vanished before he could finish raising his hand. One moment it was there and the next it seemed to fold in on itself and was gone.

All around him the Sa'ba Taalor climbed back to their standing positions.

The things they had been fighting were too fast to allow pursuit. They moved too quickly for the escape to be completely natural.

Not far away Tarag Paedori cursed and spat.

Even closer in, Tusk shook his head and said, "They run faster than the Fellein."

Kallir Lundt rose more slowly than the rest, it seemed, a deep gash running from his right shoulder down to his left hip. He stood unevenly and staggered to the side before collapsing to the ground. A moment later Tarag Paedori was at the man's side and pulling iron from a pouch at his waist, praying to Truska-Pren even as he laid the metal against the wound. Iron flowed like water into the gash, burning brightly as it cauterized flesh and sealed the massive slash. Kallir Lundt thrashed, his hands digging at the rough soil, but he did not scream despite the very obvious pain.

That was good. He honored his king and his god with his silence. Flesh burned and in seconds the metal cooled off and began to change, becoming flesh and leaving a scar that would be impossible for anyone to ignore. Truly the gods could be kind.

All around him the people of the forges tended to their wounded, some using metal to heal serious wounds and others cleaning the damaged areas using more mundane methods.

"What was that?" Tuskandru stood next to him and scowled at the spot where the robed man had been.

"A sorcerer."

Tusk shook his head and scowled. "This is not the way to fight a war."

"They want to win. They were not winning."

"They were not losing, either." Tusk spoke with an edge of admiration in his voice. "They fought well."

Drask nodded. "Perhaps they were testing the waters. It is said the War-Born changed shapes in the past. Maybe they will come back with even deadlier forms."

Above them the volcano roared, and the skies grew bloodier as the flames within Paedle surged. Drask looked at the mountain and considered the sound. Paedle was not pleased. The battle had ended before it should have, and the god wanted war.

CHAPTER FIVE

Whistler

The activity in the area told Whistler what he needed to know. The camp was about to become a settlement. The land had changed overnight and the mountain that had risen was gone, replaced by rich, dark soil. He was not a farmer, had no interest in becoming one, but if he were interested, he guessed this would be exactly the right sort of place to establish a farm.

The air around him smelled of promise. Even with his minimal knowledge of what made a place good for farming, he would have been able to sense the changes in the ground. The fact that everyone around him was speaking about the soil and the promise of good crops merely cemented what he already believed. The land had been made over, by the gods, perhaps, or by sorcery. He did not know and did not care.

The people around him understood that the world was being changed. He only understood that the creatures who had saved him were annoyed by the transformation. He could hear that much through the voices in his head.

"Why am I still here?" He spoke aloud and ignored the

sounds of activity around him as easily as he ignored the people who stared at his ruined face.

The smile that stretched his features was uncomfortable, and his eyes twitched in the glare of the day. Whistler stared back at a man who was staring at him until the man grew uncomfortable. He was contemplating whether or not he should kill the bastard when the voices responded. "You will leave here soon, Whistler. The man you watch for will be leaving here soon."

The man he watched for. Darsken Murdro. The Inquisitor. That thought elicited another chuckle from him. The very thought that he would ever willingly pursue an Inquisitor was like the start of a good jest in his eyes. He wasn't sure how the jest was supposed to end as yet, but he'd find out in time.

For now, he watched the construction going on around him. Tents were being replaced by more permanent structures. Soldiers were moving into the area, and he knew why. Farming was a business and the Empress of Fellein wanted to make certain the businesses were properly handled.

Darsken Murdro stepped out of a tent and held the opening for a woman who was striking enough to catch Whistler's eye. He moved back into the shadows without even thinking. He wasn't wanted by the Inquisitor, but the ruin of his face meant that he stood out now and he would be remembered if he were spotted. If he needed to follow the man, he did not want to be recognized easily.

Better to move in the shadows, to let others stand between him and his prey.

Better not to be seen, or at least not recognized.

He had never been the sort to hide his face away, but

Whistler was wise enough to know that had to change. As the Inquisitor and his female companion moved on, Whistler raised the hood of his new cloak and followed.

All around him activity continued. A town was being born before his eyes. He did not care. It was not a place where he would be living, and so it mattered very little to him. Whistler was a man who believed in the immediate. The future, whatever it might bring, was a problem for later.

He could not hear the words of Darsken Murdro, or the woman who walked beside him. They were too far away. Whatever the Inquisitor, said, however, was enough to elicit a laugh from the woman beside him.

The winds howled along the Wellish Steppes and rustled the canvas of several tents. A man nearby let out a gasp as the cold caught him and blew his cloak open. Whistler nodded amiably as the man looked his way then scowled as the stranger reacted to a better look at his face.

He'd have killed the bastard, but the Inquisitor was too close by, and like all of his type actually paid careful attention to his surroundings. Better not to risk catching the attention of an Inquisitor under any circumstances even if all he wanted to do was express his rage and anger.

Around him a hundred people moved in different directions as the sun descended in the west. A town was being born. An Inquisitor was still walking with a beautiful woman, and all Whistler could do was watch it all, dampening down his powerful desire to hurt all of them. He wanted to make them suffer for his misfortune. He wanted to carve away the faces of anyone who looked at him and cringed – and he knew that was most of the people.

Soon enough. That thought brought another smile to his face. They would pay soon enough.

Distracted by the thought, he almost failed to notice as a man who was fast with his fingers tried to cut the ties to his purse. Whistler barely felt the touch, but he did feel it and that was enough.

For that moment he forgot about Darsken Murdro of the Inquisition and focused instead on the petty thief whose wrist he had taken in a grip so tight the man must believe it was caught within the fires of one of the Seven Forges.

Whistler did not give the man a chance to scream before he killed him. Much as he loved the sound of a good scream, it was true, there were too many people moving in the dusk. His pleasure would have to be taken swiftly. But taken it would be.

The new smile on Whistler's face did not improve his grotesque features.

Darsken Murdro

Tataya laughed once more and rested her long, delicate fingers on his arm. Darsken smiled and let himself chuckle. The Sisters were witty and charming, and he did his best to keep up with them when it came to banter. It was not an easy thing for him. He spent most of his time on any given day seeking truths and, as often as not, killers. Humor and charm were not a part of his regular world.

But the Sisters gave him reason to try, just the same. They reminded him that there were people in the world who did not have to be questioned, who could be trusted to a degree he sometimes forgot existed. The biggest problem with being an Inquisitor was simply that he spent most of his time doubting everyone around him.

"I am looking forward to getting back to Canhoon." Darsken's eyes shifted around the area and he studied the faces moving past him. Some were eager with the promise of new things. It hadn't taken long before the word of the changes in the area became common knowledge and with the news came that most elusive of all things, hope. Winter was well and truly upon the land and the snows were starting to fall, but eventually the cold would fade away and lead to the promise of ripe, fertile lands. With most of the area open and inviting, entire families were arriving, eager to claim the properties that Empress Nachia was already promising to new claimants.

"Do you think Jeron will return to the city?" Tataya asked, matching Darsken's newly serious mood.

"I think Jeron will do what he can to disrupt everything Fellein wants left in peace," Darsken said. "I think he will do whatever he can to make certain these Overlords get their way. But I have to return to Canhoon to see what, if anything, the Inquisition plans to do about him."

"Do you think you can find him?"

"I don't even know if I will be asked to pursue him, Tataya," Darsken pointed out. "We Inquisitors do as we are told when it comes to hunting down murderers, but this is an unusual circumstance, and one very likely left to your people and not mine."

Tataya's smooth brow grew troubled. "Because he is a wizard?"

"Just so. Neither I nor any of the other Inquisitors is ready to take on a sorcerer. We do not have the powers to defend ourselves, to say nothing of attacking an adept wizard."

"I don't know of many who are capable of handling someone of his skill levels." Her eyes drifted around the area, studying faces just as he had been doing. "Jeron is powerful, more powerful than he should be if he is raising mountains."

"Perhaps it was these Overlords who created the mountain." Darsken frowned. "I do not understand who changed the mountain however, and decided to benefit the empire in the process."

Tataya smiled. "Someone with a love of plants? The soil is very fertile. Plants are already taking root, and the cold is enough to stop almost anything, but the scrub grass and weeds of the area are hearty stock and quickly thriving in this rich earth."

"And all of these people want to farm the land?"

"All of the people coming here are looking for a better life," Tataya corrected. "They are hoping for a chance to improve their circumstances."

"We would all like to improve ourselves, I think."

"Well, yes, I suppose that is true. But the chance to own land is a rare thing, and the Empress is offering the land for free."

"The Empress is offering a chance to earn the land through hard labor," Darsken corrected in his turn. "The farmers must pay higher taxes, yes?"

"I studied sorcery, not math, but yes. The land is paid overtime from higher taxes and people are pleased with the notion."

Darsken nodded again and paid attention to three figures moving behind them. All were half-buried in shadows, and heading in the same direction as he and Tataya. It was his nature to be suspicious, and perhaps all of them were merely moving along the same stretch of open path, but it seemed odd that they moved at the same relative speed.

"I think we are being followed."

"I think the same thing, Darsken. Do you have anything else you need to retrieve before you leave this area?"

"I carry all that I need on my person."

"Then we shall leave anyone following us behind." She had a teasing smile on her face. Her hand pressed on his arm and urged him to the left and, being an agreeable sort, he moved to the left. They slipped behind a wooden structure that was halfway finished and a second later the world around him twisted and warped.

And two heartbeats later, they were walking in the Imperial Gardens at the edge of the palace in Canhoon.

If anyone had been following them, they currently followed little but shadows.

Tataya let out a small laugh and Darsken, who was used to traveling quickly along the pathways offered by the Shimmer, let out a gasp and then laughed along with her. His stomach felt as if he were falling from a great height, but the rest of his senses understood that they had stepped away from the world for a moment, and then had reentered that world in a different spot. How long since he had genuinely been surprised by anyone? He could not say, but the wonder of the moment filled him with child-like awe.

"That was spectacular!"

"I'm glad you approve." Her eyes were momentarily unfocused, and he wondered how much that leap through space had cost her. Sorcery had a price, as she had told him more than once, and to travel so many leagues in an instant had to carry a large price indeed.

"Are you well, Tataya?"

"I'm as good as can be expected." Her smile was as bright

as ever. "But now I should head back to Desh with the latest news."

"And I should report to the Inquisition."

"Be safe, my friend. These are dark times." Her expression changed as completely as their surroundings had changed. Her concern was real and obvious.

"On this we agree." He nodded. "And I must insist on seeing you safely to your home. It is on my way."

"I can hardly turn down the offer of good company on a cold, dark night." Her tone lightened as she spoke, and Darsken smiled. The walk was brief, and the company was pleasant. It would be the last light moment the Inquisitor knew for a while.

Desh Krohan

The Sooth were not responsive, and even when they finally answered his questions, the words were vague and, he suspected, actually lies.

The world was not cooperating, and that annoyed him a great deal. He held ten small stones in his hands, spell stones that he had put a great deal of time and energy into. They were all that stood between him and exhaustion as he sought the answers to questions again and again.

"Are you well?" Goriah asked as he left his summoning room.

"Not in the least. The Sooth are being stubborn."

"What was it you always said to me? 'The Sooth are only stubborn if you ask the wrong questions'?"

"Obviously I was mistaken."

"How refreshing. Desh Krohan admits he can make

mistakes." Even as she said the words, she handed him a heavy ceramic bowl of clear broth. He took it gratefully and sat down at the table where he and the Sisters often ate.

"I'm hardly without flaw, Goriah. I just like to keep the worst of my bad habits to myself." He blew on the broth and then picked up a spoon. The steam rising from the bowl was aromatic and made his stomach grumble. He had forgotten to eat again, a common problem when he was looking for knowledge – and he was always looking for knowledge. "Have we heard any news on the Overlords?"

"Nothing good. There have been attacks on several towns in Morwhen. There have also been very few survivors."

"Why Morwhen? What is going on in that country that makes it a target of the Overlords?"

"Near as we can tell, that seems to be where most of their warriors were living. These stories of the Tolfah. The creatures that haunted the Dark Passage." Goriah frowned. "Desh, you already know this."

He waved her words aside and took another spoonful of the broth, grateful for the taste and the nutrients alike. "I am entitled to be absentminded after all of these years, Goriah."

"I worry about you, Desh. You've been very distracted lately."

"I'm trying to keep an empire from falling apart." He took more broth and then sighed. "It takes a great deal of my concentration."

"The empire will survive, my friend."

"Not without a great deal of work on my part, and on yours."

"Tataya has come back with news. It seems very likely that Jeron is behind whatever is happening."

Desh closed his eyes and considered that fact for a moment.

He had known Jeron for centuries, had considered the man a good friend at one point, and even now he wanted to think of the man as an ally – but that was looking less likely all the time.

"I think we'd have been better off if he'd died in that damned fire." His brows pulled down and his face settled into a scowl that was becoming far too common. "If Jeron is using necromancy, we have a serious problem on our hands."

"How so?"

"Jeron has always longed for the easy answer. Necromancy is easy. It grants power with remarkably little effort."

"How can he know necromancy? It's been forbidden for centuries."

"Jeron was one of the first necromancers." He put down the spoon and finished off the bowl of broth before continuing. "Believe me, he was very resistant to the notion of outlawing the art. He had ways of dealing with the dead that were outrageous long before I arranged to banish the school from the records, and I suspect I would have found several volumes of research on the best ways to feed on the dead if I'd ever gone to that tower of his."

"Is that why you didn't go?"

"No. I wasn't invited. We'd been very close before I outlawed necromancy. I don't think he ever quite forgave me."

"He never seemed that bitter about it."

"Jeron was always good at masking his darker emotions." Desh leaned back in his seat and Goriah snatched up his bowl, pouring more of the broth and setting it down in front of him. "Thank you." His eyes looked into the bowl, at his distorted reflection. "Jeron is a very serious threat. He's a threat I need to take care of personally, frankly. He's too powerful to be left to soldiers, and he's too good at what he does to be left alone. If he is behind the work of the Overlords then we have a very serious problem on our hands, and one that scares me."

"You're scared of Jeron?"

"No. I'm scared of what he'll do if he's left alone. If he no longer follows the rules established by the council, he could cause a great deal of damage in a very short amount of time. If he is doing the work of the Overlords, then they might well be encouraging his worst habits."

"I have found very little information on these Overlords."

"That's because we didn't know all that much about them. They arrived in Fellein in the early days, they established themselves peacefully in the Wellish Steppes, and then, when we very nearly forgot about them, they attacked. Their armies were not human. They corrupted everything they ran across, Goriah. The people who served them were bent out of shape, broken and twisted until they no longer looked human, and the armies they raised slaughtered everyone they encountered. They did not leave survivors. Mercy was not a concept they even considered."

Goriah stared at him in silence for several seconds and then asked, "When did you start remembering all of this, Desh?"

"I have read over my old notes. They were enough to remind me that the Overlords were a very real threat. To this day I'm not certain why they retreated."

"The Sa'ba Taalor tell stories of them. I've asked Swech and some of her people about them."

"Well, then maybe they can handle the situation for us."

"According to what we know, they have already had a few encounters with these War-Born."

"And?"

"So far there are no clear winners."

"You heard about Merros and the mercenaries?"

"Oh yes. I heard about the number of mercenaries who died horribly, too." Goriah shook her head. "Only a fool would charge down into a combat with the Sa'ba Taalor."

"To be fair, they were expecting Fellein soldiers."

"Well, there is that."

Desh grinned. "I imagine that's rather like expecting a few alley cats and encountering a pack of wolves."

"Have you ever crossed a feral alley cat? Not a wise move."

"And yet less likely to be fatal than the wolves, my dear."

"True, but days could be spent tending those wounds." She pushed his bowl closer. "Eat before it gets cold."

"I think I'll need something with more substance."

"You'll have it, but drink the broth first." He nodded and took a spoonful of the stuff, grateful for the Sisters who reminded him to eat and tended to his needs.

"I don't know how this will end, Goriah, and that bothers me."

"You never know how things will turn out, Desh, despite your beliefs."

"I can usually make a fairly accurate guess, but not in this case. The Overlords have been gone too long, the Sa'ba Taalor who follow them are an unknown variable, the Sa'ba Taalor who are aligning themselves with us are too unpredictable, and the Fellein armies, while vast, have to spread out over too large an area for us to quickly assemble any large-scale fighting forces. Until we know more about what the Overlords have planned, we are effectively moving around a campsite without any supplies."

"We need to find Jeron."

"No, my dear, I need to eliminate him." He sighed. "He cannot be allowed to break the rules of sorcerous engagement so causally."

"He doesn't seem to care about the rules at all," Goriah sighed too and brought a tray of meats and cheeses into the room from where she had likely prepared them while he was trying to find answers to his many questions. Desh's stomach made rude noises as he stared at the platter, and he once again lifted the bowl of broth to his lips and drank down the nearly scalding liquid. There was a selection of sliced breads on the platter and Desh took full advantage.

"Jeron is a dangerous enemy to have, Goriah. If there is any news about where he is, I need to know *immediately*. I cannot risk him being out there any longer than necessary."

"The moment I hear anything, I'll let you know."

For a time that would have to be enough. He needed to find Jeron. He needed to eliminate a threat that very few people could comprehend because they had never known a true fight between sorcerers.

But, for the moment, Desh needed to eat and that was what he focused on.

Jeron

The cold barely fazed Jeron, but beside him Roledru was shivering.

"What's wrong?"

"It's winter. I need a thicker cloak." The man's teeth were chattering.

Jeron reached out and touched the cloak around his assistant's shoulders and immediately the man's face changed to a smile of gratitude. There was a faint distortion where the air around the man grew warmer. It was a simple enchantment that he would have never considered before the Overlords granted him power. The math was quite simple: the Overlords made it easier for him to use sorcery. There was still a cost, but a simple enchantment that would have exhausted him before, like the one he had just used, seemed nearly effortless in comparison.

"That's amazing. Thank you, Jeron."

"For all you do for me, my friend, it is my pleasure." And it was, but still he considered the ease of the spell and was pleased. Desh Krohan's limitations on sorcery had nearly crippled him for years and he hadn't even realised until now.

The Overlords took a great deal of power. Every death their War-Born caused was siphoning the life force of the victims, drawing it into their bodies and from them, through their Godless generals, through Jeron himself and finally to the masters of this new changing world, the Overlords.

It was not an easy process, and it was hardly the most efficient. The paths the energies took likely left a lot of those precious energies dispersed into the universe, but there was power to be had and Jeron was getting a good enough portion of it along the way. In the process he was growing more powerful than he had ever been, than he could imagine any sorcerer being.

All of which was a nice way of realizing that destroying Desh Krohan would be easy when the time came, and he knew the time would soon be upon him. Jeron was many things now, but he was never, and would never be, a fool.

"Sooner or later Desh Krohan will learn that I'm behind everything happening here. When that happens, he will come after me, Roledru."

The man stared at him with wide eyes. To Roledru, to most people, Desh Krohan was a nearly legendary figure. Either he was so far removed from their lives that he was little more than a name, or he was the source of nightmares. Roledru had seen the man, had been witness to the destruction of the army of the dead that Desh Krohan accomplished in one masterful stroke.

Jeron frowned at that memory. How long had the First Advisor been preparing himself for casting a spell that powerful? The energies used to destroy that army must have been massive. There had been the odd time when Jeron had possibly had enough stored energies to destroy an army, but seldom. That sort of energy required months or even years' worth of spell stones collected and gathered into one place.

"He's a dangerous enemy."

"I can't even imagine." Roledru shivered. "When he destroyed the army, I saw the lightning come down from the skies and burn everything. I thought I'd be blind for the rest of my life."

"So you've said." He nodded. "It must have been an amazing spectacle."

Roledru ignored the comment. "The sound," he continued. "I thought the world would end."

"When the time comes, I'll have to strike fast and hard."

"Do you really feel like you can best him, Jeron?"

"I assure you, I'm at least as powerful as Desh Krohan. He is a potent opponent, but I have been changed by the Overlords, made stronger than I have ever been before." He would not have to save the energies that Desh would have to save. He was powered by godlike beings. He no longer had to play by the old fool's rules, not ever again.

"Will you wait for him to find you? Or will you look for him?"

"I think it might be best to find him, my friend. Better by far to choose the time and place." He considered the Sisters and nodded. He could take Desh Krohan by himself, but the notion of fighting the four of them together did not sit at all well. Besides, it would be possible to recruit them to his side if he was careful. Better to have the Sisters with him than against him.

The winds roared around them and he blocked them with a simple enchantment, pushed them away.

Not far away he could see the tents of the Godless. Winter was truly upon them and he was grateful for the Sa'ba Taalor that had aligned themselves to his cause. They did not cry over the cold weather. They did not complain about sending the War-Born back into the sleeping stage, where they were even now becoming different creatures, better prepared for the winter weather.

He looked into the darkness, studied the shapes of the War-Born in their cocoons, and smiled to himself.

Soon enough the creatures would emerge once more, altered by his will and the power of the Overlords. They had been a threat before, but now they would be so much greater at stalking their prey.

Roledru spoke, but Jeron didn't hear the words. He asked the man to repeat himself.

"I said I think the Dark Passage will be buried in snow if we're not careful."

"Let the snows come. I'll drive them away."

"Shouldn't you be saving your sorcery for Desh Krohan?"

"No." He smiled again and shook his head. "You worry too much. The Overlords have been preparing for this for hundreds of years. Nothing is being left to chance, my friend. We will win over the First Advisor with ease, and the War-Born will destroy Morwhen."

"Why here? Why Morwhen?"

"Because these are the best that Fellein has to offer when it comes to soldiers. When they fall, Fellein will fall as well." A lie, but not one that Roledru could know. In fact, he'd chosen Morwhen because that was where he'd been born, oh so very long ago. He wanted to remove the memories of his youth, and the people he had known back then. They were all long in the dust, but he hated them still.

"What about the Sa'ba Taalor?"

"They will be elsewhere. I've arranged a proper distraction for them." Jeron smiled at that thought. There were more of the War-Born than Roledru understood, and they were clay to be sculpted, formed and shaped and made all the more dangerous.

"When will you attack, Jeron?"

Jeron looked up into the skies where snow fell lazily toward the ground, and smiled as the cold air caressed his face. "Within the hour. All is finally ready."

Asher

Surviving the Dark Passage had been a blessing, Asher supposed, but considering how much of his crop he'd lost, it hardly seemed that way. A year's worth of farming and he'd be truly blessed if he could break even after the Tolfah had attacked.

The one thing that worked in his favor was simply that there weren't that many farmers growing Pabba fruit. The cost would be much higher now for anyone who wanted some of the already rare treat.

Daken Hardesty was once again leading the mercenaries who would travel with him. They were still considering the best path to Lake Gerheim and Goltha. The river route or the ocean – each still had their advantages and their pitfalls. The Sa'ba Taalor were everywhere in the area, and though they were in abundance, none of them had caused any actual troubles as yet. If anything, their presence was actually beneficial. They had battled some sort of monstrous things on the Dark Passage, from what he was hearing. Something worse than the Tolfah. That was a thought that offered little comfort.

"What do you say, Asher? Which way do we turn the caravan?" Daken was as patient as he could be, but the day was not growing longer, and they wanted to be a fair distance away from the area before the Tolfah roused from their slumbers. There were fewer reports of the beast-men of late but that didn't mean the area was clean of them. It simply meant they'd fed on his Pabba fruit enough to sate their limitless appetites, he supposed.

"The ocean paths are blocked by the gray skins." Asher sighed. "But there are worse things on the Dark Passage. So we go for the ocean and take the extra time."

Daken nodded. "That's wise. The Sa'ba Taalor can be reasoned with."

Asher snorted, but nodded as well. "Aye. One supposes."

Daken called out to his men, and they formed a rough line on either side of the wagons. The mercenaries were more seasoned this time around. Not a one of them young enough to avoid shaving. This was a serious business, and it was the difference between whether or not Asher survived the winter with any fortune worth noticing. They'd be paid handsomely but, chances were, each one of them would earn that pay.

With a nod, Daken moved forward and the mercenaries followed. The wagon drivers did their part and the whole train of them headed out, traveling east toward the ocean harbors in Danaher and the ships that would take them the long way around to the capital city.

The snows were growing worse, and Asher pulled his cloak in closer, trying to preserve as much body heat as he could. Heavy blankets covered the horses, keeping them safe from the worst of the elements. He had never travelled this late in the season before and hoped to avoid doing it again.

Daken rode on, unimpressed by the weather. He was a soldier and had been stuck in far worse situations, Asher supposed.

That was far enough away to avoid the nightmares that came to Morwhen while they were gone.

Sometimes the gods are kind.

Mallifex Krous

In Darrow, the capital of Morwhen, Mallifex Krous looked upon his father's likeness and scowled. Theorio Krous had been a hard man and, even years after his death, Mal found he could not mourn him with any sincerity.

He sat on the throne and considered what to write to his distant cousin, the Empress of Fellein. Much as he hated to ask for help, it looked like Morwhen would need to beg a favor. The only good news on that front was that his father had answered the call to war during the battles with the Sa'ba Taalor, and now he could expect a proper response to his requests.

He was a king. He ruled the country as fairly as he could, while asking as much as he could of the citizens who lived there. The armies were vast, the soldiers well-trained and ready for any event that might come their way. In all of Fellein there were none better prepared for war.

Dester, his best friend, and the man he trusted most in the world, stood nearby, reading over his shoulder. "Maybe try not to sound so much like your father."

"Alright. Who should I sound like?"

"Try sounding like you, Mal. You're actually very eloquent when you want to be, and your cousin likes you."

"My cousin barely knows me."

"She knows you better than you think. It's part of her duty as Empress to know what you are doing and what you are capable of."

"The last time I saw her was when we were celebrating Pathra's birthday." He sighed. "I think I was ten or so."

"Well, you must have made a good impression. She's spoken of you several times and always favorably."

"How would you know that?"

"I have spies everywhere." Mal wished the man was joking but knew better.

"Why do we need spies?"

"For moments like now. To make sure we know who we can count on when the time comes to borrow favor."

"And there's the problem. Why must we borrow anything?"

"Soldiers insist on being paid and you do insist on having the largest army in the empire."

"It's tradition."

"I'm not saying it's a bad thing, Mal, but it works better if there's a war going on."

"Wars cost even more money."

"Not if you win them." Dester sighed and poured them both a glass of sweet ale. He drank too much. They both did. It was a fault Mal needed to remedy and he damned well knew it.

"Highness. My king, we are attacked!" Drosmod was the bearer of bad news, as was often the case. The man had served his father and grandfather before him, and while he looked his years, he was still able bodied and sharp of mind.

"What are you on about?"

"We are attacked." The old man looked genuinely worried, which didn't happen very often.

"Where?"

"Here. My lord, in the city."

"By whom?" Dester fairly growled the words.

"We don't know. Whoever they are, they come out of the storms and disappear as quickly back into them." The man stomped closer, entering the chambers proper instead of talking from the doorway. Mal was reminded of exactly how tall the man was, and how short the man made him feel. "They are taking the people they've slaughtered. They are stealing bodies, rather than let them die in peace."

"Savages."

"Or worse." The old man shook his head. "What sort of man takes the bodies of the dead?"

"I'd rather not find out. Call on the City Guard to back up the army. Sound the alarms and seal the city down. I want the gates closed against further forces."

Drosmod nodded. The likelihood was that everything he'd just commanded had already been done, but the man was wise enough not to mention that fact. A king likes to feel useful, even to the man who had handled most of his training.

Out in the streets of Darrow, alarm bells began to ring. The soldiers would be called into battle formation, the great gates to the barrier walls of the city would be sealed, and the people would prepare for whatever came their way. Morwhen was a land where warfare was a way of life, and that would likely never change.

"If it's time for battle, let's be about it." Mal shook his head and called to his valets. He had armor to wear, and it was far too much to put in place without assistance.

Soon enough he was mounting his horse and preparing for battle. He did not revel in war as his father had, but he was ready for it. At least he thought he was. This would be the first real battle he had ever been in and all the training in the world hardly made a difference when the enemy was upon a fighter.

By the time he left the stables with his entourage, battles were already happening in what seemed every possible direction. Reports came in from the riverside, where a full battalion of cavalry had ridden out and not returned. Several horses had found their way back to the stables, but they did so without riders.

To the west of town a massacre had taken place near the orchards. Several farmers were taken from their land, and while there was blood aplenty, there were no bodies to find. Not a one; only destruction in the form of ruined doors and overturned furniture.

In the barren slums in the south the locals were fighting

against whatever it was that attacked them, but it was a disorganized mess, and the soldiers who came into the area to add protection arrived too late. That did not stop more battles from commencing however, as whatever it was that attacked the people in their modest homes and apartments once again took the bodies of every single person they defeated and either had no losses or took their own fallen as well.

Mal rode north, to the battlefields that had long stood as the marker of Morwhen's royal families. The finest soldiers in the land had trained there, and the area was open and held few secrets. Best to be able to see the enemy when they arrived, best to fight them where the advantage of surprise simply did not exist.

Snow fell heavily over the area, deep enough already to reach the knees of the horses. Deep enough to limit the benefits of riding as opposed to walking. A stuck horse was at least as bad as standing in the drifts, but it was not quite deep enough to make him want to dismount. Here the horses still offered speed and mobility over the foot soldiers who followed behind. He could see the men wading through the snow and was grateful for his ride.

If he were truly lucky, the enemy would be on foot.

Dester rode beside him, directly behind the flagbearer leading the way. He stopped, stood straight in the saddle, his dark eyes studying the area around them. "I see no one."

Drosmod spoke up. "From what I've heard, no one sees an enemy until it is too late."

Mal said, "You are hardly adding to my comfort."

"Live through this, my king, and I will have done my duty."

The sounds that came from the north were as chilling as

the weather itself. Hissing noises slid from several different areas in the vast field where soldiers stood, ready for conflict. It was a sound like a hundred whispers, or a strong breeze blowing through autumn leaves.

The sound grew until it was nearly all that could be heard. The roar of the wind was nearly deafening – and unsettling as there was nary a breeze to be felt.

Mal sat straighter in his saddle and urged his horse to remain calm when it danced skittishly.

He raised his voice to be heard over the cacophony. "What in the name of the gods?" Halfway through his question the noise abruptly ceased, and he was yelling over silence.

Dester shook his head and stared out into the fields. The sun was close to setting now and Mal felt a deep dread settle into the center of his chest.

"I think I see something." Dester squinted. "I can't be certain."

"Where?"

"To the left, maybe twenty yards out." He pointed as he spoke and Mal followed the tip of his finger. He saw nothing but snow.

"There's nothing out there, Dester, not that I can see." But even as he spoke, something moved to the right of him, ahead of them in the field. He did not see what moved but there was a wake in the snow, a sense of motion.

"Wait…" Drosmod stared into the distance. "No, there is definitely something."

The creatures came charging across the snow, running on the top of the heavy drifts, sending small sprays with every step. Whatever they were, they were the same color as the snow.

They were also very, very fast. By the time Mal could see that there were dozens of the things, it was too late to do more than call out a warning. The first of them to reach him swatted Mal hard enough to knock him from his saddle and send him sailing.

The impact was soft, he landed in snow.

The creature that immediately attacked him was ferocious and sported thick claws at the ends of very wide feet. It was lean and hard, covered in white fur and very nearly seemed made of teeth. Mal pulled his dagger from the sheath at his waist and crawled backward in the deep snow, trying to stab at his enemy. To block the teeth that lunged and snapped and–

The teeth clamped down on his left hand and tore three fingers away. For one heartbeat Mal stared in disbelief, and then the pain ripped through him, a wall of agony that smashed into him and stole away all thought, replaced it with a blind wave of panic.

He stabbed at the thing's head again and again, and the teeth lunged forward in a face that would haunt his memories for as long as he lived. Which he suspected might not be that long.

Not a dozen feet away from him, Dester fell back into the snow, his fists beating at the thing trying to chew through his defenses and rip away his face.

And then Drosmod was striking at the beast trying to kill his ruler. Mal had no idea how the old man got off his horse and moved to defend him so quickly. One second he was lost in a world of pain, wailing out his agony as blood spilled freely from his fingers, the next the head of the thing attacking him hung sideways from a deep wound to the neck. Drosmod's axe dripped blood as he shifted his body to attack another nightmare that came for his king.

Mal felt the hot breath of the next creature as it landed on his legs and scurried forward, eager to tear his throat out. And then the world went truly mad. A hand clutched at his head, fingers dug at his hair and the monstrous face before him vanished in an instant.

Nachia Krous

The great hall was filled with dignitaries and royalty from half the empire. Again. Figures she knew all too well moved about in small islands of conversation, discussing the mundane and the recent events that kept the busiest tongues in the empire wagging on about every possible danger that could be faced. Lanaie, the queen of Roathes, held on to Brolley's arm and the two of them smiled as if the entire affair was designed just to help them look like a perfect couple. Several of the most powerful men in the military moved about in their dress uniforms and made certain that they carried themselves like officers, fully aware that Merros Dulver was watching all of them.

Oh, how she hated these social events. There was a time when she had fairly well lived for the moments of social gathering, but those days ended shortly after she ascended to the throne. All of the fun had been drawn from gathering with her friends when they were replaced by dignitaries or, as had happened lately, by suitors.

Desh Krohan insisted that she needed to have an heir and to that end he continued sending her as many possible suitors as he could find in all of Fellein. Nachia tolerated the influx, but she did not enjoy them.

Most of them were as exciting as watching wine ferment.

Still, some of them were at least handsome, and others were unintentionally amusing.

Currently the crop of would-be husbands around her were doing their best to keep her attention and they were, universally, failing. She had an empire to run. To that end she was discussing matters of import with Merros Dulver and completely ignoring the attempts of Kerris Hopgood to regale her with tales of his adventures during the war with the Sa'ba Taalor. The man was doing his best to talk of his battles with the people of the forges while actively trying to ignore Swech and her entourage only a dozen feet away.

For her part Swech seemed to completely ignore all the suitors, including the ones who looked at her and the people with her as if they were exotic animals on display. In all her years, Nachia had never met a woman who made that feat look as easy.

"There's not much to tell, Majesty." Merros stood next to the throne and conversed with her in soft tones. "We have no idea where this sorcerer, Jeron, might be, and all of the efforts by Desh Krohan and his wizards have failed to turn up a sign of him."

"If he's declared war on the empire, he'll show up eventually. Pathra always said troublemakers never stay away for long. It's against their nature."

"Your cousin was a wise emperor."

"He was a man who preferred to avoid troubles."

"Like I said, wise." Merros smiled as he spoke, and his face seemed younger.

There was no sudden fanfare. There was simply, suddenly, the presence of the man who stood before the throne and Nachia alike. He was tall in his drab brown, hooded cloak and he immediately made her think of Desh Krohan, simply because virtually all of him was hidden away in the dark robes he wore.

On the ground at his feet was the king of Morwhen, her cousin, Mallifex Krous. She recognized his face despite their years apart. He was unconscious and bleeding on the marble floor.

"What is this?" It was all she could think to say.

Merros moved forward, hand at the hilt of his sword, and stepped between her and the man looming over her cousin.

Swech looked her way and moved, sliding away from easy detection by the stranger even as the other Sa'ba Taalor spread out around the throne. Desh Krohan was nowhere to be seen, which was not a comforting thought as a sorcerer obviously stood before her.

"Your cousin has failed you. Morwhen is now mine." The voice coming from the hooded shape was deep and soft, but carried easily in the sudden silence. "Your empire crumbles before me, Nachia Krous. Surrender to me and be spared the pain of watching while I destroy all you hold dear."

Merros moved in quickly and brought his sword's blade down with a resounding crash on the man's head. By all rights the man should have died right then, but the well-honed blade bounced as surely as if it had struck a stone wall. Merros withdrew and repositioned himself as quickly as he could. A moment later he was striking a second time, thrusting the tip of his weapon toward the open hood of his enemy.

A quick gesture from the stranger and the general was cast through the air, knocked back as if kicked by a horse. Merros crashed to the ground and slid a dozen feet to a halt.

Four guards moved in to take his place, bringing their spears around as they surrounded the stranger.

Nachia shook her head. She wanted to rush to Merros' side but could not. She addressed the figure before her. "Are you Jeron?"

The man didn't even bother to look her way. Instead, he moved slightly, the better to keep all the guards in his view. "I am. I offer you the chance to save yourself the agony of losing an empire to war. Surrender the throne, save your people the pain that Morwhen endures at this moment."

At the far end of the great hall two of the Sisters swept into the room and froze when they saw the situation. Nachia could not see the man's smile, but she could damned near feel his smug satisfaction. "Tataya. Goriah. Step closer, please. You should hear this as well. The Overlords have risen, and they would see Fellein bow before them."

"Jeron, why do you do this?" Tataya stepped forward, her eyes scanning as if they might find the face hidden beneath the shadows of the sorcerer's cowl. She frowned and shook her head. "No. You're not Jeron."

"I am wise enough to send a message without revealing myself yet." The man finally looked up enough to reveal part of his face. All she saw was a strong chin with a heavy dark beard.

Tataya stepped closer, frowning deeply and concentrating.

The man slid back, apparently wary of the close scrutiny. The guards around him made noises and the one he came closest to lowered the tip of his spear as if daring the stranger to walk directly into the point.

"This will be your only warning, Nachia Krous. Surrender before I am forced to make an example of you."

Tataya stepped closer still, but it was Goriah who attacked. Whatever it was she did, all that showed was a gesture of her arms and the sudden twisting of the man's body. His legs buckled and he screamed over the sound of bones breaking. Whatever he might have done, whatever he might have said, was lost in an instant as his form fell to the ground, broken and warped. Blood flowed freely from the robes that only moments earlier had easily stopped a sword strike.

Tataya ran across the polished ground, her dress flowing around her, and Goriah stepped closer to the man she had just killed. An instant later Pella was in the room as if she had been there all along, though Nachia had not seen her until that moment. Two of the guards stood over the broken body of the brown cloaked man and the other two moved with Pella to examine Mallifex.

Pella sighed. "King Mallifex is alive, Majesty."

Nachia nodded and cast her eyes toward Merros, who was already climbing weakly to his feet. The gods smiled on the man. She had feared her friend was dead.

"Where is Desh Krohan?" she asked the Sisters, for if anyone would know his whereabouts it was them.

"He prepares himself, Majesty." Tataya spoke loud enough for her to hear and no one else. "The Sooth say he will do battle soon for the empire."

"Against this Jeron?" She shook her head.

"It's likely, Majesty. Jeron is powerful."

"More powerful than his messenger?"

Goriah answered, "Jeron is as powerful as any sorcerer who has ever walked the world."

Though she had been impressed enough by his sudden appearance, Nachia was not particularly worried by the display she had just seen.

Tataya spoke softly to her again, reading her expression easily enough. "Don't let yourself be fooled. We came running because that man was moved from Morwhen to here in a matter of seconds. Sorcery of that level is not easily achieved, and he brought your cousin with him. And that was not Jeron, but he's the one who cast the spell. This was meant solely as a warning, Nachia."

"I want him found, Tataya. I want this damned sorcerer found and brought to me. I don't care if he's dead or in manacles when it happens."

"That is what Desh prepares for." She did not sound confident.

Pella stepped closer and spoke softly. "Your cousin will need care if he's to survive, Majesty. He has lost a lot of blood and he is weak."

Merros came closer as well, favoring his right leg as he walked. He pointed to the closest of the guards. "Summon the healers."

All around them people were talking now, in voices that were louder than polite. The Sa'ba Taalor in the room remained far apart from each other and alert and Nachia understood that they were waiting for any other possible threats. They were under orders to obey her and keep her safe. She found that thought oddly comforting as she looked at the dead body on the ground not a dozen feet from her.

The corpse sat up. "Hear me, Empress. This is but a trifle, a pawn in my employ. When next we meet it will be you and yours who suffer. Make peace with your gods if you have any. Your empire will fall to the Overlords and to me."

One of the guards stepped forward and grabbed at the dead man's shoulder as if to shake him into submission. A moment later he screamed and staggered back, looking at the hand that had touched the dead man with wide, frightened eyes.

Merros' jaw clenched and he took a step toward the palace guard, but he moved too late.

The guard – a man named Sercal – let out a loud scream that ascended into a shriek as his hand burst into flames. He stepped back from the corpse, which laughed and fell forward. Sercal shook his arm and managed one more deep breath and scream before the fire ran from his arm over his chest and head, swallowing him greedily. All around the room people backed away as Sercal took three steps back and then fell to his knees, already dead.

Thick black smoke rose into the air and painted the ceiling above the dead guard. The corpse of Jeron's servant rose on shaky boneless legs and stepped closer to the throne and continued to laugh. "I will show you unimagined pains if you do not surrender to me, Nachia Krous! You will suffer every conceivable agony you have ever dreamt."

Pella spoke words the Empress could not hear, and the body fell to the ground a second time. Still, it moved, crawling toward Nachia, pulling itself with lifeless hands and the face in that hood craned toward her.

Nachia Krous was a strong woman. She had to be, but enough was enough. Even with the certain knowledge that she would be safe on her throne, fear seized her. She knew a dead man when she saw one and she had no doubt at all that the thing clawing across the ground for her was dead.

The spear that pinned the thing in place drove through the moving dead man's head. Nachia heard the bones break with the impact. Swech stepped forward and leaned her weight into the thrust. One of the other Sa'ba Taalor, a man named Fesk, used a second spear to hook the body, and both of them hauled the corpse toward the funeral pyre that had been Sercal moments earlier.

The dead man laughed as he burned, a manic sound that sent shivers through the Empress's body.

People backed away even further, most with wild eyes and horrified expressions. Merros Dulver stayed by her side, eyeing the burning bodies. Pella stepped closer to the conflagration and a moment later both of the burning bodies vanished from sight, taking the flames and a good amount of the greasy smoke with them.

Nachia looked at Pella and offered a weak smile of thanks. Swech and Fesk looked on, seemingly unaffected by the horrors they had just seen. Then again, their people had once commanded an army of the dead. Perhaps they were more prepared for facing new horrors.

Trigan Garth

The War-Born were interesting creatures, and leading them was a fascinating experience. Trigan Garth opened his eyes and blinked several times as he adjusted to the darkness of the cave.

Jeron had found the place and settled the Godless within its darkness. He had altered the structure, added the odd seats where they settled themselves, and taught them how to lead their servants with their minds alone.

Trigan's body was relaxed, and his limbs rested casually on a bed of heavy moss that was oddly warm and comfortable. The cave was lost in semidarkness, a room lit only by a few distant torches. It was easy to fall into a sleeping state in the calm of the quiet darkness. Not far away the other Godless continued to rest, lost in their own missions.

For all the world he felt like he'd been sleeping.

When he was in command of the War-Born Trigan simply closed his eyes and felt the world drift. It was a strange dream he'd had, where his mind was fragmented into a hundred bodies, each a separate part of a larger whole. He felt each body, moved within them, and commanded the different forms as easily as he moved his limbs. They were separate entities, but they were connected, and he was the line that connected them.

It was like nothing he had ever experienced before. It was an oddly intoxicating feeling, and he found he liked it. His entire life he had fought, sometimes as part of a group and often as an individual. He was Sa'ba Taalor and that meant he was a warrior before he was anything else. The people of the forges were bred for war, raised to serve gods of war. Combat was as much a part of life as eating or sleeping.

Ah, but controlling the War-Born, that was something else entirely. His mind fragmented when he was in charge of his War-Born. It broke into a hundred different lights, a constellation of senses that were his, not one body that was a part of an army, but rather one army that worked together to form his body.

How was it possible? He did not know, but he reveled in it. He had fought against the Sa'ba Taalor as a dozen of the spider creatures at once and it had been an awakening of his senses unlike anything he had ever known. The Godless worked together, learning to control multiple bodies, multiple limbs, and now they did the work again, but with a hundred forms under their individual command, each connected not only to the War-Born but also to each other in ways Trigan would have never thought possible. There were members of his species that felt a special connection to their mounts, but he had never been given that gift. He wondered if what he felt with the War-Born and the Godless was something similar.

The sensation was powerful, and even now he wanted it back.

Around him the other Godless stirred. They woke from their odd, dreamlike slumber and looked around with eyes that barely saw the cave they inhabited.

The sorcerer was wise. They needed this place with its odd beds of stone and moss and the torches in their sconces.

Not far away Roledru cooked for them. The man stirred a cauldron worth of stew and when he saw them moving, he began filling bowls with the stuff.

Trigan rose to his feet and moved toward the sorcerer's manservant, suddenly ravenous. He did not know how long he had been gone from his body and moving among the many bodies of his personal army, but he sensed it had been days, not hours.

Roledru smiled briefly and handed him the food without saying a word. Trigan took the stew eagerly and half ate, half drank the contents of the bowl, ignoring the heat in order to consume it quickly. He sat down in the dry of the cave and lost himself in the feast.

By the time he was sated the others were eating and Jeron had entered the cave.

"You are well?" The wizard loomed far above him. The sorcerer was taller than he had been and oddly angular under his robe. He was no longer truly humanoid in shape. He had changed even more, though Trigan would have thought that nearly impossible after the changes that had taken place already.

"I am well." Trigan's voice was rough from disuse.

"What do you think now of what the Overlords did to you?"

"I do not understand all that they did, but I must admit, I find the changes rewarding."

"They have remade you in their image, Trigan Garth." The hooded face looked toward him, and he sensed more than saw the wizard's smile. "Your mind has been adapted, altered so that you can look through a hundred sets of eyes, speak with a hundred tongues at once."

"I have always been a warrior, but I have never been an army."

"The Overlords have made you what you should always have been, my friend. You are a natural leader and the War-Born are designed as weapons. They are not meant to think. They are meant to serve."

"To have a hundred bodies at once is invigorating."

Jeron nodded and laughed. "Soon you will have more. Soon you will rule over a thousand bodies, but you must first crawl before you can walk, and you must walk before you can run."

"A thousand bodies?"

"The War-Born are many, Trigan. They have been growing in number for centuries and, like their creators, they have slept. The time comes when the sleepers awaken, and the hidden armies of the Overlords will be yours to command."

"Where do they rest?"

"Beneath the ground in the bodies of the dead. The Overlords have their ways, and their secrets are many. They're awake now but, even as they move, the Overlords continue to gather their powers."

Trigan pondered that. He had ruled a dozen forms. He had ruled a hundred bodies and sometime soon he would command an army of a thousand or more. That thought alone was enough to make him smile. Each experience had been better than the last. He was more alive with his army of bodies than he had ever been in his entire existence. He had walked. Soon he would run. He would fly!

Trigan Garth considered the possibilities and could barely contain his enthusiasm.

CHAPTER SIX

Andover Iron Hands

The winds along the shoreline were bitterly cold, and though it was daytime the skies were near dark as night. Paedle's mantle was hidden behind clouds of ash, and that ash bred storm clouds that hid the sun. The god of the forge was brooding, and the world matched the god's mood.

Thinking about that made Andover smile grimly.

Beside him three kings stood united. Tarag Paedori, Tuskandru and Donaie Swarl talked with each other in the shadow of the volcano, speaking of matters that meant little to him. He was aware of the conversation, but mostly his thoughts were lost in recollection of the recent battle against monstrous things with too many legs and scythes for arms.

That had been glorious, indeed. They had fought well and died well. He had never seen their like before and neither had any of the Sa'ba Taalor.

Waves crashed along the shore, slammed themselves to death against the rocks and the sand, with a sound like hissing thunder. The waters were as rough and bitter as the wind and the sky above.

Not a hundred feet away, Drask Silver Hand stood looking out at the waters, but Andover already understood that he was in silent communication with others. He spoke with Tega and with a man named Nolan March. They had been with him when the gods changed Drask. They had been changed as well. The last time he had seen Tega she had already gone on her strange journey and come back with power that seemed utterly impossible, that would have baffled Andover if he had not been touched by the same gods and altered. He was forged into a weapon, a champion of the Daxar Taalor. Drask and Tega and Nolan had been made into something new and wondrous, and not for the first time Andover found himself contemplating the difference between the gods of the Seven Forges and the deities worshipped in Fellein. Gods who spoke and acted versus gods who seemed far removed from their worshippers.

Of course, that wasn't completely true. The gods of Fellein had acted as well. They had raised the Silent Army when all seemed lost for Canhoon. Stone warriors who did not speak but who fought with incredible strength, and could walk through walls as if the walls did not exist. He had marveled at them more than once, and wondered whether or not he could best one in singular combat. Hard to fight a creature made of stone, but he was willing to try if the need ever arose.

The notion of gods was one he found fascinating, but in a vague way. Gods were gods and he was mortal. The Daxar Taalor spoke to him and when they asked him to do something he did it without question. They had given him so much, how could he possibly deny them?

Drask shook his head and then stretched, his Great Scars pulling into what Andover knew from first-hand experience was a smile of sorts. Or possibly a grimace.

"Tega offers you her regards, Andover." The man moved closer. "She is glad that you are well."

"I hope she is well, too." Which was truth. There had been a time, a lifetime ago in many ways, when he had dreamt of the woman every day and imagined a world where she was his wife. He had thought her the very center of everything in his world back then. They had seldom spoken words, but he had believed he loved her. A lifetime ago, indeed.

"She is. Currently she has gone back to where we were changed."

"Why?"

"The gods of the forges have never deigned to speak to her and so she sought answers to questions that do not leave her at peace."

"Has she found her answers?"

The response came softly. "The Daxar Taalor still do not speak to her."

"You could ask for her."

Drask chuckled and shook his head. "I would if she wanted me to, but she studied sorcery, Andover. She seeks answers to riddles beyond what the gods want."

"What do you mean?"

"Tega wants to know the answer to why she has power, not necessarily why the gods gave her power."

"I don't understand the difference."

"That is because you never sought to learn sorcery."

Andover considered that answer for a moment and then nodded. Tega did not seek answers from gods but rather sought to understand the gods.

"It seems a strange way to seek answers, does it not?"

"Sorcery is a strange thing. Wizards do not see the world as we do."

"No?"

"No." Drask held out one hand in front of him and mimicked the waves in what was effectively a shrug for the Sa'ba Taalor. "It is not enough to understand how something works. They must understand how it works, and what individual processes make it work. Wizards seek not only answers, but every possible question that can lead to that answer."

"Why?"

"There are a thousand mysteries linked to each riddle the world has. By understanding as many of those mysteries as they can, they believe they better understand the universe."

Andover frowned.

Drask continued. "There are seven gods of war for my people. Each shows how to fight a war, but each has different rules for how they feel war should be fought, yes?"

"Yes."

"It is like that. If they understand all of the possible questions, the wizards believe they learn secrets that would never be revealed to them if they simply asked the gods. They seek the answers they believe the gods would never offer them."

"They seek to be like the gods themselves?"

Drask considered that carefully before replying. "No. I think they seek to be closer to the gods, but they do not realize that fact."

"Then wizards are very strange."

"We Sa'ba Taalor seek all possible knowledge of war. It is how we have been raised by the gods themselves."

"Yes."

"If we thought the gods hid knowledge from us, we would seek it in other places."

"Do you think so?"

"Oh, yes. I know it." Drask made his arm wave again. "Why do you think I went to other lands?"

"Did you learn many secrets in your travels?" Andover stared into the bigger man's eyes. "Did you learn new ways to fight?"

"I learned different ways to consider combat and discovered there are people who spend lifetimes trying to find ways to avoid fighting."

"Truly?"

"Oh, yes. And some of them find ways to make evasion a weapon."

"Sometime I might ask you to show me that."

Drask grinned again. "And when you do, if we have the time, I will do so."

Andover grinned back. The idea of learning a new style of combat was one he could not resist.

"Evasion as a weapon? Truly?"

"Wrommish teaches us some of this, yes? How to use an attack against the attacker, how to evade and then strike back using the force of the attacker's strike." Andover felt himself nod in agreement. "It is the same, but there are more complex possibilities that I had not considered before I traveled."

"Yes, I will ask you to teach me."

Drask smiled again.

Behind them, the great volcanic mountain that was Paedle roared and threw fire into the heavens, lighting the clouds in shades of blood. The very air smelled of molten metal a few seconds later and, in their heads, they heard Paedle scream in agony.

The sound was in their ears and in their minds alike, and

all around them the Sa'ba Taalor collapsed as the cacophony filled their senses like water fills a drowning man's lungs.

Behind them, Paedle shook, and the ground around them heaved in sympathy.

Swech

A god screamed.

There are levels to the communication between the Sa'ba Taalor and their gods. Once one of the children of the forges earns the first Great Scar, they are forever changed. It's not just the marking, it's the voices of the gods themselves that mark the transformation. To hear a god is a powerful thing, indeed.

The gods speak directly to their followers; they can hear their children and they can be heard. The most devout followers hear more often. Those, like Drask Silver Hand and Andover Iron Hands, who have a full seven marks hear from all of the gods directly. They are marked by each god as a sign that they have earned the trust of the Daxar Taalor, and seven signs means that they are trusted by all seven gods. That does not mean they are the only people who can hear the gods. The Sa'ba Taalor are fortunate enough to hear from their gods in times of need, even if they have not been marked, for the gods believe their children always need guidance. The Great Scars are marks that also allow the gods to hear their children more directly.

The kings of the Sa'ba Taalor hear the most from their gods. It is said that the kings hear secrets not meant for any others. They rule over the people who follow the gods as their emissaries; their words are not merely their own but are very nearly sacred simply because they are trusted more by the gods than any other followers. There are no false kings. The idea is impossible. There can be no false kings when the gods themselves make the appointments. To be a king is the greatest sign of respect a god can offer to a follower, and once chosen, it is virtually impossible to lose the favor of a god. The connection between god and king is the very height of intimacy among the Sa'ba Taalor. When the god speaks the king acts, and all who follow that god obey the king as if the Daxar Taalor have given an order, because they have.

Swech knew this and accepted it. She knew that Nachia Krous did not fully understand her connection to her gods, because the Empress of Fellein did not speak to her gods and they did not speak to her. To the ruler of the empire the gods were an abstract concept.

The Empress was blind to the will of her gods because her gods chose to remain aloof and distant.

Swech pitied the woman.

And then Paedle screamed.

It was not a sound as such to Swech. It was a sensation that overwhelmed her. All of Paedle's followers heard the noise, felt it with their bodies as surely as if thunder had detonated nearby, but Swech felt that thunder as if she were the storm cloud that birthed it.

Paedle screamed, and every part of Swech's body shook with the force of that pain.

She was standing in the throne room of the Empress, as she did every day, when her god cried out in pain, and that pain reverberated through Swech as surely as if she had been standing in the heart of the god's mountain.

The world around her disappeared in an instant, and pain

cut through her, made her muscles shake with the violence of that agony, drove her to her knees and threw her body across the polished floor.

She could not see. She could not hear. There was no taste, no scent or sensation. For one moment the world around her was gone completely, replaced by pain that dwarfed every sensation she had ever known. In comparison to that, the pain of giving birth had been as easy as taking in a breath.

Swech did not lose consciousness. She did not scream, because the act of exhaling was too much for her body to endure in that moment. For three heartbeats Swech knew only the most brilliant agonies of her life and nothing else, except a sudden fear that she would lose her god.

She understood instinctively that the pain was not truly hers. She felt the pain in exactly the same way that she felt Paedle's presence, as a part of her that was both all-encompassing and simultaneously removed from her.

She knew it was her god that suffered, and felt rage surge through her body.

"No!" Her scream broke in her throat.

Desh Krohan

Locked in his private chambers, in the room he used for dealing with the Sooth and other strange entities, Desh Krohan sat on the ground and shook with feverish exhaustion.

It was not easy to search for Jeron. The man knew how to hide himself, and his sorcerous powers were at a height that Desh could barely believe. Jeron, who was like a brother to him, who was certainly one of his closest peers, was hiding from him. Had betrayed his trust, and now seemed determined to destroy the empire for his own reasons.

Jeron was making him angry, and Desh did his best not to let the anger sweep him away from his goals.

Sometimes it was not easy to be patient. Sometimes anger was a blessing.

Exhausted and irritable as he was, Desh summoned his power and reached out, pushing through the ether, moving his mind across the distance that separated him from his target.

This time, finally, his mind found Jeron and seized hold of his enemy's awareness. Jeron's eyes bulged in his skull, and he turned as quickly as he could.

Before Jeron could say more than, "How did you…" Desh attacked.

He shoved through the other sorcerer's defenses and forced the man to his knees, and then to look away from his followers. In that instant, Desh became fully aware that the creatures around his nemesis were no longer quite human. Their skin was as dark as if they'd painted themselves with a paste of ashes, darker by far than the darkest Sa'ba Taalor, but he could see that they had once belonged to that people. Everything about them, from the way they stood to their choice of clothing, indicated the gray-skins, but they were no longer what they had been, any more than Jeron was still just human.

This was a consideration for another time. Desh kept his focus tight.

Jeron fought back, tried to force his way back to a standing position, and Desh fairly growled as he shoved the man against the wall of the cave where he was hiding, and then pushed harder, still using his magic as a battering ram to crush Jeron down as hard as he could.

The other sorcerer screamed in frustration, his hands catching the wall, fighting to break the grip that Desh held him in – and failing. Desh had to keep him off balance, physically and mentally. He knew that if he let his enemy concentrate the fight would end differently, so he pushed, forced himself against the struggling form and crushed down.

Jeron screamed, and his body bent and collapsed toward the stone of the cave's side, bones creaking, breaking as Desh Krohan continued his assault. Long, unnaturally thin arms buckled under the force, and though Desh heard bones breaking he was unrelenting in his attack. A part of him wanted to spare the man. Jeron had been a friend, but that had been five years ago. Five years since he'd heard of Jeron's death. He had mourned the man long ago and now he pushed, strained to end the life of a man who had broken every rule of sorcery, who had stolen souls from the living and the dead alike.

Jeron shrieked in panic as his body crumbled and his face was slammed into stone. He cried out and then cried silently as the air was forced from his lungs.

Exhaustion tried to creep into the First Advisor's body and mind, but he was prepared for that and took the power he had long since stored away and drained more of it into his being. Magic had a price, but he was well-prepared to pay it.

The flesh of his enemy broke and bled. Bones pushed their way through skin and muscle alike, but still Desh pushed, strained. Finally, as Jeron's skin ruptured and blood spilled toward the ground of the semi-darkened cave, he changed his tactics and sent a cascade of intense heat into the sorcerer's still struggling form. The wall beneath his ruined body glowed first red and then white. Flesh hissed, sizzled and then ignited. Cloth and meat burned, and hair shriveled before flames rose across crisped follicles.

All around the cavern where Jeron had tried to hide, those who followed the dying sorcerer backed away from the burning body and nearly molten stone of the wall.

Jeron desperately wanted to lash out. Desh could feel his mind seeking a way to get to him, but he defended himself against the possibility and pushed his advantage. By now, the body of the necromancer was little more than a scorch mark on the wall of the cavern.

At last, after a battle that had seemed to last for the ages, Jeron died. Desh could sense no trace of the sorcerer's spirit in the shattered remains of his corpse. His devastating assault had obliterated it from existence.

Exhausted, Desh sank to the floor, the gravity of his victory pressing down on him with the same weight he had just exerted on Jeron.

"Enough." He barely recognized his own voice.

Sorcery of the levels he'd used were more draining than attacking an entire army. He knew from experience. But whatever it cost, it was worth paying the price.

Desh Krohan closed his eyes and in moments was asleep.

Trigan Garth

How did magic work? Trigan had absolutely no idea. He could understand so much of the world, how the gods granted gifts, how metal changed as it was heated and cooled, but sorcery was a mystery he doubted he would ever understand.

One moment he was speaking to Jeron, and the next Jeron was pinned to the wall and dying.

In ten heartbeats the man was dead, his body burnt beyond recognition and pressed into the half-melted stone of the wall.

It was as if a god had crushed the man down and incinerated him. The air reeked of cooked meat and heated stone, and all around him the Godless looked on as Roledru screamed. For Roledru this might have been a new thing; for the Godless, who had seen miracles both light and dark delivered by the gods, the sight was disturbing, yes, but truly not the strangest thing they had ever experienced. The Daxar Taalor were unforgiving, and they had punished many of their followers over the centuries. Stories of those punishments were known to all of the Sa'ba Taalor, even those who had turned away from their gods.

Roledru looked at the meager remains of the sorcerer and shuddered, horrified. A moment later the man shook, fell to the ground, and crawled away from the remains of his master.

And Trigan saw the transformation take place. It was a subtle thing, really, a twist of familiar features. One moment Roledru was terrified and the next he was smiling to himself and looking at the ground before he sat up on his haunches and stared at his hands.

Trigan did not have to guess.

"Jeron."

Roledru turned his head and looked toward Trigan with dark eyes that showed no regret, no fear. "Very perceptive, Trigan."

"How did you do that?"

Roledru's face smiled with an expression that the man

had never shown in the time he had known him. "I've been preparing Roledru for a long while. It's regrettable. I truly liked the man, but I needed a ready sacrifice, and he was available."

Trigan nodded. "If I ever feel you are preparing me to be his replacement, I will carve out your heart and your eyes."

Roledru/Jeron rose from the cave floor and dusted off his knees. "There are rules to sorcery. What I did takes a great deal of preparation."

"My answer is the same. If I think you are trying to prepare me for use as a body, I will kill you."

With that he moved away from the sorcerer and frowned. How would he know if Jeron decided to do anything at all? He doubted that he would.

He would have to consider that carefully. He had liked Roledru well enough. The man had been efficient and friendly. It was not the way of the Sa'ba Taalor to mourn or to grieve. There had never been a loss in his life that had caused Trigan tears, save for when the gods were silenced from him, and that had been more a betrayal than anything else.

He appreciated all that Jeron had done for him. The man had given him a purpose that felt better than merely serving as a mercenary from time to time, and the ability to command the War-Born was a gift, but that did not change his beliefs, and his instincts told him simply that a man who would kill a faithful servant once would do so again to protect his self-interests.

That was not a man who should be trusted.

For the Sa'ba Taalor, Godless or not, that was a poor thing indeed.

CHAPTER SEVEN

Darsken Murdro

The alleyways of the city were dark and twisted around themselves in ways that were confusing. Darsken was familiar with Goltha, but it was not his territory and the serpentine roads left him confused. The only good news was that Daivem was with him, and he always enjoyed any opportunity to spend time with his little sister. Also, he was more familiar with the city than she was, which meant he didn't feel a complete fool.

"Where exactly are we?" Daivem's voice carried in the narrow passage that wound around the whole of the city as best he could tell.

"I do not know." He squinted and tried to remember the last of the statues they had passed. Most of the city's courts were named for one old king or another. The problem was that everything looked different at night. Also, he had the strong sense that someone was following them, though he had seen no one.

Daivem seemed to sense nothing of the sort, though it was hard to say exactly what was on her mind through the heavy fog creeping along the streets closest to the lake.

The face he knew so well was very nearly hidden from him.

"How does anyone ever see anything in this town?" she muttered

Before he could answer, a blade cut into his arm. It was a well-honed knife and the point easily sliced through his outer coat and jacket alike before driving into his bicep. Had he not been turning to look for any recognizable landmarks it was likely the knife would have pierced his ribs.

Despite the fog, Daivem moved quickly, her eyes looking past the blade and her hand lashing out. The walking stick blurred and struck a solid blow against a form that Darsken barely even saw. The shadowy figure slid back into darkness without a single sound, and Daivem moved after it, teeth bared and eyes wide.

Darsken looked at his arm for half a moment as the pain sank teeth in the wound. Daivem let out a small cry and caught his attention back to where it should have been all along. As the shadows moved again, his little sister uttered another noise. The sound of her stick hitting a solid target was clear enough, and Darsken charged toward the form that staggered back from his fellow Inquisitor.

There was a reason that they traveled together these days. By orders of the Grand Inquisitor, no one traveled alone any longer. He had moved with the army before but now that he was once again seeking answers to where the necromancer might be, he stayed with his sister, hoping to keep her safe.

The shape came out of the shadows and swept toward him, knives in both hands. Darsken dodged back from the first blade and then the second, narrowly avoiding having his face carved open.

When he stepped back again, he moved into the Shimmer, stepping across the open courtyard with one stride. The shape that had attacked him recoiled as if hit with scalding water, looking for a target that was simply no longer there.

Daivem stepped into the Shimmer for a moment as well, moving further into the alley behind the knife-wielder. Each inquisitor carried a walking stick made of heavy wood, and she used hers as a bludgeon again, the carved wood striking his attacker in the head hard enough to stagger him.

The darkness hid details, but surely there was something wrong with the stranger's face. A mask, perhaps – but Darsken could not be sure.

"Daivem, enough! We should leave here, there might be more than one." He spoke in their native tongue, knowing few who were not from Louron would understand the words.

His sister nodded but said nothing, and pursued the same figure again.

Whatever their abilities, the stranger seemed to have his own. Daivem looked for Darsken's attacker but did not find him.

Warmth ran down the length of his left arm, and Darsken hissed.

Daivem moved closer, her face set in a scowl. "Agreed. Enough for tonight, brother. For now we get you mended."

He nodded. It was always best to assume an attack on an Inquisitor would be an attempt to kill. Best to find out if the blades were poisoned and to treat the wounds carefully.

Darsken looked around one last time and sighed. It seemed there would be no answers, not tonight at least.

Whistler

The second blow had opened a wound on the right side of his forehead that bled a stream of blood into his right eye. The wound also hurt enough that he didn't trust his fool head hadn't been broken.

"You let him live." The voices were not amused.

"I did not. He turned before I could open his heart."

"You said you could kill him. This is why you have travelled here."

"And I will, but not tonight." Whistler rolled his eyes and wiped at the blood burning into his right eye.

"You are hurt."

"Nice of you to notice." He hissed the words as he stumbled down the Avenue of Echoes, his footsteps bouncing off claustrophobically close walls. Hard to believe that a carriage could wend its way down the narrow streets, but he'd seen it himself on many occasions.

After Darsken had vanished virtually from within his grasp, Whistler had thought his hopes of regaining his proper face had vanished entirely, but the voices still had use for him. They knew – how, he neither knew nor cared – where Darsken had traveled to, and where he had gone thereafter, and – by dint of intimidation of a suitably cowed merchant – Whistler had made his way across country to Goltha.

The town was a massive, sprawling affair, and that suited his needs. Hard to remain hidden when his face was so badly scarred. His looks tended to make him obvious in the daylight which meant he preferred the nights. He should have been following the Inquisitor, but he knew where the man would go. He would either sleep in the city's Inquisitor's Tower, or he would stay in one of the inns near the lake.

Either way, Darsken was from Louron and finding him was easy. His skin was dark and most of the people in the area were pale, especially in the winter months.

It was cold enough that very few people were wandering the streets at night. The snow had partially melted during the day and then frozen again, leaving the streets and walkways treacherous.

Whistler moved toward the tavern where he'd rented a room. It was clean enough and warm enough and the price was right. It was also the sort of place where most of the people did their best to ignore their neighbors and go about their own affairs as quietly as possible.

The man who slept one room over looked at him and stared. Whistler ignored him but he was tempted to carve the bastard's eyes out of his head. He did not like being ogled by men, no matter what the reason, but it was doubly annoying knowing the man looked at him with disgust and pity alike.

Still, better to ignore the stares. Whistler was memorable for all the wrong reasons. If the Inquisitors had managed a good look at him, it would be impossible to hide away as completely as he'd like.

He looked at the scars on his face and shook his head. The marks were deep. Flesh had burned away in some areas and, though there was no pain, though he had full function, he was distinctive enough that hiding was not an option. So long as people could see his face, he would be easily identified. What remained of his mouth turned up in an odd leering grin, and his eyes were nearly all pupil, it seemed, with little of the iris to be seen amid wells of darkness. He could see as well as a cat in the night but had to squint his eyes nearly closed in the full brightness of a sunny day.

"Better to go out at night in any event with a face like this."

"Kill the Inquisitor and your face is yours again. We have discussed this." The voice rang as clearly to him as if someone spoke into his ear, but he knew better. There was no one talking to him, at least no one that others could hear.

"If you have this power then you should use it now. I can kill the bastard if I can get close to him. I cannot get close if he recognizes a ruined face."

There was a moment of silence, and then, to Whistler's amazement, pain flared along his scarred face. First it was a dull itch, and then it raged into a hot explosion along his nerve endings and Whistler fell away from the dull looking glass where he had caught his reflection and dropped to the ground, biting back the screams that tried to slip past his ruined lips.

Having his face burned half to nothing had been painful, but having it grow back was worse. Whistler crawled across the ground, whimpering, eyes watering and flesh and muscles stretching in ways that defied his ability to fully comprehend. For several minutes the pain soared through his senses and dwarfed every other thought and sensation.

When it finally stopped, when he had recovered enough to think coherently again, he carefully let his hands probe the regenerated flesh on his face. Familiar curves and planes were all he felt and, though he knew it was vanity, Whistler wept with joy.

He waited a few minutes before finally daring to look in the reflective surface of the cheap mirror, and risked a grin as his old face looked back.

"What has been given can be taken away." The voice in

his head spoke like a strict parent, a fact that was not lost to Whistler. Nor was it appreciated. Still, what choice?

"I will find him, and I will kill him." Whistler spoke to his reflection, pleased with the way his lips moved, marveling at the differences he felt. "You have my word."

"Be swift about it. We are not patient. We have waited too long to be thwarted."

Whistler said nothing but he nodded, mesmerized by the appearance of his nodding reflection. He had never considered himself vain, and yet he would kill a dozen people to keep his visage, and he knew it.

Out into the darkness he slipped, the knives at his hips as sharp as could be, and the need to keep his restored looks driving him to please the voices that had haunted him for years. The Inquisitor was as good as dead.

Merros Dulver

Merros looked at the shape of Swech in the bed where she lay. Her skin was too pale, and though she slept she did not rest easy. Her eyes rolled under closed eyelids, and the Great Scars on her face opened and closed, uttering small nonsensical noises. Her arms moved. Her legs twitched.

Valam stood near his mother's bed and stared at the wall when he was not studying the sleeping shape of the most important person in his world. Merros wanted to offer the boy comfort but didn't know what to say.

She had collapsed the day before and had not recovered yet. Every one of the Sa'ba Taalor had suffered, but none quite as much as Swech. Though he did not understand everything that had happened, he knew that something had happened to their god, Paedle. The notion that a god could be injured was unsettling but the thought that all of the followers of that god could suffer as well was even worse.

Merros looked at the woman he had once just possibly loved and worried his teeth across his lower lip. He did not like to think about her, but thoughts of Swech distracted him from every thought he should have been having.

Goriah swept into the room, moving with the liquid grace that marked all of the Sisters as surely as their nearly unearthly beauty. She nodded to him and then moved to Swech, frowning as she studied her patient.

It was not common for the Sisters to work as healers, but then Swech was not suffering from a normal affliction. It was not her body that was injured as far as anyone could tell, it was her mind, or possibly her spirit. Many of the healers in Canhoon were affiliated with the religious sects, but Swech did not follow their gods. Her demeanor hid most of her contempt for the gods of Fellein, but he understood how very little she cared for the silent gods. Their ways were very nearly the methods of parents who had abandoned their children in her eyes, and therefore they were contemptable.

Besides. There were ten Sa'ba Taalor who were now incapacitated. Swech was the king of her people and, as far as Merros was aware, the companions who had been with her were not as severely affected as she was, but they were not well.

"How is she?"

"She's the same, Merros. What you see is what I see." They both spoke in the common tongue of Fellein, and he did not know if Valam could understand them, but Merros suspected he could despite his quiet demeanor. Swech was a woman who believed in being prepared for all circumstances and teaching her son the words of the people she saw as an enemy or a friend made sense to her way of thinking. It was one more fraction of Valam's life where he could have control. For a boy his age, he already seemed enough like his mother that it was very nearly haunting.

Before he could ask Goriah said, "The others are still the same. They are conscious, but they are weak and easily disoriented." She shrugged. "It is not all of the Sa'ba Taalor and as far as we can tell not even all of the followers of this Paedle, but some of them are just as… weakened, I suppose, is the best word to use here." Merros nodded. That was what he had expected. The people closest to Swech were close to her god, and Paedle was the god closest to her heart. Some of them suffered almost as much as she did, and some, he expected, were not hurt at all.

"What can fight a god, Goriah?"

The woman looked very tired, despite her unnatural beauty. There were no bags under her eyes, no noticeable blemishes, but she moved differently than he was used to, and her focus seemed less.

"Desh thinks it's the Overlords."

"Truly?" he frowned. That was a disconcerting notion. "How powerful are these things?"

"Strong enough to harm a god, apparently. Strong enough to raise a mountain."

"Then how are we supposed to fight them?" He looked around the chamber as if the shadows might have an answer, or perhaps Swech could reveal secrets from her sick bed, but there were no mysteries solved in his scrutiny.

"That is precisely what Desh is considering." She shook her head and sighed. "He has us looking for notes about how they were defeated, in books written centuries ago.

There is so little written down and most of what we have found is conjecture. We have two separate sorcerers who are old enough to have lived through the conflict and neither of them remember what happened or even what the Overlords truly are."

"That cannot be coincidence."

"What do you mean?"

"I can accept that there are blank spaces in their memories, but I cannot believe that two sorcerers have completely forgotten what these Overlords are capable of. From what I've heard this was a vast chapter in the history of Fellein. Surely one of them or both of them would remember well enough what happened, or at least they would have when they wrote their passages in the books you seek to study." He shook his head. "Exaggeration be damned. I don't care what time has done to their recollections. Something has happened to stop them from remembering the Overlords or, as a lot, sorcerers are fools."

She looked ready to argue with him, not surprising as he had just insulted all of the sorcerers in one comment but then she stopped and thought hard about his words.

"You think the Overlords have done something to Desh and Corin alike?"

"I'm not saying I remember every detail of my childhood, Goriah, but I remember the big events. I remember the first time my father punished me, and I remember why. I remember the first time I trained with a sword and how bloodied my knuckles were by the time that session was done. Those were important things. If two of the smartest men in all of Fellein have both forgotten what happened with these Overlords from when they were younger, then I have to think someone has willfully cursed them to forget. You said yourself these

Overlords have magic of their own and if they can fight gods, they can surely cause mortals a problem or two."

"Sometimes I forget how wise you can be, Merros."

He wasn't sure if he found those words comforting or insulting, but they were uttered now and could not be unspoken in any event.

"I'll talk to Pella and Tataya. We will investigate this possibility. If something has been done, perhaps it can be undone as well."

"If that's the case, then kindly restore Swech. She has a son to attend to."

"Fortunately, the boy has a father as well." She couldn't have startled him more if she had slapped him in the face.

Merros looked toward the boy, who stood as he had before, looking at his mother and studying her as if she might suddenly sit up and attack. Considering her history, Merros supposed it was always possible, but seeing her and how she seemed to have shrunk in on herself, he had his doubts.

Drask Silver Hand

Three kings paced around the bonfire, each looking ready to attack and kill any possible threat.

Drask understood their mood all too well. He felt the same restlessness in his breast, brought on by the simple but impossible fact that someone or something had attacked a god and caused that deity grievous harm.

Not far away, Andover Lashk stood in silent contemplation, his silvery eyes flickering at every sound. He could guess what the boy was thinking: here he stood unharmed, when he was supposed to be the champion of the gods. Trained by the gods themselves, yet somehow, he had failed them. Like the kings, he was chosen. Like the kings, he felt he had failed.

Somewhere among the Fellein, Swech was surely raging at the thought of being forced to stay in Canhoon instead of fighting for her god.

Somewhere, Paedle suffered and languished, wounded but not dead.

Drask contemplated all of that as he considered where he stood in the grander scheme of the Daxar Taalor's plans. He had been gifted with incredible power. He had been trained in the use of that power. He had, quite literally, leveled a mountain for the gods. Like the people around him who doubted themselves, he had been given a gift by the gods, had been chosen by the gods for a reason.

There had been a moment when he considered consulting the kings, but he pushed that thought away and spoke to the gods themselves. "What would you have me do?"

Ganem replied. "We would have you honor us with your actions."

Drask looked back at Paedle, the mountain, the home of a wounded god, and considered the words of another deity.

How does one honor a god of war? That was simple enough to answer. One went to war for the god. Drask closed his eyes and considered the possible enemy of Paedle. He had to find that enemy before he could attack and, to do that, he used the sorcery he had learned from Tega to reach out to her, to speak to her directly.

"Tega, remind me, how does one scry for secrets?"

She spoke, but her voice sounded distracted, and he knew his timing was poor. The directions she offered would have made no sense to him five years earlier, but she had taught him well. The instructions were simple enough to one who had been trained in the art of sorcery. Drask kept his eyes closed and reached out with his senses, feeling through the air, until he reached the heart of Paedle and sensed both the god's pain and the source of the injuries Paedle endured.

There, hidden within the volcanic heart of Paedle, he found one of the Overlords, coiled like a serpent wrapped around the god, binding the Daxar Taalor and crushing inward.

"Tega. Nolan. I need you both." He spoke to them, pushed through the defenses they had up. They were far away; they sought to understand the source of their power, of the gift they had been given by the gods, uncertain as to how or why they were chosen.

Nolan March, through the broken mind he had received when the gods gifted him, had decided long ago that his blessings were an accident. He was never supposed to have the power as far as he could tell, but Drask suspected otherwise and always had.

Tega did not worry about why she was gifted, but instead used those abilities to expand her mind, her own powers, and to contemplate the seemingly endless energies that each of them had absorbed from the very gods.

"What do you need?" Tega's voice was calm and confident.

"Power. I fight an Overlord."

Without another word he willed himself into the fray, uncertain as to exactly what it was he was about to fight.

Tuskandru

Tusk looked around as Andover Iron Hands let out a gasp.

Ten feet away from him Drask doubled, nearly tripled in size and then vanished like a cloud dissipating in a hard wind. He was there, he grew, and then was simply gone as his shape turned completely toward Paedle.

A moment later, the mountain shook, and the top of the volcano belched forth a great tongue of flame that licked the sky and lit the clouds with fiery brilliance. All three kings felt the change in Paedle, and heard their gods roar their approval.

Whatever it was that Drask had done, the gods were pleased by his actions.

Drask Silver Hand

War is not about a fair fight, it is about advantages. Drask knew that, and took care to keep every advantage he could. He had never encountered the Overlords. He did not know what they looked like, or what they were capable of – but then, he barely understood his own powers since the Daxar Taalor had changed him. He merely knew that he was more than he had been, and that had to be enough. He had traveled the world and tested himself and he thought he knew his limitations and his strengths well enough.

He attacked while the Overlord was busy trying to wound Paedle again. The god of liquid metal roared and fought back, and Drask took advantage of the rejoined combat, striking the Overlord as quickly and brutally as he could.

The Overlord did not have a simple form. It was not

human in shape, nor was it truly solid. He did not know if the thing reflected back the liquid form of Paedle, or if it simply did not have a single form, but it changed again and again even as he struck his first blow. One moment the creature was solid, a powerful shape not unlike a Pra-Moresh, with powerful limbs and rending claws, and the next it flowed into a serpentine thing that wrapped around Drask and crushed him with coils of muscle and scales.

Had he been untouched by the gods the attack would have killed him, but Drask had abilities far beyond what most of his people understood. Like the Overlord, he flowed into a new shape, becoming a flood that dissolved around the writhing form of his enemy and coalesced into a heavy wave that surrounded the twisting, writhing form, enveloped the creature and then squeezed, crushing down with power enough to shatter stone.

The Overlord reacted instantly. Exploding outward into a hundred stabbing shards, ripping through Drask's body, forcing him to rethink his attack. Had he been solid at the moment, he would have been cut to shreds.

Rather than attempt to change shape again, Drask concentrated on stopping his enemy from continuing its onslaught of new forms. He froze the Overlord, forced it into one solid form, pushing with the power he had been given by the gods. He felt the very cells of his enemy solidify and freeze, crystallize at his will, and felt the potent hatred of the Overlord as well. It was not used to being defied. Whatever the creature truly was, it had long-since grown accustomed to simply changing itself into new forms as it wanted. If the world was solid, then this creature was plasmid, ever changing. It moved like fluid between rocks, filling in gaps and crevices to reshape as it needed.

The thing moved like mercury, the liquid metal that defined Paedle. The fluid silver was poison. The Overlord was venomous. They had that much in common.

Drask forced that unstable flesh into a frozen mass, aided by Tega and her understanding of matter and liquid and energy. She had taught him much over the last five years.

The Overlord tried to fight back. When it was captured inside the shapes Drask willed, it grew angry and struggled desperately to be free, but Drask would not permit that. He had learned new methods of fighting over the years of his travel, had developed his mind in ways that were new to the Sa'ba Taalor, that would have puzzled Tusk and Tarag Paedori. The combat was not completely physical. In a very real sense, he fought with his mind as well as his body.

The thing he fought had spent a much longer time preparing to fight in different ways. Where Drask had opened himself to the possibilities of combat beyond the physical realm, the Overlords had spent literally centuries exploring with their minds, well beyond the physical realms. Drask fought tenaciously, but to the Overlord he was almost a child. He fought with enthusiasm, yes, but he lacked skill and finesse.

Had he been alone in his combat, Drask Silver Hand would have been easily crushed. The Overlord would have swatted him aside as casually as he himself might strike down a toddler. All of his strength would have been wasted and he knew that.

Like a toddler, he counted on his parent to be with him. In this case, he counted on Paedle to fight beside him as the gods had always fought beside him. He had come to Paedle's aid, yes, but that did not mean he expected a war god to sit idly by and watch him fight. He expected the god to join him, and he was not disappointed.

Paedle struck back at the Overlord and struck true. The god of silent combat attacked as an assassin should, waiting while the Overlord fought Drask and striking at the first vulnerability with a precise and deadly blow. It was not a physical attack, nor was it entirely spiritual, but rather a combination that would have meant nothing to anyone who could only see in one realm or the other. Drask was fortunate enough to see in new ways, as gods and Overlords see, perhaps, or merely in ways that his people could not properly comprehend. In any event he got to witness a god striking an enemy and it was as miraculous and incredible as anything he had ever witnessed.

Paedle drove a thousand venomous strikes into the shadowy form of the Overlord and the creature shrieked in agony as those venoms tore through its body, its mind, and its spirit, withering all of them as surely as a flame incinerates paper.

Drask watched as the Overlord died, and moved back cautiously as it tried to strike at him several times, like a wounded beast.

Paedle writhed, injured by the battle that only Drask had witnessed even in part.

How badly was his god wounded? Drask did not know and dared not ask, for fear he would hear an answer he could not stand.

No child likes to find that a parent is not indestructible. For the Sa'ba Taalor, the gods were parents in many ways.

CHAPTER EIGHT

Jeron

The Overlords were not gods, not truly, but they were godlike, and feeling one of them die shook Jeron to his core. He had only just escaped dying himself, and he remained hidden from the other sorcerers only because he had arranged a misdirection. Now, only barely confident in his ability to hide, he felt one of his newly chosen deities slaughtered by the gods of the barbarian Sa'ba Taalor, and he was unsettled deeply by the change of situation.

Normally he would have looked to Roledru to offer him a calm word or two, as the man was almost always levelheaded, but Roledru was dead and Jeron found himself without the benefit of a confidant.

In the cavern where he hid himself, the Godless lay in slumber as the War-Born prepared for a grand battle. Snow drifted silently down in heavy flakes and buried the world in a white caul. The silence around him was deep and abiding. It should have comforted him, as silence had always been a comfort to him, but now it left him too much time to think.

He contemplated the face he wore and the new body. It was simple vanity, and he should never have considered it under the circumstances, but he found Roledru's form did nothing to comfort him. He remade his new body in his old image, carefully reshaping his face until he once again looked like Jeron and not a peasant servant. He kept the hair on his head, however, as he had grown tired of the cold, and the thick tresses offered a modicum of warmth.

Unsettled and not truly wishing to be alone, Jeron shifted into a comfortable position and pushed his mind outward, seeking his plaything again. The boy called Whistler was under the delusion that he had been chosen by the gods themselves. He believed that because Jeron wanted him to believe it. In truth he was a trinket, a toy and little more. But he was a useful plaything, a pleasant distraction that could be manipulated, and so Jeron looked to his living weapon and pointed him back in the right direction.

"Go," he whispered into the boy's mind. "Seek out the Inquisitor and kill him. Make his death painful and you shall be rewarded. Fail me, and your pretty face is once again forfeit."

Whistler cringed mentally at the very idea, which put a smile on Jeron's newly restored features. Perhaps his new masters had made him in their image in other ways because, before the Overlords, he had never been so randomly sadistic. It might have been the sort of thing that would have worried him once, but he found he liked the change. He liked the fear he created in his pet.

Still, there were other matters to consider. The savages, the Sa'ba Taalor, needed to be broken before they could regroup. For that he needed the War-Born to continue their brutal assaults.

The weather was to his benefit, as it should have been. He had bent the world to his will and increased the cold and snow until most of Fellein was nearly buried in a blizzard. Most of the roads, even the highways that were nearly constantly traveled, were impassable. For the gray-skins that was hardly a challenge. They rode through worse storms constantly in their Blasted Lands, but the empire suffered as a result of his actions. One of the two enemies he faced for his new masters was very nearly crippled and the other would soon be badly wounded. He'd make certain of it.

He found himself missing Roledru again. The man had been a faithful servant, and he handled many of the mundane details, like finding the proper victims for his necromantic needs. Now he either had to trust someone else – a doubtful and risky proposition – or he hunted for himself. He needed fresh kills. The War-Born helped sustain him, a portion of every wretch they killed fed directly to him, but he needed more.

Easy enough, really. With a thought he shifted himself to what remained of Morrow. The people there were cold and destitute, few daring to leave their homes for fear that the nearly invisible War-Born would attack them. He only had to look for the signs of a fire burning in a hovel to know where he would find good hunting.

The smoke from such a fire carried into the starry skies, and he moved to the home with little concern. His robes kept him warm and safe from very nearly any attack. The door to the domicile was barred, but that too was of little concern. A gesture and a thought and the door collapsed. He heard the scream of fright from inside the structure and entered, hood drawn up over his head, face lost in shadows that were far from natural. He had learned that trick from Desh Krohan a long time ago. The garments he wore caused those who saw him to be afraid, deeply frightened of what might be lurking within that cowl.

Four women of different ages waited inside near the fire, shivering with a cold that could not be pushed aside with heat. They were terrified and he in turn was amused.

"Boo!" He roared the word and the women shrieked. The youngest of his targets wept and tried to crawl into the shadows as if they could possibly hide her away. Part of him wanted to toy with the women but really, there was no time for games. Instead, he pointed the tip of his spear at the closest and sent his power writhing across the ground until it bit into her very life essence as a serpent might strike.

The old woman let out a gasp and fell back, dead. The second of the women raised up, a dagger in her hand and would likely have attacked if he gave her the chance. Instead he made another gesture and ripped her soul away from her body, taking in that energy as easily as a Pra-Moresh might eat an infant. The third fell as quickly, and that left only the youngest, a girl no older than ten, who stared at him from the shadows with bulging eyes and mouth agape.

She almost cried out before he pulled the life from her. Her corpse hit the ground and Jeron shivered as a wave of pleasure moved through his body. There was little in his life that had ever given him greater pleasure. That hadn't been the case before but now as he worked the sorceries that had been forbidden to him by Desh Krohan and his ilk, and as the power rippled through his being, he had to admit that forbidden fruit tasted sweeter.

When the attack hit him, it came as a surprise. He was still reveling in the sensations he'd taken in, basking in the afterglow of his feast, when the very power he'd absorbed was ripped from his body.

One moment he was smiling and the next Jeron was screaming in pain and shock, completely unprepared for the assault. Had he been a lesser sorcerer, he'd likely have been killed, but his defenses were always at the ready.

Had his victims felt the same sort of pain as he siphoned away their lives? Very likely yes. He knew such agony from Desh Krohan's assault mere hours earlier and had not thought to experience its like so quickly. The cold that replaced his warm glow was like icy daggers carefully inserted under his skin that carved into nerves and muscles alike. His eyes ached, his teeth hurt, and his blood felt as if it had been frozen within his veins.

And that after he knew he'd been warded against even worse attacks.

The sorcerer who came for him was hidden in shadows, draped in darkness and anonymity. The blast crippled him and left him on his knees, but he fought back just the same lashing out blindly and following the trail of the very power that had been pulled from his body. He had an advantage over his enemy: he could borrow more power from his masters, and he did. The Overlords granted his power without any hesitation and Jeron lashed out, sending a wave that rippled across the air and seared the ground for a hundred feet or more around his enemy.

The figure waved his attack aside as easily as a shield might deflect a pebble.

Jeron was not prepared for that. His enemy had stolen his power and wielded it easily. Whoever his attacker, there was no warning and no boasting, merely the assault. The air around Jeron shifted and constricted, crushing down on him like the pressure of a lake falling over him. His robes held back the worst of the attack, but he felt it more than he expected and he gasped out a breath, truly fearing that it might be his last. The blow likely would have killed him, but the Overlords were angered that yet another sorcerer had attacked him so swiftly after Desh Krohan, and moved to defend him with more of their own powers.

He groaned and lashed out, casting blindly toward the enemy he fought and sending a barrage of force through the air. The side of the hovel he stood in exploded outward, revealing more of his enemy.

Sunlight spilled into his eyes and the shape of his enemy staggered backward as rocks slid through the air and then bounced against a sorcerer as well defended as he was. A hundred men would have been crushed under his onslaught but the wizard he fought still stood, though he retreated.

"Enough of this, Jeron. You have betrayed your every trust and defied the empire. Surrender before I am forced to kill you."

Fear caught him as he recognized the voice. It was Corin who attacked him. Corin, who was older than he was, and whose morals were not as simply defined as Desh Krohan's. Desh Krohan had written the very laws that defined what sorceries could be used, and he would follow those laws. Corin was not the same. Corin was quiet, observant, and relentless. He could remember times when the man had faced other sorcerers in combat, and he had crushed his enemies with ease. For a moment, Jeron regretted returning his features to their familiar pattern – had he not done so, he might have had a brief advantage.

"Corin, stop this."

The man did not answer, but instead pushed against him again. He did not make grand gestures, or reveal what he planned to do by speaking his sorceries aloud. Instead, he cast the sort of spells that Jeron himself preferred, the subtle sort of powers that struck as hard as falling stars. A wave of force ripped across the distance between them, and the air grew dark as shadows reached out and surrounded Jeron, digging at his defenses, carving into his robes and shredding them. A hundred arrows would not have touched his flesh had they been fired by the best archers in the land, but Corin caught him and cut him, slipping past the powerful wards surrounding him as if they simply did not matter.

Skin peeled away from his muscles, his nerve endings and his very bones. Jeron watched the flesh of his right arm stripped aside and shrieked in pain, overwhelmed by the unexpected agonies. Corin did not stop, but continued the assault even as Jeron fell to his knees and tried to defend himself.

He should have died right then, but the Overlords were not done with him. He felt their interference, watched the waves of shadow bend and ripple around him as surely as if he wore heavy plate armor. The flesh on his arm slipped back up his torn limb in a nauseating wave of healing that hurt exactly as much as being attacked had hurt. It was not a kind soothing balm, but another assault of blinding pain.

He should have lost. He should have died.

The Overlords would not allow it.

Corin moved closer, walking across the snowy fields and the ruins of a home without owners, power surrounding him like a heavy cloak. How long had the old bastard been preparing for combat? How effortlessly he gathered still more energies. Corin did not waste time with false bravado or threats. He simply came on, the power around him ripping a hole in the fabric of reality. The darkness of the space between the stars swirled around the man's hands and head, his face lost in the folds of his hood. Had any man ever looked so terrifying? No. He had let himself think he was an equal to Corin and Corin had allowed him to believe it, but now he knew better.

Still Corin said nothing as he attacked. The ground under Jeron vanished and he fell, dropping as if he'd toppled from a mountain top, the earth falling away in a thousand broken shards.

Jeron reached for anything to save himself and found nothing there. He tried to gather his thoughts, but everything happened too quickly. He had let himself grow soft over the years, while all along he thought himself clever and prepared.

Heat washed over him and burned the air away. His hair crisped and his beard ignited.

The Overlords saved him again, caught him in their powerful grasp and pulled him back from the fall that would surely have ended in his death. Jeron stood in the air, untouched, his skin no longer burning, and wept as the pain that had started to tear at him vanished.

And then, finally, the Overlords attacked his enemy.

They had the power to combat gods, to wound deities.

Next to that, Corin was defenseless.

One moment the sorcerer was moving closer, preparing another attack. The next he imploded as if little more than a bug crushed in a giant fist. Bones were pulped, muscles torn apart. Corin did not so much as scream before he was dead. Painted in a spray of his own blood he was folded over himself again and again.

Jeron drifted slowly to the ground, dazed. The great cavernous hole Corin had summoned was still there, but he fell near it, not into it, and he looked around wildly, expecting another attack that did not happen.

For several seconds he felt the power of the Overlords wrapped around him and then that essence was gone, leaving him standing in the potent cold of the ruined town. He willed himself home. The cave was still there. The Godless rested on their beds of stone and moss, though now they woke from their slumbers.

Safe. Somehow, he was safe.

Jeron fell to his knees in the snow and thanked his new gods. Those gods said nothing at all and offered no form of comfort.

Whistler

The voices said to kill the Inquisitor or lose his face again.

Whistler decided to listen.

He moved through Goltha as a shark cuts across the seas, aimed unerringly at the place where the Inquisitor waited unknowingly to die.

As he had anticipated, the Inquisitor was in the tower where many of his kind lived. There was no chance that he could enter the building without being seen. And so, despite the bitter cold and the falling snow, Whistler waited. It was almost a day before the man left the building. He once again walked with the woman who was half his size but bore a strong resemblance facially, which was inconvenient as the Inquisitor had to die. There was simply no choice in the matter. Whistler had lived with his ruined face and would not suffer it a second time. If that made him vain then he was vain, but he would not live as a monster in the eyes of the people around him. Better to be anonymous than nightmarish.

The snow kept falling, and Whistler slipped into the street behind the Inquisitor and his companion. He kept back a distance, and cursed the cold that ate at the edges of his fingers and feet after so many hours outside. The only saving grace he'd had was the heavy cloak that protected him from the worst of the weather and had kept him warm even when he napped while waiting.

Now his consolation was the blade he carried in his right hand. This time it was tipped with a thick coating of ground parva seed oil and raw garlic. One strike, one deep cut, and the Inquisitor was as good as dead, though it would take a few hours for his heart to stop. He intended a clean death for the man, but he would take whatever sort of victory came his way.

The Inquisitor moved onto one of the main roads. His companion had left him, but she was not his target. Where wagons rolled past in both directions and people walked on foot between busy shops. The snow might stop many things, but it would never prevent people from buying the food they needed, or stopping at a pub for an ale or a goblet of wine.

As the crowd moved, Whistler stepped in closer to make his strike. Too busy for an easy kill, but one good thrust of his blade and in a few hours…

The Inquisitor's broad back kept a steady pace and Whistler moved forward, and got a firm grip on his blade.

Merros Dulver

"Corin is dead."

The First Advisor looked as if someone had struck him a telling blow across the back of his head.

"What?"

"Corin is dead." Desh Krohan was staring at him with shocked eyes and speaking in a voice barely above a whisper. "By all of the gods, Merros, I thought the man nearly immortal. He was older than me, and twice the sorcerer besides."

It took Merros a moment to fully understand. He had been contemplating Swech where she lay on a bed and offered little besides shallow breaths. It was three days since she had made any significant motions, and he worried that the woman might well die before she ever woke again.

Valam, his son, her son, still waited by the bed, seldom leaving except to relieve his bladder. He concentrated on his mother with the same sort of devotion that she offered to her gods, and Merros felt for the child. Jo'Hedee, another of the Sa'ba Taalor and second to Swech, watched over the boy and made certain he ate and slept, but could not get him to leave his mother's bedside.

Much as Merros wanted to hate her, Swech still haunted his thoughts on any day, and now more often as she lay in a state that showed little hope for positive change.

Desh's words finally crawled through his thoughts with enough force to penetrate.

"Gods, Desh. I am so sorry."

"I have no idea what he found, but something killed him. Merros, he was the strongest of us, and he's gone." Desh looked ancient in that moment, and on the verge of tears, not from sorrow, but from a quiet desperation.

"What could have killed him?"

"Corin was the most cautious among us. He never left his chambers with his hood down, never went anywhere without wards and protections that would stop a sword or a bear for that matter."

"What was he doing?"

"Looking for the Overlords and their servants, the same as all of us, really. There are threats that cannot be ignored, and they are chief among those dangers."

Merros had seen the sort of damage the wizard's robes could withstand, and he was unsettled by the idea that anyone could so easily kill one of the sorcerers strong enough to create the garments.

"He was my friend, Merros. I have known him for as long as I can remember." Desh lowered his face into his hands and sighed mightily. "For nearly my entire life."

Valam stepped closer and stared at Desh as if he were studying a statue that suddenly moved. The sorcerer looked up and stared into the child's eyes and managed a weak smile though he said no words except, "This one, he has your eyes, Merros."

The boy frowned. It was clear now to Merros that his son did not speak the common languages of Fellein. He did not understand the words.

Jo'Hedee answered the silent question Valam cast in her direction. "He says you look like your father."

Valam nodded and stepped toward his mother's bed.

"She is gone." The boy's words caught Merros off guard. He looked toward the bed fearing the worst, that Swech had died while he was distracted. The thought sent his stomach into a storm of worry that felt like he was falling from a great height.

Her bed was empty.

Swech was literally gone, no longer on the bed where she had been resting for days on end.

"Where did she go?" Merros stood so quickly that the world tilted for a moment, shocked as he had seldom been surprised before. Jo'Hedee shook her head and said, "If my king decides to move quietly, no one will see her or hear her."

"Where would she have gone?"

"Wherever the gods send her." Jo'Hedee made a wave motion with her arm, and they moved closer to the empty bed.

Merros stared, shocked and worried. If she moved so quietly on the hunt, he pitied her prey and hoped that the target of her hunt was someone he did not know.

Nachia Krous

This was not the sort of news that made the Empress of Fellein happy. Swech was gone and one of her most powerful wizards was dead. She would have preferred to hear that the Overlords were dead, or that the winter was calming down, or that the Sa'ba Taalor wanted peace.

No. Instead she got disappearances and death. Oh, and more fanatics begging for her to speak with them so that the gods would have a voice in her court.

Theor waited patiently for a chance to speak with her – a chance she had promised he would have as soon as she was done handling the business of running an empire. He was a handsome enough man, older than her by two decades at least, but charismatic and friendly. Unlike some of the others he did not push for her attention, but merely waited his chance to speak on behalf of Entrilla, the god of cities. Here, in Canhoon, Theor was a powerful man indeed. He was in the second largest city in the empire, and while he did not rule over the Silent Army, the living statues offered him a quiet deference that they offered to very few others. When he walked past them, they lowered their heads and watched him as he moved past. The only other person she saw them act that way with was her, and she was the ruler of the entire empire.

Swech had vanished. That thought bothered her a great deal. Swech had killed her predecessor and had told Nachia with complete candor that she would murder anyone the gods told her to kill. She had heard from Merros on several occasions how very good the woman was at slaughter; how she, along with only nine other Sa'ba Taalor, had killed over a thousand people in one night, a task she never wanted to see repeated. He once feared that Swech would be hurt in one of the worst parts of Tyrne before the Summer City was destroyed. By the time he reached her, determined to warn her or protect her, she had killed half a dozen men without so much as breathing harder. Simply put, the woman was a terror. With or without a weapon in her hands, Swech was deadly enough to warrant her being worried.

Who knew what her gods would say to her? Nachia knew she was safe on her throne from almost any attack, but she had no intention of sitting on her throne for the rest of her life. The damned thing was uncomfortable, and enchanted to remain that way. If she could have, she'd have summoned the Silent Army to protect her.

That was another concern, and one she tried not to think about. Her maid and secretary, Gissamoen, stood nearby as she always did, ready to do as requested at a moment's notice. The woman annoyed her constantly, seldom had much to say and tutted and fretted about as if every move Nachia made was derelict of finesse. To be fair, she was probably quite accurate in that silent assessment, as Nachia had never cared about appearance so much as she did substance. Nonetheless, she would have been lost without her.

She looked to her secretary and said softly, "Make certain the palace guards are notified of the king's disappearance."

"Already done, Majesty."

Nachia nodded. "Find Desh Krohan and have him come to me. My First Advisor has been occupied with other things lately, and that has to come to a stop."

"Yes, Majesty." There. Right there. That tone was the one that made Nachia want to grit her teeth. As if criticizing the man she looked to for advice was the very height of political error Perhaps it was, but she was the Empress and would do as she pleased.

"I'm hardly speaking to the court, Gissamoen."

"I'm only a servant, Majesty. I should not hear criticisms of your finest aides."

"You're nearly the only person I can speak to."

"Granted, but why do you trust me?"

"Because if you betray my trust, I'll have you executed, or locked in irons, or flayed alive as an example to others."

"Fair enough, Majesty." She sniffed and moved away as quietly as she could, a skill she had long since perfected as surely as the assassins of the Sa'ba Taalor.

Nachia closed her eyes and said a silent prayer to the gods of Fellein.

To her surprise, they responded.

CHAPTER NINE

Jeron

The winds howled outside of the wall of the caves and the Godless slept in their death-like slumbers, moving the War-Born to new places and preparing for the next strike against Fellein and the Sa'ba Taalor. Mostly against Fellein. The creatures they commanded were adept hunters, but against the followers of the war gods they were not quite as useful. To that end the Overlords were planning to handle the gods by themselves, striking against the Daxar Taalor as they had already struck at Paedle.

The Overlords were powerful. They were very nearly gods themselves, as evidenced by the fact that they had wounded one of the Daxar Taalor and left Paedle nearly crippled. The gods of war relied too much on their human servants, it seemed, and not enough on their own abilities. Not that Jeron could judge too harshly; if not for the Godless, he would have little control over the War-Born. He had been given great deals of power by his new masters, but when it came to fighting another mage, he had fallen short of his goals and nearly been killed.

For the first time in as long as he could remember Jeron

was truly afraid. His failures could well lead to his dismissal by the Overlords, and that likely would mean his true death. It was time to prove himself to his new gods before they decided he was easy to replace. Jeron was powerful, yes, but even with Corin dead, there were others who could come close, especially were the Overlords to offer them the same sort of power they had given him.

"No." He spoke only to hear a voice in the cold, bitter caves. "Not the Overlords. Necromancy." And it was true. He was powerful now because he broke the rules of his kind. Perhaps that was what he should have understood from the conflict with Corin. The other sorcerer had either saved up a vast reserve of power over the centuries, holding it for if he ever needed it in combat, or he had found a different source of power, much as Jeron had.

All of the physical changes that had taken place within Jeron had been erased when he possessed poor Roledru. There was no choice. It was die or move his spirit to another body and Roledru was the man he'd prepared for any such emergency. Still, his perceptions were once again human, and his body was sadly weakened. His power? That came from the lifeforces he stole, not from the Overlords. That didn't mean they weren't with him. They had quite literally crushed his enemy in combat.

Still, best to consider where he would get his power from when he needed it.

Not far away one of the Godless moved and sighed in his sleep. Jeron turned to look at the shape, uncertain if the woman were waking and would offer a report. No. Silence greeted him.

He frowned and looked to the shape on its stone and moss bed and moved closer. Something was wrong, though he couldn't have said exactly what. She was still. She...

Wasn't breathing. Her chest did not rise and fall. The delicate pulse he should have seen on her scarred neck did not show itself. Her mouths hung slightly open, and her eyes stared at the ceiling but saw absolutely nothing from fixed pupils.

Jeron stepped back, his eyes flying wide, and looked at the next of his servants. Vendtril, called Unbroken by his peers, was just as dead as the woman, just as useless.

"Trigan Garth! Trigan! We are attacked!" Jeron's voice broke as he called out to his general. Trigan stayed in the same position, but his head rolled to the side and Jeron saw the deep slash that opened the man's neck. Thick blood spilled from the wound, but it spilled slowly, and it steamed lightly in the dank air. He smelled – or imagined he smelled – the man's blood from where he stood, and his heart hammered in his chest.

He'd have bet many a coin on Trigan Garth being impossible to kill… and yet the man was dead. Murdered!

Jeron backed away and his hands clutched at his chest as he considered the possibilities. What, or who, could kill three of the Sa'ba Taalor and not be seen?

The next body in line did not move either. His Godless all seemed to be dead, or dying at the very least. Jeron stepped back and drew his hood over his head, desperate for his sorceries to protect him against possible harm. The robes served him well as they always had, but they did not cover every inch of him, and any exposed flesh was potentially a vulnerable spot.

"Wake up, you fools! Wake up! We are attacked!"

None of the Godless stirred. His generals, the leaders of his vast army of the War-Born, were all dead.

Impossible!

Jeron wept as he retreated from the bodies laid out around him. His first line of defense was gone. The Godless were all dead, and they'd stolen away his hopes in the process of letting themselves be killed.

Swech

She did not hurry. Instead Swech used her skills to move through the shadows and carefully kill each of the traitors who slept before her.

When Paedle rose from his struggles with the Overlords he called to her, and she responded. Her god told her to rise from her bed and leave the palace and so she had. She rejoiced when she heard him speak, for she'd feared that somehow one of the great gods of her people had been slaughtered. She'd felt every blow delivered upon him, had collapsed into her own pain as a result, for her connection to Paedle was greater than any connection she had to any of the other gods. She was close to most of the gods, certainly to Wrommish and Durhallem, but she was Paedle's King and that was more than an honor. They were bonded.

Paedle did not have time for pleasantries. He told her what he wanted and where to go and so she stepped into the Blasted Lands as soon as she reached them, and was lifted by her god and transported to a desolate area where the Godless and their vile master waited.

The Godless died first, for that was Paedle's command. They had abandoned the gods, and the Daxar Taalor were not kind to their wayward children.

The wretches had hoped that their location was enough, apparently, but Paedle, as all of the gods, saw with more than mortal eyes, and found the fallen where they tried to hide themselves. After that it was a matter of patience and a blade or two.

And the right poison.

Their deaths were not a kindness. Mound crawler venom and the crushed seeds of dorah berries guaranteed that the death she offered each of the Godless was painful and lingering, as the gods demanded. They were paralyzed. They could not stir, they could not scream, but their wounds felt as if they were being eaten from the inside, and the agonies they felt were amplified hundreds of times over before they died.

Death took seconds, but felt like decades. It was enough to please Paedle.

Swech watched the sorcerer discover the bodies and kept her place in the shadows. His voice broke as he called out for Trigan Garth, a man she had met several times in her life. He had been a faithful follower of the gods at one time, and now he was dead by her hand.

Paedle was pleased. It was enough.

She had never fought a wizard and was uncertain how to proceed, but it was what Paedle wanted. His rage was a line of fire drawn across her soul. It burned brightly and directed her towards his desires.

The man-made demands of his dead followers. They did not respond.

Four darts slipped into Swech's hand.

Her target retreated from her, though she didn't think she'd been spotted. He sought to protect himself from any attacks, perhaps, or to hide himself in the shadows.

Swech moved closer and stepped into the light of the closest torch.

"Who are you?" His voice cracked and the hood shifted as

he tried to see her better. Swech answered with a dart that flew effortlessly from her fingertips, and was rewarded with a hiss of pain as it struck flesh.

"I am King Swech Tothis Durwrae of the Sa'ba Taalor." She spoke softly and prepared herself. He would retaliate soon, and she could not be caught unawares if she wanted to survive.

"You are dead." Strong hands came from within the robes of the sorcerer, gesturing, catching the air as if to force it to move in certain directions. She could see the air around those fingers begin to blur.

Two more darts slid from her grasp and moved through the air in seemingly effortless arcs. One sank into the web between the thumb and index finger in his left hand, and the other stuck in the skin between the knuckles of his right index finger and the next finger over.

Swech moved as she felt the power around the man come into focus. She dropped low and pushed herself backward, rolling across the floor as quickly as she could.

The air where she had been standing burned, and Swech threw the last of her darts toward the sorcerer's hood opening but saw it slide off as if bouncing against a steel plate.

None of the wounds she had given him were large, or the sort that could kill a man. It was the poison that mattered. The toxins had to get past skin and into blood to work.

Swech backed away carefully, her eyes never leaving the shape of the man before her. "Your eyes give you away. I can see where you stand, even in the darkness." He spoke softly, but there was an edge of triumph in his voice.

Swech offered a prayer to Paedle as the wizard

gestured again, this time hitting her with the power at his command.

Tendrils of fire swept from his fingers, burning away the darts stuck in his flesh and sweeping toward her. She was not fast enough, and flames caught her cloak and her clothing, burning hotter than natural flame, it seemed.

Swech pulled her clothes away as she retreated, not allowing herself to cry out as the fire scorched her skin. Flesh blistered, but the worst of the attack was delivered to her clothing instead of to her. The cloak fell away, her vest dropped to the ground and the heavy fabric over her arms burned. It took her mere seconds to get out of the clothes and lose herself in the darkness of the cave again.

"There's no escape." The voice of the sorcerer sounded more confident.

"You are right." Swech moved quickly after speaking, keeping to the shadows, and the wizard tried to kill her again. The wall behind where she had stood moments earlier cracked as a peal of thunder escaped the man and shattered stone.

And then there was silence. Not the silence brought by the powerful noise, but the silence of inactivity.

The silence of the grave.

The wizard fell to the floor of the cavern and let out a slow, weak sigh.

The poison was taking effect.

Swech stayed where she was for several minutes, listening and watching. She had no idea what the limits of sorcerers might be, and she had no desire to die. She was not afraid of death, but neither did she seek it out as she had seen others do in her lifetime.

Darsken Murdro

"We are followed once more."

Daivem kept her voice cheerful and conversational, as befitted a pleasant discussion between two close relatives while they walked through a busy marketplace. The shops and stalls around them were well populated by crowds and, though most people might have worried about pickpockets and cutpurses, the two Inquisitors were not concerned. Very nearly everyone was far too afraid of catching their attention to ever consider trying to steal from them.

There were advantages to being thought of as monsters.

"Yes. I have seen him. He lacks subtlety."

"He is hard to miss once you've seen him."

"Does he not know how badly he's disfigured?" Darsken spoke with the same cheer as his sister, safe in the knowledge that the man with the ruined face did not speak their native tongue.

"I truly do not think he does." The face of the man who followed them was a mass of scars, nearly skeletal with the remains of skin and muscle, yet he walked along as if he could not see the people who recoiled from him in horror. He was young and wiry, straggly blond hair, a strut of a fellow who knew he was attractive to the ladies. He was almost familiar in his gait, but the face was a horror.

"He is mad, I think."

"Or the victim of sorcery, perhaps. I have heard tales of such things," Daivem shook her head sadly.

"We could capture him, I suppose."

"If his plan is to attack us, then we defend ourselves. If he wants to steal a purse, then we keep our coin and give him to the City-Guard."

"If he is mad?"

"Then the madness is beyond my abilities to treat and there are too many other issues I must deal with, including finding this Jeron before he kills again." Darsken sighed and shook his head. "Either way, I will go down the alley to our left, and see if he follows you or if he follows me."

Without another word the Inquisitor broke away, and found he was happy when the small man followed him. Better that someone try to kill him than his sister. They were both Inquisitors. They were always at risk of being targets, but he was not at all surprised that Jeron might find a cutthroat to end his prying ways, and the notion that Daivem was as safe as could be from a malignant stalker was a comfort. He would not insult her by thinking her untrained in defending herself, but he would also not stop being a protective older brother.

He plodded on and pretended not to notice that he was followed.

The man crept closer.

Daivem struck long before the stranger could make a move on Darsken. One hard blow to the back of the head ended the pursuit.

His sister shook her head and frowned when he wheeled on her.

"You would have done the same."

"Yes, but I'm your big brother. I am supposed to keep you safe."

She laughed and shook her head as she took several knives from the unconscious man's body. Up close his scars were even worse. His lips were drawn into a parody of smile that was unsettling. While she was occupied, Darsken found the closest of the City-Guard to find a cell for the would-be assailant.

As Darsken led the very nervous City-Guard back to the scene, the snow stopped for the first time in over a week.

First the necromancer, then he would attend to the scarred man.

Merros Dulver

The sorcerers watched the white-furred monsters as they approached the Dark Passage and several towns around it. They were almost invisible to human eyes, especially considering the snows, but for sorcerers they were easily seen.

In the throne room Merros listened on, pleased despite the sorcery involved, as Desh Krohan explained the situation. "There seems to be a hierarchy of some sort. There was Jeron, then a gathering below him, and under that gathering there were these vile creatures. When Jeron was killed the ones who were following his orders stopped doing their bit and now these things have stopped moving at all. They simply stand there as if waiting for new commands."

Merros frowned and considered that. "Didn't you report Jeron killed several days ago?"

"I'm assuming that these followers of his have only just realized that he's dead. It's possible they had no choice but to do his bidding and once they no longer received new orders, they simply stopped."

"What sort of creatures would these be?" Nachia, the Empress, spoke casually enough but only because there was no court in session. This, like many of their gatherings, was an informal thing between people who were friends. It just happened that they were also some of the most powerful figures in the empire.

Also, Merros had no doubt at all that she was holding something back from both him and Desh, and that was unusual but not unheard of. She would speak when she was ready, and until then he would wait. That was the way of the woman. If she sought advice, she would ask him. If she wanted to consider something on her own, she would remain silent. He hardly took offense.

Desh sighed and shook his head. "I've absolutely no idea. Sorcery can cause the creation of many things."

"Then why haven't you just created an heir apparent and left me alone about the whole courtship thing?" Nachia raised an eyebrow archly and leaned back in her throne.

"Don't even jest. That sort of power would require I take up necromancy." Merros snickered, despite his attempts at self-restraint, and Nachia actually laughed, a sound he loved to hear. Desh was noticeably more relaxed with his enemy dead and the unnatural army of the pale things frozen in place.

Though they had not yet reached the things, his soldiers, led by General Kransten, were on their way to the white forms of the animals that Jeron had created with intentions to destroy them. The plan was to cut their throats and burn them. There would be no souvenirs for the soldiers.

Sorcerous creatures were not to be trifled with under any circumstances.

"Have you found your necromancer's body yet?"

"We're still looking. There are a lot of the Harkennen mountains to look through and the snow has slowed down any attempts at a physical search. He may be dead... no, he *is* dead, but his sorceries are still around."

"Be a lot more convenient if the magic died with the sorcerer."

"I'm not going to live forever, Nachia. There would be disasters aplenty if my sorcery died with me."

'You'll outlive us all, old man." Nachia waved his words away, as she always did, but Desh frowned as she did it, and then sighed.

And Merros wondered, not for the first time, if the man knew something that he was not saying. Everyone seemed to have their secrets these days, and he didn't like to think too much about that.

He might have said something on a different occasion, might have asked his friend what was on his mind, but he was distracted, too. The mother of his child was missing, and the boy he barely knew was staying with the other Sa'ba Taalor while she was gone. Not for the first time he wondered what would happen to Valam if his mother was dead.

He wondered what would happen to him if Swech were truly dead this time. He had avoided being around her too much, but part of him still longed to get to know her again. He was like a drunkard seeking wine and that notion irritated him deeply.

"Merros?" Nachia was looking at him.

"I'm sorry, Majesty. I was distracted."

"I asked where we stand with reclaiming Morwhen."

"If those beasts are truly dead then it will be an easy situation. Once General Kransten has burned the bodies, we have won."

"That easily handled?"

"I have battalions of soldiers who will restore order as needed in the cities and towns, Majesty."

Nachia nodded. Merros offered a tight smile that felt false to him but was heartfelt. The idea of an easy solution was lovely and, so far, the Sa'ba Taalor seemed fine with leaving well enough alone. He could hope.

"Where are we with the religious factions?" Desh spoke and Merros rolled his eyes and felt a headache immediately begin to form.

Nachia answered, "I've called for a meeting with the leaders of the various groups in three days."

"Truly? Whatever for?"

"Because I've had a discussion with at least two gods, and I'll see this resolved."

Merros turned his head so fast that he felt muscles flare with sudden heat from the back of his skull to his left shoulder.

Desh Krohan gaped at the Empress. He expected his own expression was nearly as goggle-eyed.

"You've been talking with gods?"

"No. They've been talking with me." Nachia looked at her First Advisor and stared hard, daring him to doubt her word.

"When did this happen?"

"It happened. That's all you need to know."

"Nachia..." Desh got that warning tone in his voice and Nachia shook her head.

"Don't."

"It's my duty, Majesty."

"Your duty is to serve me. Not to scold me if you think I'm making a mistake."

Desh stayed where he was and kept his mouth sealed against any possible words. Had it been within his powers Merros would have willed himself to another location but, as he had said more than once, he did not trust sorcery. He certainly wasn't planning on learning new methods of escaping from his duties, even the ones that made him extremely uncomfortable.

"No, my duty is to serve the empire by offering you wisdom and advice."

"I've literally had gods talking to me, Desh. If I need advice, I'll ask for it."

"The last member of your family who claimed the gods spoke to him was referred to as mad by more than one of his advisors."

"I'm not mad, Desh. I've been talking with gods, and we're in discussion about how the empire should be run."

"Are you listening to what you're saying? The gods have suddenly come down from their silent heavens too talk to you?"

"I'm the Empress of Fellein. Now and then I find powerful people want to talk to me. Imagine that."

"That's not what I mean, and you know it."

"The gods of the Sa'ba Taalor talk to all of their people, old man. The Mother-Vine shares a unique relationship with Queen Tully of New Trecharch. What makes you think the gods of Fellein might not want to reach out?"

"They haven't tried for hundreds of years."

"Now that's not necessarily true," Merros interrupted, against his better judgement. "They brought about the Pilgrim, and he brought about the Silent Army. It's not as if hearing from the gods is unheard of in recent times."

Desh frowned. "Well, there is that."

"And as we have already said, better to hear from the gods than to hear from their local leaders."

"And as I have recently said, and as Kanheer pointed out when he spoke to me, if the gods wanted to talk to me, they should speak to me directly. I invited this."

Desh slowly closed his mouth with an audible snap, and then just as slowly, just as carefully, he nodded. "That makes an unsettling amount of sense."

"I certainly didn't expect the gods to communicate with me, old man, but I assure you, it was not the sound of an entertainer throwing a voice at me." She shook her head. "It also didn't feel like those rare occasions when one of yours talked directly in my head. It felt stronger."

"How much stronger?" The sorcerer sounded dubious about her statement.

"A burning city against the light of a candle's flame."

The First Advisor to the empire frowned at those words.

"What did the gods say to you, Nachia?"

"Not yet." She shook her head. "I'm still trying to understand all that they said."

"They spoke a great deal?"

"They spoke enough. What they said was… troubling."

Merros considered those words. Really, would the gods ever say anything that wasn't troubling? He had his doubts.

"Troubling in what way?" Desh stared at her, his eyes drinking in the details of her expression as greedily as a young lover stared at the woman he desired.

"They told me this much for certain: the Overlords have not yet finished with us."

Desh Krohan relaxed fractionally, which Merros also found just as worrisome.

"Then they only say what I already knew."

Nachia said nothing, but turned her attention to the fire burning in the hearth. Flames crackled merrily and offered a warmth the general could not feel at the moment. Unlike the sorcerer he was not comforted by the news that the

Overlords were only just beginning their assault on the empire.

What else, he wondered, were they capable of? There would surely be sorcery involved, and so he dreaded the possible answers.

Asher

The caravan had done its work and Asher was on his way around the Blade of Trellia with his goods. The ship was sturdy, the captain was honest enough, and in another few days he would be in the capital and selling his Pabba fruit for a decent sum of money. Daken Hardesty and several of the mercenaries were with him and he was grateful. More of his livelihood depended on the delivery than he cared to think about.

The stories coming from Morwhen were bad, bad enough that he feared he would return home to find his family estates ravaged by more than the horrible weather. Bad enough that snows were still falling on the orchards and across his lands, but the thought that war could once again see his fields bloodied and his crops crushed by horses and worse? The very stuff of nightmares and he had endured enough of those to last him a lifetime.

"Have they truly made peace with the Sa'ba Taalor?" Daken asked yet again, as he eyed the volcanic mountain they could see to the west and the distant plumes of smoke from the mountain to their north. They were between two of the damnable homes of the gray skins, and the man was justifiably nervous. Making matters more unsettling, there were storms at the base of each of the mountains, and those heavy clouds were ripe with violent winds, and even the occasional flash of lightning that shouldn't have existed at that level.

"Captain Pumanta assures me that there is nothing to fear from them. They have reached an accord and traded horses for peace."

Hardesty shook his head and continued looking to the north and west alternately. "Gods watch us all."

"I've no doubt they do." He thought of the stories he had heard about the Silent Army, and the four separate times he had seen the moving statues that wandered through the older parts of the city.

As he watched the horizon, Asher saw clouds come from out of nowhere, rising above the odd clouds around the forges. Natural clouds simply did not rise that quickly – not that he had ever seen in his entire life.

These were dark clouds, nearly as black as a bitter night, and they rose as high as the clouds near the volcanoes and then rose higher still, blocking the bright sunlight and sending forth a bitterly cold wind that came howling along the water and bringing with it a scattering of snow in an area that was known for warmth.

"What gods watch this, I wonder?" Hardesty scowled and rubbed at his arms.

Asher had no answer to that and so he stayed silent as the ship's captain bellowed out orders to his crew to compensate for the sudden change in the weather. Whatever was happening, he doubted it bode well.

General Kransten

The assembled soldiers moved carefully among their prey, uncertain what to make of the nearly endless pale white figures. They had looked for these creatures, had sent out scouts, had followed the messages and directions offered by the sorcerers who used their magic to find the beasts, and finally discovered several clusters of the creatures that had been hunting their men.

They were not at all what was expected. For one thing the beasts were as still as carvings. They were alive, that much was obvious; they breathed, they had eyes that stared into the distance, unseeing, and they had claws which looked like they could rend leather and flesh with ease.

There were so many more of the things than they had expected. Not dozens. Not hundreds, but a frozen tableau of the beasts that stretched as far as the eye could see.

Small wonder they had taken Morwhen so quickly. Morwhen was known for its fierce soldiers and military precision. They had been half the reason that Fellein survived the war with the Sa'ba Taalor. Truly the soldiers from the area fought with more discipline during the war than any other group had managed. When they arrived on scene for any battle the leaders of the army, Kransten himself included, thanked the gods. Seeing them overtaken so easily had been a cause for worry, indeed, and seeing the cause of their quick demise firsthand, particularly seeing how many of these beasts there were, was a cause of great stress – until they were examined and discovered in their unnatural state.

The things did not move. They did not hunt. They merely stood still. They did not react to being touched or even wounded, they merely stood in place and breathed and blinked occasionally, and so a very relieved Kransten sent off his queries and waited to hear back from Dulver. The leader of the combined imperial armies was a solid leader, a good man and wanted to be kept apprised of all unusual situations for obvious reasons. He had the ear of the Empress, and he did not like unpleasant surprises. Neither did the young woman who ruled over all of Fellein, or her First Advisor for that matter.

Like Merros Dulver, Kransten was not overly happy about the use of sorcery. The world had changed, however, and sorcerers had become a part of the army, or at least part of the chain of communication.

Clenainn Wellem was a sorcerer. He was young and he was polite, but he carried himself with the same calm reserve of most of his kind and seldom seemed to be in a hurry. The man's dark curls fell around his round face and his gray eyes, and if he hadn't been able to grow a proper moustache Kransten would have mistaken him for a waif. He was short and soft skinned but had proven himself several times to the general.

Currently the man was sitting on a large rock that he had dusted free of snow, and he softly swayed, his eyes closed, as he communed with others of his kind, getting feedback from General Dulver.

The man's eyes opened and he nodded, his young face splitting into a smile. "Excellent news, General." His voice was older than his face, and as always threw Kransten off his mental stride when he first spoke. The voice did not fit, it was exactly that simple. "General Dulver says you should handle the situation as you see fit but he would encourage the elimination of your enemies in all haste, lest they awaken."

"May all the gods forgive that notion." Kransten nodded and gestured to his signalmen. They had hoped for that answer, and he'd prepared for it. The signal was given, and one hundred and fifty men waited with ready blades. They struck quickly, driving their blades into the necks of their enemies' frozen forms, opening wounds that bled heavily. They might have stood still as statues, but as they bled out, the pale, furry creatures dropped to the ground and died properly.

Not far away another dozen men lit pyres even as still more soldiers grabbed the dead or dying creatures and unceremoniously hurled bodies onto the growing, oil-fueled blazes. They burned the dead and dying, removing the possibility that the dead might ever rise again. Once had been quite enough and Kransten still remembered the army of corpses that had marched on Canhoon in the not distant enough past.

Still had nightmares about it, too.

Clenainn watched on, his face a bit sickened by the military efficiency. Kransten understood but would not have changed a thing.

There were literally thousands of the creatures around them, unmoving, as still as stone and as alive as anyone he had ever seen. If they chose to sleep through their efficient murder, so much the better.

His soldiers moved toward the next cluster of the damned things, swords dripping with blood. They would see Morwhen freed of the damned beasts, brought back to Fellein as a free country again, and they would see their enemies dead as quickly as could be arranged.

Kransten had little doubt in recognizing that had such a plethora of creatures been animate, he and all of his men would be dead now.

The things were nightmares – broad jaws; wide mouths filled with fangs; great, thick claws on hands and feet alike; and long, muscular limbs that were surely designed for running fast and striking even faster. Despite their sheer numbers the things would likely have never been spotted if the storms had continued.

Whatever made the things move and hunt had gone silent. The gods were kind and Kransten was grateful for that.

"General Kransten!" The voice was loud and startled. He turned to see one of his signalmen, a sergeant named Leeds, running his way.

"What is it, sergeant?"

"They're starting to awaken. Some of them are stirring."

"Then kill them faster!" His heart raced at the notion. Should they truly start to react, there were far more of the beasts than there were soldiers on the field.

Clenainn clambered down from his rock and shook his head. "Something is happening I can feel it. We are in very severe danger."

Leeds raised his horn and sounded an alarm, and all around, the soldiers moved quickly. They all understood the danger. They were vastly outnumbered even with the three hundred or so of the beasts that had been killed.

Above them the clouds roiled and Clenainn shook his head. "This is sorcery. This is powerful sorcery!" The man sounded frightened.

Heavy snow began to fall from above, and in the distance something growled. Several somethings.

Whatever had quieted the pale hunters had changed. Somebody screamed not far away, and Kransten shivered as he looked in that direction.

Jeron

Jeron was dead. His body lay slumped across the ground where it had fallen, and his muscles atrophied even as gasses bloated his insides. It was bitterly cold, yet still flies found their way to the body and feasted.

When he opened his eyes, they were milky but still they saw. When he moved, muscles pulled and strained and tore; still, he moved.

Jeron groaned and slowly crawled into a sitting position. Every part of him hurt, but in a distorted way.

"Ahhhhhh…nuh." He wanted to speak clearly, but his tongue stuttered inside a mouth too dry, and his jaw did not want to work properly. He closed his eyes and focused as best he could through the pain.

"Duh-dead." Yes. Dead. He had no heartbeat. He worked his lungs and drew in a breath, but he did not breathe. Not far away Trigan Garth sat up and groaned. He, too, was dead. His dead eyes blinked, and his dead mouth moved and worked idiotically, the muscles in his dead face twitching. Jeron could see the curiosity in the dead man's expression through the muscles that twitched and moved without rhyme or reason.

Dead. Dead. Dead, but moving. Jeron and the Godless alike.

"What is this?" Jeron asked the question aloud and called out with his mind, seeking the masters he had served as faithfully as anyone had ever been served.

The Overlords spoke, and Jeron understood.

Their answer was simple and direct. "You are needed. The War-Born are not finished and they need you and your Godless to lead them."

He wept at the thought. He would never be freed from this servitude. He would not be rewarded with eternal life, nor would he be granted great knowledge and power. The proof? He was dead, an object to be used as needed. The Overlords demanded service so he would serve. His head turned hard to the left and he looked on as the Godless moved, adjusting to the same sort of pain he felt in his own rotting cadaverous form.

"So be it." He hissed the words through ruptured lips and sighed a breath from his filling lungs. His mouth twitched; his eyelids fluttered. Jeron moved very little, only enough to capture his spear again and draw it to him. There was power in the old spear, a weapon he had carried with him over centuries. It had been preserved and cared for, handled and used for as long as he could remember. It held a part of him that was beyond death.

He was grateful for that fact as he fell back against the stone wall of his cavern dwelling.

His body ached. His mind was too busy. He closed his eyes and focused on the Godless. They did not think as he did. They were empty of thoughts, really, but there was something there, something he could feel and reach for and touch with his mind.

They saw nothing at all in the cave, but they saw with so many eyes! Trigan Garth looked through a hundred pairs and managed to make sense of the view. So too, the other Godless. Jeron focused himself and tried to concentrate hard enough to understand the views from a thousand or more sets of eyes. It was a cacophony of sights, of sounds that was overwhelming.

"No. If they can do this, I can do this." He would not be bested by savages, even the sort of brutes that he had, himself, helped transform into the new shapes they had taken before their deaths.

He was a necromancer. The Overlords were necromancers. They would do this together. He would serve if he had to, but not as a mere slave. Death would not be his end. He would see to it.

The Overlords moved in his mind, slithered through his thoughts, and he let them. They sensed his desires, perhaps, and that was just as well. His needs were simple. He had need of power, and they, being the creatures they were, provided for him.

Darkness slowly pulled itself along his dead body and wrapped around him in a cocoon of soothing shadow.

So be it. He was dead. That would not stop him. There were tasks ahead of him and he would see them done. He had no choice, really, but if he were to be a slave to the Overlords, he would do all he could to make his own position better in the process. The shadows tried to change him, and he let them do their work, directing the transformation as best he could.

The darkness wrapped around him, touched his dead flesh, and brought a revitalizing energy with it. Necromancy was a weapon to be used.

He did not try to breathe any longer. He did not have to.

Jeron leaned back for a moment and then stood, moving his cadaverous limbs slowly and carefully, as if he were fragile, when he was not. He reached out with his mind and forced his will upon the dead around him. They were dead. So? He did not care. Death was nothing.

"Nothing!" He roared the word. His hands moved for a moment, and he forced his will upon the stones where his body had bled and died, spending energies that should not have been his, that were stolen from the Overlords. He shaped the stone, as easily as a sculptor shaped clay, and drew a crude throne from the ground, where he settled his dead body.

"Obey me!" he called out to the Godless, and they moved, shifted, sat up on their moss and stone death beds until as one their corpses faced him, their lifeless eyes seeing because he willed it, demanded it.

"Call your War-Born, bring them to life and prepare them to hunt."

His words echoed in the cold cave.

And slowly, the dead listened, and obeyed.

Drask

Drask considered his options carefully, understanding that they were fewer than he might have hoped for.

The Daxar Taalor called to him and he responded as he always had, as he always would, as a child of his gods. His entire life had revolved around the simple fact that he served the gods, and they, in turn, made him better for the efforts. He was a warrior. He was a soldier, and he was a follower of his gods.

Tega and Nolan March looked his way as he came closer, moving through the rich, verdant forest of New Trecharch to the depth of the Mounds which lay buried under trees, ivy and shrubs. Both smiled to see him, and he smiled back. It had been too long, yet they had only been apart for a few days, really. Long enough for him to reacquaint himself with his people and his gods alike.

He had never been apart from the gods, that was true, but to be in their presence was not the same as to have them in his head as the whispers he always heard.

"It's colder here than I expected," he said in greeting.

Nolan nodded. "We've been discussing that. Though it is still winter, Trecharch has always been made warmer by the Mother-Vine. Something fights to change the weather here, but is held at bay."

Drask studied the trees around him, all extensions of the great Mother-Vine that ruled this domain. Something powerful indeed would be required to change the weather substantially.

Tega squinted past a beam of bright light that filtered down through the canopy of leaves from the sun above. "I thought you'd be busy with your people."

"I was, but the Daxar Taalor have tasked me to end the Overlords for them. I'm to destroy the creatures before they can cause any more harm, and for that I might well need your help."

"You'll have it, of course." Tega stood from where she had been crouching against a lip of rock. The Mounds were in front of them, buried in shadow and covered in vines, lifeless now as they had been ever since the three of them had descended into the strange and forbidden place.

They had crawled into the very bowels of the Mounds, seen the odd creatures that lived there, and the wells of power waiting in the depths and then...

Nothing. There were no memories of exactly what happened down there. Five years he had tried to remember and still what exactly they went through was lost to him.

"What do we do first?" Nolan offered his lopsided smile and also stood. His hands were painted in shades of dirt that had run through his fingers. The lad was a trained fighter, but he was most certainly not a warrior. He had been a part of the Fellein army, meant to guard Tega when they both descended into the Mounds. For years he had said nothing and had walked around in a broken form that he could have easily fixed. He was, simply put, insane.

"First we finish what you are doing here, if you have not already finished."

Tega looked at him and smiled again. Her smile was a light that warmed him. He could not say if he loved her, but she was good for him. "We are finished. There is nothing left here but stone. Whatever the gods did here, they do it no longer."

Drask nodded. "Then we have to leave. The Overlords are building their powers – they are preparing to strike against Fellein and the Seven Forges alike. They have already wounded one god, and they intend to maim or kill all of the gods of my people and yours."

"No," Nolan shook his head. "That'll never do. The gods need to be here, if only to keep Tega humble."

Tega drove her elbow into the boy's ribs, but it was a playful dig. She was already the humblest of them. She had power enough to level mountains, just as Drask had already done. The difference was she understood the power they had better than either Drask or Nolan, and she almost never used it.

"We have great power, but it is finite. I will use it only when I must and if I must use it on behalf of the gods, then I will do so. They gave us the power for a reason, of that much I am certain."

Drask nodded and then looked around carefully. "The Overlords have already attacked me once. They are very, very powerful."

"You said your people know where they come from?" Tega looked up and stared into his eyes.

"My people have tales that were told to us by the gods. They say that the Overlords came from the stars in the time before the Blasted Lands, before Fellein was an empire. Before the gods were fully formed or had names."

"That would make them ancient."

"They are not human. The Fellein, the Sa'ba Taalor, we can trace ourselves back. We have common roots, even if we are now very different peoples, but the Overlords have nothing in common with us. Not even their bodies."

Nolan shook his head and frowned. "How can we fight them?"

"With swords and hands, with the power the gods have given us. I have fought and killed one of them already. We will fight the others."

"How many of them exist?"

Drask frowned. "I am not certain. Enough that they are confident they can attack gods and survive."

"Are they that strong?"

"They struck at Paedle and wounded him. He recovers now but he was injured, and that has not happened before."

Nolan shook his head, his brow clouded by doubts. "Then what can we do?"

"We find them. We kill them. However we must." Drask made his hand wave, shrug gesture, an expression that was very familiar to both of his companions.

Tega put a small hand on his arm. "Do you fear them, Drask?"

"No." He was resolute. "The gods say this must be done and so we will do it. They would not say this if it could not be accomplished."

All around them New Trecharch grew verdant and lush, but the chill in the air still worried Drask. The Mother-Vine was powerful enough to raise a forest from the arid grounds that had been the Blasted Lands. The soil at his feet was rich, alive with plants and teeming with life. He could feel that life around him, everywhere. The cold was shocking in comparison.

"This cold, Tega, it feels unnatural."

"I think that your Overlords might be working here, Drask," she said quietly.

He nodded. If they were at work in New Trecharch, they were being far more subtle than they had been with Paedle. He would consider the possibility and consult with the Daxar Taalor. The gods had their needs, and he was their servant.

To that end, he did what he had been called to do, much as he disliked the notion.

His silver hand struck Tega hard at the base of her skull and she dropped to the ground, knocked unconscious by the blow.

Nolan March barely had time to register that Tega had fallen before Drask's stiffened fingers drove into the side of his head and broke through his skull in a killing blow. Nolan collapsed, his body twitching, and then died.

By that time Drask was already siphoning the power from the man's dying body. Tega never had a chance to recover before he was pulling the energies from her unconscious form. If he could have, he'd have left her alive, but in the end, there was no choice in the matter. The energies she had absorbed from the Mounds were too much a part of her, and so he ripped them free from her body and took her life force at the same time.

Paedle was injured and needed to be restored. The same

energies that had changed his entire body over time had changed the two people he murdered for the gods. He mourned them, in his way, but their deaths were not a tragedy to him. He would miss their companionship, true enough, but the will of the gods was all, as it had always been. Even when he acted against the Sa'ba Taalor, his actions were influenced by their gods, the Daxar Taalor. His gods. His masters.

It was a simple matter of thinking and speaking to connect with Paedle where he rested in his mountain home, several days travel away.

"I have done as you've asked, Paedle. Your will is mine." Even as he spoke, he focused on the god and offered up all of the power he had taken from his long-time companions. Nolan March and Tega were dead, as the gods commanded, but their lives were not wasted. Their essence went to Paedle and fed him, invigorated him, allowed him to heal from the wounds that had very nearly crippled a god.

The god's voice, when he spoke, was restored and powerful. "YOU HAVE DONE WELL, DRASK. YOU HAVE SERVED ME AS FAITHFULLY AS EVER."

Drask raised his arms to shoulder height and turned his open palms towed the skies, before bowing at the waist. "I am honored by you, Paedle."

"YOU ARE A FAVOURED SON."

Drask felt the god's gratitude and knew peace in his soul.

Had it been required of him; he'd have killed a thousand people.

He placed the bodies of Tega and Nolan carefully within the Mounds, a silent memorial to the woman he had loved and the young man he'd looked at as a brother. They would be remembered and honored for as long as he lived.

"The weather here is colder than it should be, Paedle, but I cannot see why. Is this the work of the Overlords?"

"IT IS LIKELY."

"Should I hunt your enemies even here?"

"NO. THE OVERLORDS WILL SHOW THEMSELVES SOON ENOUGH. UNTIL THEN YOU SHOULD REMAIN PREPARED TO STRIKE WHEN YOU ARE NEEDED." The god's words were soothing, a balm on his turbulent spirit. He would have hunted the Overlords here had he been asked, just as he would strike at the Mother-Vine if it were required of him, but for the moment there were other concerns.

There were other enemies who needed watching, and he would do as he must.

Whistler

The cell was small and dark, and Whistler paced the room seeking a way to escape. The only light came from the small gaps around the door, which was locked and barred by means he could not see. Despite his best efforts, it would not yield to his attempts to break through.

After a few hours, Whistler stopped trying, and settled himself on the small cot which was the only furniture afforded him. His stomach rumbled, his mouth was dry, but no food or drink had been offered as yet.

If there were jailers, they had not yet answered his calls or his jeers.

Finally, just as he was drifting into an uneasy sleep, the door to his cell opened. He recognized the woman who came into the room. She was the woman who had been with the Inquisitor he was supposed to kill. Her dark eyes regarded him in the perpetual twilight of his cell, and her hand held a short, heavy walking stick that he expected could crack his skull as easily as he cracked a raw egg.

"What is your name, boy?"

"Whistler." He had no reason to lie, and from what he'd heard it was best to answer an Inquisitor's questions honestly, lest they see the lie and peel the truth slowly and painfully from the body.

"Whistler. Why did you attack Darsken Murdro, Whistler?"

"I was told to kill him."

"Who ordered this?"

"The voices."

"What voices?"

He wasn't sure quite how to answer that, so he tried for the truth again. "I've had voices telling me what to do as long as I can remember. If I don't do as they say, they get louder and louder until I can't hear nothing else." He shrugged. It was the best he could offer.

"What happened to your face?" His hands reached up and touched his smooth features.

"I was burned, but the voices cured me. They took the scars away."

The woman moved closer to him, and Whistler felt himself relax. He had to be relaxed, because otherwise he would alert her if he tried to strike.

"I would offer you a mirror, but I don't think you could see what I see." She spoke softly. "You are not well. I think you are under a spell, and I will send someone soon to see if that spell can be broken."

Whistler looked at her, puzzled. "What do you mean?"

She stared at him in silence for several heartbeats, and

then said, "Your face is scarred still, Whistler. You are not healed."

He said nothing but felt a cold dread in his stomach. Treachery. His ears rang and his mouth tasted of cold metal. He had never considered that possibility.

"What do you mean?"

"You followed me and my brother on two occasions," the woman said, and although he tried to school his features, Whistler was unable to prevent his shock at her realization of his actions. "You attacked my brother. We saw you coming this time because your face is marked by scars. Whoever told you they had cured you of your affliction lied to you."

Whistler ran his hands over the skin of his face and felt a cold crawl through him. Impossible. She had to be lying, or making a jest. His face was clean of scars, though he felt a bit of stubble. She was mad, she had to be.

Or the voices were liars. The very thought drove spikes of doubt through him.

Before he could say anything else, the woman Inquisitor was leaving his cell. He thought of rushing past her but knew it would be pointless. He would have to bide his time. And contemplate the possibility that someone had used him as a tool, no more significant than the knives he used in his daily life.

Whistler sat in the near dark and considered that. And then, just as suddenly, he was enraged by the notion, more disheartened than he would have thought possible.

It wasn't long before the Inquisitor returned, bringing with her one of the most stunning females he had ever seen, a woman with dark red tresses and the sort of finery saved for ladies of the court.

The Inquisitor ignored him and addressed her companion. "Darsken said you would be able to tell."

Whistler started to move, and the newcomer made a simple gesture with her hand. His muscles froze, his body as still as a statue. Although he tried mightily to move, his body refused him.

"Oh. Yes. Definitely." The woman moved around him, and though he was aware of her even his eyes refused to move in his head. He could not stare at her, nor even manage to blink. He caught the scent of her perfumed flesh, heard the rustle of her finery, but could not clearly see her face.

Long delicate fingers touched his face as if he were nothing more than a wooden sculpture. "This is serious sorcery. He has been touched by it many times, I fear."

"Can you fix him, Tataya?"

"Well, yes, but I don't know if I should."

"He should know the truth, yes?"

The redhead moved again, standing tall and looking down on him, as he struggled to raise his head and failed. "He should, but he might not want to know. These sorts of things are best handled gradually, and I'm not known for my subtlety."

"I would want to know."

"You are not scarred this way." For a moment the woman bent at her knees until she was staring into his eyes. "Sleep now," she said to him.

And Whistler slept.

CHAPTER TEN

Desh Krohan

Clenainn Wellem stared at Desh Krohan and shivered, but said nothing.

Desh let him stare for a long moment and then finally turned toward the man. "Go. You've done enough and I know you're exhausted.

"I…" The man paused. "It was all I could do, Desh."

"I know. You've earned your rest. Take yourself from harm's way and get the rest you need." Clenainn had held the creatures at bay, frozen in ice, while Desh moved from the palace to the barren stretch of land where he now found himself, locked in the cold and snow among the hundreds of creatures.

"Are you certain? I could stay and help."

He walked the long stretch of road that was called the Dark Passage and, as he did, Desh Krohan considered the creatures around him. They wanted to move. They wanted to attack. They surely would have, if Clenainn had let them. Instead, the white-furred beasts stood as still as trees, shifting slightly in the winds and doing little else.

Desh reached out with his power and took control of the

situation. It was an effort, but not impossible. They were not fully awake, could not wake up as long as he took the right precautions and continued Clenainn's good work.

The other sorcerer bowed his head and looked around one more time before he stepped away. A moment later he shifted into the form of a storm crow and took flight. Likely he was desperate to get far away from the creatures he had held at bay for hours. Clenainn's abilities had been sorely taxed, and he left the area in a state of exhaustion that would require either more magic or a great deal of rest. It was fortunate that he'd come to the area prepared for a long and serious struggle. He would sleep soon, and probably not awaken for days.

"How do you manage this?" General Kransten asked with a nearly religious fear on his face.

"I'm the First Advisor to the empire, General, and I was a sorcerer long before your father was born." Desh Krohan said the words casually. It was true, he was old, and he was one of the most powerful sorcerers in the world, though he seldom showed it.

The general and his men would have likely died if Clenainn hadn't intervened, Desh knew. They had been losing. While it took remarkably little effort for him to put the creatures down – the spell wasn't all that complex, he effectively told them not to wake up – the energy the younger man used was different.

Clenainn had been better prepared than Desh would have expected and stopped the War-Born at the first warning that they were moving, ending their threat with surprising ease.

He would recover in time. But time was something that Desh suspected they did not have. If the War-Born had awoken, chances were that meant that somewhere, somehow, Jeron was still alive. Desh could feel the threads of sorcery weaving through the air here, a pattern that was discernable to one who knew how to look for them, and Desh Krohan knew better than most. That wasn't arrogance, it was fact.

"I thought we were certain to die, First Advisor." He barely knew the man. Kransten looked older than Desh did, but of course he didn't have the advantage of wizardry to keep his appearance.

Desh did. He used it to his advantage as he always had. He also wore his robes, and had his hood drawn up, knowing full well that his appearance would be enough to inspire, if not fear, at least a healthy respect for the unknown.

Literal centuries of practice and the best I can do is hide myself behind a cloak and put a scare into the masses? He shook his head. Alright, he could do a lot better but still, sometimes he felt like a charlatan.

"I can maintain this for a while, but have your men resume their duties, please, General."

Kransten nodded and called out to one of his soldiers. The man nodded and barked an order that was passed along by others in short order. Within minutes the soldiers were once again cutting the throats of the paralyzed demons and quickly dragging the dead and dying to their funeral pyres

Desh ignored them all. His concentration was better focused on the source of their troubles. Jeron was nearby, he could feel it.

"How many of these damned things are there, General?"

"Hundreds at the least. Thousands more likely."

Desh considered that and the mounting danger, and then broke the rules. He needed power to hold the creatures at bay yet did not dare deplete his own resources. So he used the War-Born's own fading life forces to grant him that power. The simplest form of necromancy, but it was enough to stave off a powerful exhaustion that would have cost him more than he wanted to think about.

Each life that ended gave him strength, and despite his full knowledge of what he was doing and how it broke the very laws he'd helped establish, he took advantage.

He'd need the power soon enough. He had to fight Jeron and he would do so very soon. Just as soon as he finished with his grisly work.

Enough. He pushed the thought away and maintained his control over the War-Born even as he sought out the other sorcerer again. Jeron had survived despite his best attempt at killing him from a distance. No, he *had* killed Jeron. Had felt him die. Still the man lived.

Simple enough with sorcery, with necromancy. Death was only as real as the necromancer wanted. At that moment, ironically, Desh was the perfect example of that. Power flowed into him with each death occurring around him, and the soldiers rapidly killed more than a hundred of the War-Born. They were efficient and deadly.

Desh took in that energy like a sponge, feasting on the power as he had not permitted himself to do in years. It was a heady sensation, and he felt nearly drunk with the energies he stole.

The men said little as they did their grim work. The General seemed torn between watching his men, regarding the War-Born stand still and die, and staring at Desh himself.

"We are nearly finished. Your assistance is more than we would have ever expected, First Advisor."

"These things cannot be allowed to live, General. I'll not see you or your soldiers killed by these creatures."

"We would surely be dead if not for Clenainn Wellem and you. I intend to let General Dulver know as much."

"He already acknowledges the benefits of sorcery, much as he does not always appreciate the notion."

"Just the same, you both have my gratitude."

"Thank you for that."

Around them the slaughter continued. Soldiers cut throats, and more soldiers burned bodies, and in some cases the dead and dying let loose groans of pain but most did nothing. It was hardly a fair fight – it wasn't a fight at all – but Desh was fine with that. The damned things were designed to kill, had eliminated half of the lives in Morwhen, enough to leave the country suffering for a long time to come.

Not far away the volcanic mountain of the Sa'ba Taalor raged on, spewing clouds and fire into the skies above. Desh found himself wondering what, if anything, the gray skins had done about the threat.

How long did he wait for the soldiers to finish their dark work? He could not say. Long enough for the sun to descend behind the closest hills and night to come fully to the Dark Passage. The air was redolent with the scent of roasting meat, but he was not the least bit hungry. Even if he hadn't known the source of the scents, he was too stressed to consider eating.

The Sooth told him that he'd be fighting Jeron before the night was done. They might not understand how the other sorcerer still lived, but they were sure of this.

And Desh Krohan needed to be ready for that.

Swech

Swech had completed the task she had been given and left no one alive. And now the time had come to unite the Seven Forges in war again. Paedle was recovered from his injuries – Swech knew that simply because she was his King, and felt his vigor return.

She also felt his call, and obeyed it.

The Overlords played games with the Fellein, showed them what they wanted to see, what they needed to see in order to feel safe, but the Sa'ba Taalor were not so easily fooled. The War-Born were a threat that had to be ended.

To that end the gods called for the seven kings to join together again and Swech, like all of the kings, obeyed.

She had expected to meet at Prydiria, and that was exactly where the kings chose to meet. Prydiria was the keep at the heart of Truska-Pren, the fortress that was built in honor of the Iron God, and on this occasion the meeting was not in the throne room of Tarag Paedori but rather the vast courtyard just inside the great iron walls of the keep. There were few places where the armies of the Sa'ba Taalor could meet, and the massive staging area was one of them.

Truska-Pren was the God in Iron, the god of armed combat, and Tarag Paedori, his king, was the ruler of all the Sa'ba Taalor in times of war. Paedori stood with the other kings, with Swech and Tuskandru, with Ganem and, N'Heelis, Lored and Doniae Swarl, the seven most powerful members of their people. Not far away several of the followers of all seven gods stood together, honored in their own right for their faith among the gods. Drask Silver Hand, Andover Iron Hands, Thescrah, who had only recently earned a seventh

Great Scar, and several others, They stood as casually as any of the Sa'ba Taalor, as if their accomplishments were not nearly legendary, as if the fact that they had earned the respect of all the gods was unremarkable.

She made herself focus as Paedori spoke. "It is time to destroy the War-Born, to crush the Overlords as we believed our ancestors had done. They have attacked the Daxar Taalor, and plan to do so again."

No one spoke, but all around her the people of the forges moved and seethed, offended by the idea of anyone daring to strike at their gods.

"We will strike them down!" Paedori roared the words, and beside him Tuskandru simply roared. Swech remained silent, but she agreed with the sentiment. Those who defied the gods would be punished. They would be destroyed.

Jeron

The dead listened and obeyed.

Miles away in Morwhen the War-Born were in ruins, their corpses burned and left to rot in piles of bone and ash.

Jeron was angered. The War-Born were his to command through his Godless form, and he would have them.

The Overlords moved through the darkness, slithered their way through the world, and Jeron obeyed their desires.

The Fellein watched on as the bodies burned, soldiers warming themselves over funeral pyres and gathering their meals as they regarded the burning shapes. Hundreds of soldiers moved wearily, exhausted from slaughter, from cleaning up over two thousand bodies.

They could hardly be blamed for not noticing the shifting

bones, or the way the burning ashes rearranged themselves. Bodies fell, fires collapsed, and still they did not notice. They slept in their tents, or ate their meals, numbly aware of their environments, of the cold that permeated their bodies as the bitter cold summoned by Jeron sank teeth into them.

And then Jeron woke the dead, forced them from their pyres and made them rise again. If he would not be granted peace in death, then none would be allowed the solace of the grave.

The War-Born burned. They did not breathe, nor scream, but they rose just the same. Bones shifted, burnt meat and ash slipped along ruined bones, taking form instead of falling to pieces.

The dead rose from their pyres, and while their first steps were awkward, almost as clumsy as the steps of toddlers who'd just learned to walk, they recovered quickly. They learned to walk, and then the dead learned to kill.

And Jeron watched on, and saw that it was good.

General Kransten

Exhaustion crept up quickly, and Kransten retreated to his tent and considered how to move his troops. The worst of the slaughter was done, and almost bloodless. He was grateful for that.

The sorcerer, Desh Krohan had kept them safe and then moved on. Once the bodies were burning, he left the camp, heading to the west, where he believed his enemies were waiting for a final conflict. Despite the offers of a military escort, the First Advisor had left camp alone.

Another sorcerer had already been called to join the

general in the morning, a woman named Helias who was already traveling by whatever methods sorcerers used to travel three days' worth of distance in only hours.

Kransten settled himself at his table and looked at the maps laid out without truly seeing them. He needed rest and he knew it. With a long, slow sigh he shook his head and rose from his chair, heading for the thick bedroll he used when traveling. A few hours' sleep would make all the difference.

He was just settling himself down to rest when the screams started. They were a mix of panicked yells for help and calls to arms and Kransten was up and moving before he consciously considered the action, pulling on his cloak and heading out through the flaps of his tent even as he grabbed his sword and scabbard.

Kransten was an adept swordsman. He had trained with the best and had won several different contests over the years, to say nothing of the actual duels he had survived. Faced with this enemy, the weapon in his hand felt immediately ineffectual.

The things moving through the camp were nightmares made real, insane impossibilities brought to life.

They had no humanoid form, but rather moved on all fours, prowling like hungry wolves, amalgamations of burnt bone and ash, moving together silently as they attacked. There were no throats to offer growls, there were no lungs to breathe out roars of challenge. Instead they were simply demons of burning ash, embers made of meat and wood, wrapped around the remains that had gathered together to attack the living. Flames licked at those ashes and coals, blackened the bones, and consumed the forms even as they attacked. Paws made of broken, burnt bone slashed out and cut at human flesh, and the Fellein soldiers fought back as best they could with swords, spears and shields even as they recovered from the shock of fighting against what simply could not exist outside the worst ravings of a madman.

Earis Dunne, a captain under Kransten's command, roared orders to a full battalion of soldiers, all armed with spears and using heavy shields. The shields held back the worst of the attacks, but one of the men went down as a pillar of burning corpse slammed the shield aside and the head-like shape at the front of the creature lunged forward and bit down on a soldier's face and neck, killing him instantly. As Kransten watched, the man's body was pulled into the animated hellscape, incorporated into the burning dead thing to add more form and fuel to the living fire beast. Cloth and cloak burned, armor glowed red hot and was drawn into the shape, becoming part of the beast even as the freshly dead soldier was dragged in and absorbed.

Insanity.

There were at least twenty of the things and more were forming.

The troops were already assembling. And more of them were dying as they fought against the unnatural things forming from the funeral pyres. Fear tried to seize his stomach, and Kransten did his best to shake it away. Sorcery. It had to be sorcery, and this on the first day in months when he was without a wizard to support him and his movements.

Another man screamed as he was buried beneath an avalanche of burning bones. Even as he died, Kransten could see the poor bastard's body drawn into the fiery mess, drowning in ashes and embers, the bones of his body being pulled violently from the flesh.

Kransten moved forward and found himself praying to Kanheer, desperately in need of assistance of some kind.

He had his doubts that the god was listening, as two more soldiers were hauled into the hellish beasts that were attacking them and added to the growing mass of death.

Desh Krohan

The cave was unassuming, and he only noticed it because he could feel the dark magics at work behind the layer of stone hiding the interior of the hidden fortress.

It would have been satisfying to peel away the side of the mountain and expose the inhabitant to the same cold he was feeling but Desh Krohan was wise enough to leave the cave alone. That sort of display would have taken a considerable amount of the power he was holding onto – and he was going to need it, if the Sooth could be believed. They were not always reliable spirits, but they usually didn't directly lie to him so much as give half-truths.

The small entrance required that he duck down and hold his staff like a spearman ready to stab a boar, but he managed to slip into the semi-darkness, taking his time, letting his eyes adjust. The sun had only just started to rise outside, but in comparison to the dawning light the cave was as dark as midnight on a storm-ridden night.

He found the corpses easily enough. Over a dozen bodies lay sprawled across outcroppings of stone and moss that had been raised from the cavern's floor, created by sorcery to offer the bodies a place to rest. Near the farthest side of the cave, he could see a crude throne raised from the ground, sculpted by the same wizardry. On that throne sat the mortal remains of Jeron, his head slumped, and his face pointed toward his feet, as if studying his boots. The corpse's hands gripped the stone armrests, the fingers clutching at moss and stone, the very tips lost in the grey-green vegetation as if caressing the finest crushed velvet.

The dead man's skin was drawn tightly over bones, his features heavily shadowed in the ill-lit chamber, but Desh could see him well enough to know he was deceased and not resting. Jeron's lips peeled back slightly from his teeth and gums, and his nose was beginning to collapse inward.

"You are already dead, my friend." Desh shook his head. He'd hoped for that conclusion and dreaded it at the same time. He would never be grateful for the death of old companions, even if time had put them on the wrong side of a conflict. "I am so very sorry."

Bones shifted and Jeron's head raised slowly until the corpse was facing Desh instead of looking down.

Jeron did not speak, but dead, withered eyes moved in their sockets and Desh knew the dead man was looking at him, seeing him, studying him.

His heart slammed in his chest. He knew the man performed necromancy, but to keep his spirit locked into a dead body was potent sorcery, the sort he had hoped to never see. It was an atrocity, an abomination, and Desh stepped back in surprise.

Jeron did not rise from his throne, but his dead fingers clenched harder at his stone armrests, and his mouth moved wordlessly.

Desh managed to defend himself at the last second.

The dead man cast a spell that would have killed him had he allowed himself another second of panic. Eldritch energies moved through the air, distorting his view of the dead wizard, and Desh created a barrier that held back the impact of those energies and forced them to either side like a boulder parts the waters of a river.

There were a thousand things he wanted to say to Jeron, but in the end words would never have mattered. No curse would offend the undead nightmare, and no kindness would move his unbeating heart. Desh stepped in close and swung his staff, the rough head of his walking stick cracking across the skull of the dead man and knocking the corpse's head sideways. Had he been alive the blow might have stunned him, but it had no real effect, except, perhaps, to annoy the thing sitting before him.

Jeron rose from his stone seat, his hand moving to the spear at his side and wrapping emaciated fingers around his prize.

There were some sorcerers who imbued their personal possessions with power, and some who did not. Desh never had and, in his experience, Jeron seemed reluctant to do so, but that had been five years earlier; there were runes carved into the well-seasoned wood of the spear.

"Jeron, don't–"

Too late. The dead man hurled the spear at Desh, and the carefully sharpened tip of the spear cut through the air, sliced past Desh's best defenses as if they weren't there, and drove deep into his stomach with one powerful thrust.

Pain tore at him. He staggered back, dropping his staff, and both of his hands gripped the shaft of the spear, even as the dead man moved toward him and grabbed the other end of the long shaft.

Desh tried to stop the spear from going deeper and failed. Even dead, Jeron's muscles were stronger than his, and he let out a scream as the barbed tip of the spear drove deeper into his insides, angled upward by the thrust, moving into organs he didn't want to consider.

Foolish! What a damned stupid way to die.

Desh Kohan coughed blood up his throat and out of his mouth as he was lifted from the ground.

Jeron's corpse smiled at him, that wretched rictus turning into a sinister grin. Still, he said nothing.

Desh gripped the spear and whimpered, the pain moving through him enough to guarantee that concentrating would be almost impossible.

Almost. A thousand years of discipline is a long time to practice self-control.

Desh uttered words softly, and the spear in his hands aged a hundred years in seconds. The shaft collapsed into wood rot and dust and his body fell back toward the uneven ground of the cavern.

The head of the spear did not melt exactly, but it, too, crumbled, falling apart inside Desh Krohan's belly and chest, the point sliding into his lung before it disintegrated.

"Enough." The word was whispered. It was all Desh could manage. His chest felt bitterly cold, far colder than the winter weather could account for. The bastard had likely poisoned the spear's tip. It was what Desh himself would have done.

"Enough." He repeated the word and coughed violently.

"You killed me, Desh Krohan." So Jeron could speak after all. That dead smile stayed in place. The lips barely moved, but Desh heard the words in his head.

Instead of answering he spoke another incantation, this one older than most he knew, and one he had never once uttered in his life.

Jeron leaned forward, dead ears straining to hear the whispered words.

"No! No!"

It was Desh's turn to smile. "Oh, yes." He finished the incantation and the world around him detonated.

All of the magical energies he had taken from the War-Born as they died, all of the power he had carefully stored for years in his stone and bead batteries, was detonated in one instant. The resulting explosion tore his body apart and shattered the walls of the cavern where Jeron and his Godless worked their dark sorceries.

Desh Krohan killed himself, but he made sure to take his enemies with him.

The side of the mountain blew outward in a gigantic fireball, shattering stone and the peace of the early morning.

In Canhoon, hundreds of miles away, all three of the Sisters stifled the need to scream, as did several other sorcerers who were powerful enough to sense the death of the First Advisor.

In the Dark Passage itself, the War-Born stopped attacking. The dead monstrosities that Jeron and his Godless commanded fell apart, and General Kransten, who was expecting to die within the hour, thanked Kanheer for his unexpected salvation as his enemies crumbled into ruination.

Moments later he heard the distant explosion echo through the mountain pass, none the wiser for what the sounds meant.

CHAPTER ELEVEN

Nachia Krous

"Desh Krohan is dead, Majesty." The words rang in her ears, and Nachia sat on her throne and stared at absolutely nothing, her mind insisting that what she had heard must be someone's idea of a jest, no matter how poorly she thought that notion.

The words were uttered by Pella, who stood before her with tear-stained eyes, shaking softly with grief.

"That's impossible."

"He died fighting Jeron. He is dead, Majesty."

Nachia shook her head and forced herself not to scream at the woman, despite how very much she felt like screaming. Desh Krohan being dead made as little sense to her as the notion that the sun would not set. He had been the most stable part of her world for as long as she could remember. Her mother had passed when she was young, her father died a decade later, and she had survived those things, in large part because Desh Krohan had been there to offer wisdom and comfort to her. He had been kind when no one else was, and he had been stern when she needed someone to stop her from making a complete fool of herself.

"No." She shook her head again.

Merros Dulver stood nearby, his face unreadable as he absorbed the very same information. He was a military man, and he was used to bad news, but this? It was simply too much to absorb.

"Are you certain, Pella? There can be no mistake?"

"We have been connected to Desh for a very long time, General. I wish it were possible to be mistaken, but it is not. Desh Krohan is dead."

"Stop saying that." Nachia spoke automatically.

Tataya answered. "Nothing would please us more, Majesty. But as Desh said more than once, we are to advise you when he is not present, and he is not here. He will not be coming back."

She did not cry, but Tataya's expression showed her grief just the same. Her eyes were too wide, and her hands fluttered restlessly. The Sisters were always composed. Always. And yet here they stood, all three of them, and each looked to be crumbling under the weight of the news they shared. The First Advisor to the Fellein Empire, who had held his position for over a thousand years, was gone. An impossibility that was made reality.

"We are here to serve you, Majesty," Goriah said softly. "There is no possibility that we can ever take the place of Desh Krohan, but we are here to serve as you see fit."

Nachia looked around the room and slowly nodded. She was the Empress. She had to maintain her composure. "Yes. Of course, Goriah. The Sisters are most certainly appreciated in this time of need."

Goriah inclined her head in a small, formal bow. "Jeron is gone too. It appears that the worst of the weather we have experienced this winter might have been his doing.

The skies are clear for the first time in many days, and the days may well be warmer than they have been."

Nachia waved the news side. It hardly seemed to matter.

Desh was dead. Her Desh. Her friend and companion. The annoying man who kept telling her to have a child because–

Oh. She closed her eyes and placed both of her joined hands in her lap. *Because I will not always be around.* How many times had he said those words of late? How many times had she brushed them aside, secure in the knowledge that he would always be there for her to lean on?

She looked at the Sisters, and then Nachia turned to Merros, where he stood stiffly at attention, his gaze unwaveringly locked on the tapestry before him, where his son stood examining the details that had been woven into the ancient images.

"It's good that Jeron is dead," she said softly. "If not, I'd have the entire damned army searching for him."

The Sa'ba Taalor in the room stood together, as they often did, and Jo'Hedee moved over to Valam, placing one hand on the boy's shoulder.

Valam looked at Nachia and stepped closer to her. He said nothing and although she was sure he did not understand the exact words, she thought he understood that something dreadful had happened. It was likely he had never experienced grief, not in the way that she was now. Or Merros. Or the Sisters, who had been closer to Desh than anyone else she could think of.

Grief bit at her, stole away her thoughts and twisted her insides until she thought she might simply scream and never stop.

And then the air seemed to ring with a crystalline note

that she knew was not really there, but had to be a product of her imagination.

The gods had spoken to her recently, and she'd never had the chance to tell Desh what they had said. Guilt crawled through her insides at that thought. He'd wanted to discuss their words and Nachia had brushed the notion aside because, well, she was still trying to understand all that they'd said to her, to absorb the experience – in the same way she knew her mind was now trying to absorb that her First Advisor was gone forever.

When she looked around the room again, the light had fled from the various windows, and the fires burned brighter in the fireplaces, and the Sa'ba Taalor were gone, as were the Sisters. Somehow, she had lost hours. The only person who remained in the room was Merros Dulver. Even Gissamoen was gone from her side. Her throat was raw, and her eyes ached in her head.

Merros no longer stood in the same spot, but sat in one of the chairs at her vast table of maps. He did not study the papers there but merely sat still, his eyes focused on the palms of his hands, which rested across his knees.

She was only mildly curious about where everyone had gone. Ultimately it didn't seem to matter. There was little that seemed to matter.

Desh Krohan was dead, and she was alone.

"I hate this, Merros."

Merros looked toward her and nodded. "As do I."

It was all either of them needed to say at the time. Still, he got up from where he'd been sitting and walked over to her. It was not General Dulver who reached out and touched her hand, but rather it was her friend Merros. Her fingers intertwined with his and the grip they shared bordered on being painful. Neither said a word. Neither had to. They had lost a dear friend, and one of the small group of people they both trusted with their lives, with discretion.

There was nothing else to say.

And so they said nothing, but stayed where they were in quiet companionship.

Darsken Murdro

The First Advisor to the empire was dead. Darsken found the idea nearly impossible to comprehend. Desh Krohan was beyond powerful. Long before he ever met the man, he knew of him through the longstanding legends of what he had done in the past. He had helped shape the empire, had advised, managed and shaped the world as Darsken knew it, and now he was dead.

He pushed the thought aside. In the end it did not matter. Had he been called on to investigate the death? No, he had not. But his objectives had been changed by the death just the same. The necromancer he had sought was no longer alive.

The trail had led only to the east, and now the trail did not matter.

According to Daivem, the man who'd tried to kill him had been a victim of sorcery, but that spell was broken.

His life should have been easier, but there were always more deaths to consider, weren't there?'

"Oh, yes." He shook his head. "Always more. Always."

The necromancer was dead, but there were still several bodies that had been disfigured, marked with the same sort of markings. An examination showed that the bodies had not actually been affected by necromancy. Someone muddied the waters of his investigation with false evidence.

And so he investigated that instead, and suspected the Sa'ba Taalor had been involved for whatever possible reason. Though a war no longer was fought between the nations, he knew the ways of the Sa'ba Taalor well enough to see their efficiency in the way the bodies were killed. Either it was the gray skins, or someone who thought like them. The difference was as easy for him to see as were the differences between two painters using different brushes and canvases to paint sunsets.

Darsken walked the streets of Canhoon and tapped his walking stick on the cobblestones with each stride of his left foot. The weather had warmed up nicely, and the heavy snows were melting, leaving puddles and streams of runoff wherever he walked.

The man he sought was not a Sa'ba Taalor, or if he was, he was one of their hidden agents.

According to Merros Dulver there were members of the Sa'ba Taalor who hid among the Fellein. He had once fallen victim to one of them and though that one had long since been removed, there were others who still wandered the city streets and watched the Fellein for the gods of the forges.

The Sa'ba Taalor did not have sorcery that they knew of, but they had their gods, and it was hard to say what miracles they could commit. They replaced lost limbs with living metal. They raised mountains in different places and locked perpetual storms around those mountains. How hard would it be to change the color of a person's skin after all of that?

So he followed one of his suspects, moved through the city and observed.

And, for a change, was rewarded for his diligence.

The man named Dulcern Abesh left his apartment in the garden district and walked down the Avenue of Heroes, sauntering down the pathways with indifference as he walked past people who had money and prestige. He walked as only someone who shared those benefits ever could. People moved out of the way of Dulcern Abesh, as if they somehow sensed he had the ability to punish them, and they were wise to. Abesh was not a member of the City-Guard, but he was known to them, and they favored him. He was a man of influence among the police forces of Canhoon. He worked as a liaison between the City-Guard and the Imperial Army, an official in neither group, who commanded the respect of both simply because he had been born into a family of bankers who handled the pay of soldiers of all kinds. In all sincerity he was powerful in ways most would never understand.

In simpler terms, he was a political middleman.

Darsken knew the type. They were never quite arrogant, but they were self-important.

Abesh looked over his shoulder and frowned when he saw Darsken. For his part the Inquisitor did absolutely nothing to indicate he had seen the man. He continued on with his head down, carefully placing his feet as if afraid that he might slip on the wet cobblestones or the ice that still stubbornly clung to several surfaces.

His target frowned slightly and continued on his way. There was little chance of missing a member of the Inquisition. Most came from the Louron. Most had darker skin and all of them carried their walking sticks, like unofficial signs of their office. It had never been the intention of the Inquisition to hide. They were investigators and they took their jobs as seriously as anyone could.

Abesh did not run. He carried on, and Darsken followed him.

Abesh turned a corner, into a smaller alleyway, and Darsken gave him a minute before he followed.

Just long enough for the man to prepare an attack.

Abesh came at him at a hard charge, a long blade in his left hand and a bludgeon in his right. The heavy stick came down like an ax strike and Darsken retreated, using his own walking stick to deflect the blow. He managed to dodge the blade as it cut the air where his stomach was a moment earlier.

As the knife swung around a second time Darsken defended himself. His heavy walking stick came around in a tight arc, and the well-worn head of the stick drove into his attacker's throat. Abesh backed up, trying to cough, but the damage had been done and it was substantial. Abesh fell backward, unable to breathe through his ruined airway.

Darsken did not try to save him. He watched on as the man coughed, darkened and slowly died. Their fight had lasted seconds. Abesh took much longer to suffocate.

When he was dead, Darsken settled down next to him and began his rituals. The spirit he pulled from the body was not from Fellein. He was Sa'ba Taalor. He was also very devout in his faith, and despite Darsken's best efforts, the man would not answer his questions in death any more than he had in life.

Eventually, after he had tried several times to draw answers from the dead man, he released the spirit.

Merros Dulver

General Kransten had returned from the Dark Passage as

quickly as he could manage, bringing with him the news that as far as he knew the creatures he had been sent to destroy were gone.

Merros nodded and smiled grimly. They sat around a small table in the gardens of the palace, as close to an informal meeting as the two military men had ever managed.

"I'm glad you're alive, Caer."

"I'm surprised I am alive," Kransten admitted. "Even when they were as still as statues those damned things scared the reason out of me. They had as many teeth as a Pra-Moresh." Kransten laughed as he said the words, but Merros knew the man wasn't exaggerating. The body count left by the War-Born was still being tallied, but several towns had been destroyed both along the Passage and well away from it. Half of Morwhen seemed to have been slain and eaten by the damned things. Plagues had done less damage.

"Well, if the gods smile, we'll not see any more of the things."

"I have doubts." Kransten shook his head. "We killed well over a thousand of them, but I doubt even a thousand could have done as much damage as is being claimed. There must be more of them hidden about."

"We have sorcerers looking." Merros shrugged. "It's all we can do. The weather is getting better, but the problem is we either have the soldiers to have at the ready or to send out in scouting parties, not both."

"It's maddening."

Merros shook his head. "The Sa'ba Taalor are gathering their armies."

"Have you sent emissaries?"

"Not yet. It's a tricky situation, as well you know. Send too many and they might be seen as a threat. Send too few and they'll be a light snack for those damned mounts of theirs."

"Merros, no matter how many you send, the gray skins will never see them as a threat. More likely as a warm-up or an invitation to cause mayhem."

"We are not at war, and I want to keep it that way."

"You could go yourself. Last I heard they respected you."

"I'm supposed to lead the entire army."

"Aye. And you have others, like me, who can follow the orders you give, or who you can send to talk with the kings and their soldiers."

"It's never that easy."

"It's *exactly* that easy, Merros. You cannot do all of this yourself, just as you couldn't fight an entire war by yourself. Delegate as you see fit, but if we need to speak with the Sa'ba Taalor, you either do it or you send someone they respect. You have ten of them in the palace right now: ask them how best to handle it."

The man offered him the exact same advice he would have offered to Nachia, and it was good advice, which was the annoying part. He wanted to handle everything. He wanted to be in control at all times because ultimately the weight was on his shoulders and he was responsible, but no, he could not manage every part of the army without aid.

"Maybe I could send one of the Sisters. They travel quickly and they are very aware of the way the Sa'ba Taalor think."

Kransten nodded. "They are also powerful wizards. I hear the gray skins respect their strength."

"Anyone who has ever seen them respects their strength."

"I still can't believe Desh Krohan is dead. He saved my life."

Merros shook his head. He didn't want to think about the

dead man. Didn't want to accept his death, though he had no real choice in the matter.

"Enough. I'll ask the Empress how she wants to handle the Sa'ba Taalor and we'll move on from there. In the meanwhile, we need to consider these War-Born and whether or not they're truly finished. I do not believe we are going to be that fortunate. I have to agree with your assessment. Two thousand is not a big army. Five thousand is still too small. These creatures, these Overlords want to take on all Fellein? They'd need a much larger army."

"Then where do they hide them? Beneath the Dark Passage In the plague winds? We already know we can't send armies down into that area. They tend to die when they breathe in the winds for too long."

Merros grunted but said nothing else. It was a debate that had gone on many times before. The plague winds brought sickness to people. More than a day or two in the lower regions could cripple a man. A week or more and death was almost inevitable. It was considered a blessing of the gods that the winds did not rise from the lower areas of Morwhen. The air down below was heavy; it stank of sulfur and worse. Desh Krohan had once told him the cause was "volcanic gasses", whatever that meant. All Merros knew was that the area was bad for the health and so he kept his soldiers well away.

And that meant there was a very large area where the Overlords could well hide an army.

Merros stood up and Kransten followed suit. Kransten was older, thinner and shorter than Merros. He was also a pleasure to work with, and blessedly competent.

"Why don't you have a conversation with the Empress. I'll talk to the Sisters, if I can find one, and discuss trying to locate the War-Born with them?" Kransten suggested, looking across the gardens, where several of the local nobility were walking around and enjoying the warm weather that had finally arrived.

Merros smiled. "Exactly what I had in mind, Caer."

Caer Kransten smiled. "I seldom need an excuse to find one of the ladies to talk with."

"Few men do." With that, both men were on their way. Kransten headed deeper into the gardens and Merros watched him leave, storming across the manicured lawns like a ship on calm waters. It hardly mattered what was going on, Kransten was a man who seemed calm in almost every case. That was one of the reasons Merros liked him. Seeing the man helped him feel calmer himself.

He needed that, just lately. He didn't feel calm. He felt like an edge of panic was waiting close by at all times, ready to help him make a fool of himself. According to most people he seemed to carry off his duties well enough, but there were times he expected everyone around him to call him out, to accuse him of being an impostor.

His insecurities were natural enough, he supposed. He had gone from retired captain to leader of the armies based solely on the fact that he met the Sa'ba Taalor before anyone else had. How he managed to keep his post was one of those mysteries he tried not to consider too heavily.

He found Nachia exactly where he expected her to be, sitting on her throne and scowling softly.

He bowed formally and she smiled when she saw him.

"I expected to see you earlier."

"Apologies, Majesty. I was dealing with reports from the field."

"Anything interesting?"

"Puzzling, really. We have dispatched a large number of these creatures, the Overlords' pets, but not enough. I need to find out if there are more of them hiding and if so, where. They are too dangerous to leave alone.

"Also, I am hearing tales of the Sa'ba Taalor gathering their forces for possible war." He looked toward Jo'Hedee, who stood close by with Merros' son. "Should we ask them?"

"According to Swech, they are here to serve me. I expect that means we can ask them questions."

Merros nodded and excused himself to speak to the woman he knew was a friend of Swech.

She saw him coming and stood exactly as she had before she noticed. Like all of her kind she was always prepared for a possible attack, but hardly seemed worried that he would pounce.

"You are well, Merros Dulver?"

"I am, Jo'Hedee. I wanted to know if you know why your people are gathering together."

"Of course. The gods have called them to prepare for war."

"Against whom?"

Her eyes regarded him for a moment. "The Overlords have servants. They are called the 'War-Born.'"

Merros smiled and nodded. "Yes. We are aware of them."

"The gods have called us to war against them, not you. We are here to serve the Empress, a show of faith and trust between our peoples. You have nothing to fear from us."

"You will war against these War-Born?"

"That is what the gods desire, Merros Dulver. It is what we will do."

Merros smiled. 'Do you know where Swech is?"

"She is at that gathering. She has been called to war by the gods. She is a king."

"Why did she leave her son here?"

"Because his father is here."

Merros frowned. "I thought the Sa'ba Taalor did not follow the idea of fathers knowing their children."

"Your people do." Her eyes stayed firmly locked on his. "She wanted you to have a chance to meet your son, to know him better."

"I have not done enough to know him."

"That is not for me to say." Her words were direct and so was her tone. She agreed with him but did not judge.

Jo'Hedee turned to look at Valam. The boy was once again studying the weapons on the wall, each blade a piece of history or legend among the Fellein. Swords that had been held by great soldiers; the spear that had, according to legend, ended the life of a great serpent in the swamps of Louron over three hundred years earlier. A bow that, according to myth, had once been in the possession of Kanheer when the god walked the world. Many legends and tales, though Merros doubted the provenance of most of the pieces. Like as not they were imitations. According to what he had heard in his youth, most of the real weapons had existed in the Summer Palace, and that structure had been destroyed by the Sa'ba Taalor before the war between their people truly began.

"I will try to do better." Merros wasn't sure if he was talking to himself or to Jo'Hedee, but she nodded just the same. He returned the nod and walked back to the throne.

"Apparently the Sa'ba Taalor will be fighting against the War-Born."

Nachia chuckled. "Then that is a situation we no longer have to worry about."

"I was thinking exactly the same thing."

Jo'Hedee and the other Sa'ba Taalor did not seem to pay the least bit of attention to their conversation, but Merros did not trust that, and neither did Nachia. Whatever they had to say about the people of the forges it would wait for now.

"I need to know where you want our forces collected, Majesty. Do you want to find these War-Born? Should we be gathering our own armies for possible combat?"

"I'll speak to the sorcerers. We shall have them find the Overlords and their servants."

Merros nodded. Much as he still distrusted sorcery, he was learning to tolerate the difference it could make.

"In the meantime, General, rally our forces as best you can. I want us ready if we must go to war."

"What are we doing about Morwhen?"

"Take it back. I will not lose a kingdom."

"Your cousin? Is he well?"

"He is recovering. He is not at all happy with his situation."

"Who among us is, Majesty?"

"Few, I fear," She shook her head, and he knew she was thinking about Desh again. How could she not?

"We will endure, Nachia." His words were barely a whisper. "We will get through this."

"Of course we will." She smiled, and her face changed completely.

He ignored the fact that her smile was not genuine. Perhaps in time, but for now there was simply too much darkness.

CHAPTER TWELVE

Whistler

He sat in silence, and for the first time in as long as he could remember that silence was complete. The darkness of his cell was nothing in comparison to the darkness in his mind. The voices were silent, and that silence overwhelmed him.

Whistler had spent the night alternately pacing his small cell and crying to himself as softly as possible. It wouldn't do to have others know that he was alone and scared. There had been plenty of times when he had been lost in solitude before, and it had never gone well for him. He was used to the voices. They offered him an odd comfort in his lowest moments.

If the word were true, his voices had been the trick of a sorcerer. According to the women who had visited him, the Inquisitor, and the witch, he had been freed of that trickery, but it didn't feel to him as if he had been freed of anything.

He felt deafened and alone.

We are with you, Whistler.

The sound was unexpected. He heard the gathered voices speaking as one and his heart surged in his chest. Whistler sat up and craned his head to the side as if he might somehow hear the perfectly clear voices even better than before.

"Who are you then?" He spoke softly.

We are your friends.

"And how would I know that?"

You have been lied to. Tricked. No more. We will mend you. We will free you.

"More mind games?"

Jeron believed in trickery. We believe in better than that.

"And what would you have of me?"

Jeron is gone. He has been destroyed and with him he has lost an army. We need someone to lead our armies.

"I'm not a soldier. I never have been."

We do not need a soldier. We need a king.

There will be no lies between us, Whistler. Serve us and you serve yourself. You prepare yourself for a better world, with wealth and power. You serve us, and we reward you. There is no punishment. You do not have to fear. Serve us, and you will be a king.

"I'm a thug." He shook his head. "I've never been prepared to be a king, never would know where to start."

The door to his cell swung open, easy as you please, and the light from the corridor outside of the small space was enough to make him squint.

Walk free. Consider this your first reward. Serve us and you will know more rewards.

After a moment, Whistler stepped forward hesitantly. The thought crossed his mind that this could be the witch somehow trying to trick him, but the further he went from his cell, the more that fear receded.

The corridor was lit by occasional torches in sconces, and they were enough to let Whistler walk without fear of tripping over his own feet in the darkness. It was a matter of only minutes before he reached the doorway they had brought him through when the City-Guard dragged him to his new home.

The entrance was open and unguarded. Despite himself, Whistler grew excited at the possibility of freedom.

And then he was across the threshold and staring at the nondescript wall of the tower he had passed a dozen times before without ever knowing what was on the other side of it. There were two City-Guard not far away, but they were either unconscious or dead. Either way, he left them alone and walked away as calmly as he could, his mouth dry as ashes and his heart thudding in his ears.

Three people walked down the street not far away and not one of them bothered to look in his direction. Whistler moved cautiously just the same, expecting to see someone flinch when they saw his ruined face. One young woman looked at him and offered a smile. He smiled back.

It was only then that he thought to touch his face. The scars were gone, replaced by light stubble and the shape he had grown accustomed to over the years.

He did not dare believe. Not a second time.

As we said before, Jeron believed in trickery. We believe in rewards. Your face is easily mended.

"How do I know you don't lie to me?"

We have freed you and repaired you. What else do you need?

"A meal would be nice. A place to stay."

He felt fingers slide through his mind, cold and alien. *Find an inn where you can eat and rest.*

There was no point returning to his original lodgings – the room, and his scant belongings, would be long gone. But he knew just the place. Because he wanted to test the boundaries of what he was offered, Whistler walked several blocks until he made his way to the Gilded Swan, a fine establishment with large rooms and a good tavern besides. He asked for a room and received one, He went into the tavern and was found a table. Within less than a minute, a meal of roasted chicken, sufficient for two, was in front of him. The man doing the serving smiled and left with only a few words spoken. He came back shortly with wine of excellent quality.

Whistler sat in silence and ate the best food he'd had in a long while. When he was finished, he went to the room provided for him. The bed was comfortable and clean, far better than he was used to, and with a full belly he retired for the night.

As he lay on the bed and closed his eyes, the voices came back again.

You will rule for us, and you will serve us?

"It seems you know how to bargain, so aye. But why do you choose me?"

Jeron chose you. We accept this and you in his place.

"What happened to this Jeron?"

He died.

"So tell me what I must do.'

Rest and we will prepare you.

With those words a deep exhaustion took him, and Whistler slept.

Andover Iron Hands

They moved from the perpetual storm of the Blasted Lands and into the foothills near Paedle, and Andover felt a sense of repeating himself. The landscape was almost the same, but the weather was much better than it had been, warmer, calmer. The last time they'd come to the area winter seemed determined to stay forever, and now plants were growing from the ground and the snow was gone. After the cold of the storms inside the Blasted Lands, the calm of the day was almost unsettling.

The Sa'ba Taalor made enough noise to make up for the silence.

There were hundreds of them – no, far more than that. They were here for one simple reason: the gods wanted the War-born and the Overlords destroyed, and the children of the forges, along with a few select others, were supposed to handle the situation. Andover looked around and saw little to combat, save blooming plants and pollen motes.

The War-Born did not seem to be present.

Tuskandru rode up beside him, a grin on his broad face. "They hide from us."

"Or they are not here at all," Andover replied.

Tusk sniffed the air and laughed. "They are here. I can smell them."

There was a definite odor, Andover agreed, though he couldn't have said what caused it. An undercurrent of bitterness moved through the air of the valley.

The Dark Passage was just below them and to the west but, here, the air should have been fresher.

Drask rode past, his eyes cast toward the ground, his hands buried in the mane of his mount. The great beast lowered its muzzle and sniffed the rough terrain.

"They have been here. The War-Born, but they are not here now." He shook his head. "Brackka thinks they moved down to the passage."

"So we hunt them." Tusk started for the lower ground. If anyone disagreed, they kept silent. The kings were seldom wrong in their decrees as the gods spoke through them. Stastha shook her head and grinned, looking at Tusk's broad back and shoulders with an expression of indulgence that was almost maternal, and Andover followed without hesitation.

Andover did not question in any event. He didn't want to think, he wanted to fight. He wanted to lose himself in combat, in the ebb and flow of bodies pressed together with the simple goal of destroying enemies.

He wanted bloodshed. His body nearly twitched at the thought. Tusk grunted and then moved faster, riding into a gallop on his great mount, and the rest followed. Tusk was not in charge of them, but there was no dispute. All of them began their descent, sliding past the Dark Passage and moving lower, into the badlands of the deep valley below. Andover understood about the plague winds but did not care. He and the rest of the people with him had just ridden through the Blasted Lands, where far worse could and often did happen.

The Daxar Taalor had prepared their people for the worst of environments. Their skin was toughened against heat and cold, their eyes had a second inner lid to deflect the grit and debris cast about by the storms of the Blasted Lands. The plague winds would not cause them harm. Andover did not question these things. He understood them. He had been in several discussions with Desh Krohan and others who had studied him in an effort to better understand the changes between the pink-skinned appearance of most of the Fellein and what had happened to Andover when he was chosen by the Daxar Taalor. His skin was gray, his features transformed by the gods of the forges. He was, as he had already considered several times, at least as much like a true Sa'ba Taalor as a person could be. He had been blessed by the gods and changed by them. His iron hands were simply the most notable of the transformations.

Tusk and Stastha rode ahead of him and descended quickly into the areas below the Dark Passage. A thrill ran through Andover at the idea. The War-Born had come from the Tolfah, according to the gods. The Tolfah thrived as well as anything could in the badlands, and if the Overlords changed them as the gods had transformed Andover himself, then the Tolfah could be almost anything. They could be formidable indeed.

They would know soon enough.

Whistler

Whistler slept and dreamed.

In his dreams a vast army waited for him. They were faceless, shadowy forms that shifted impatiently from foot to foot, eager to bring about death and mayhem. He could feel their need for violence as if it were his own, and perhaps it was.

In his dreams the armies waited for his command, waited for him to decide what they should attack, what they should destroy.

And in those dreams, he saw the enemy approaching, a great horde of gray skinned brutes, mongrels riding on furry beasts or running on foot, all of them armed and all of them eager to shed blood.

And who was he to deny the warriors or his own army?

In his dreams Whistler roared out, "Attack! Kill the bastards!"

And his army replied with a salvo of screams, or bloody roars, a challenge to any enemy that might come along, and then they moved forward, a heavy wave of destruction that surged forward and threatened to flood the world in a tide of blood.

And as they moved, they *changed*. Flesh thickened, bones twisted and bent into new shapes designed to move on all fours, built for predatory hunting and destruction.

In all his life few things had ever scared Whistler. He did not fear people. He had no dread of combat. Though he was not a large man he was wiry and fast, and surprisingly strong for his size. He had killed and maimed a dozen men larger than him over the years, and never once felt a deep fear of any of them.

But there had been a time when he was younger and foolish, when he had worked as a lookout and, yes, a whistler, for the street gangs in Goltha, and had made the mistake of breaking onto the wrong estate. He'd expected human guards. What he got instead were hounds, great black dogs trained to hunt and kill anyone who dared cross their territories. He had made it off the property and over the stone gate alive, but only just managed to avoid being caught by the beasts. Tillio and Dapist, two of the boys he'd been a look out for, had not been so lucky. He'd heard Dapist scream as the hounds took him. He'd watched Tillio get torn apart by three of the animals. They'd clawed the boy's body and torn great gobbets of flesh from him as he writhed and shrieked and then died.

He had not consciously thought of those boys in several

years, and he never wanted to remember the hounds, but in his dream he shivered as his soldiers changed, became more like the hounds – large things with too many teeth and rending claws capable of peeling the bark from a tree and the flesh from a man.

And in his dreams, his army charged into battle, baying and howling their outrage into the air even as they overwhelmed their enemies.

Andover Iron Hands.

Oh, they came quickly when they attacked. The air in the badlands was murky with the plague winds, and all around him the translucent inner lids of the Sa'ba Taalor descended to protect their eyes.

The seven Great Scars on Andover's face clenched tightly, and his skin fairly crawled as the things came for them. For one moment he thought he saw humanoid shapes coming up from the lower depths to greet them, but then those same shapes dropped to all fours and charged forward at a fearsome pace.

And Andover grinned as they came forward. Here was a challenge! Here was something different, something bold and aggressive.

He dropped from his saddle and grabbed his short sword from its sheath as they came closer, low to the ground and moving at a furious speed.

And then the first of the creatures crashed into Tuskandru and staggered the king, knocking him sideways as it rushed into battle. Stastha caught the next of the creatures and her mount caught the third, tearing the creature from its path and biting down on the nightmare's head before it could cause any harm.

And then one of the things was on him, all claws and teeth and sinewy muscular attack, and Andover forgot all of the people around him as he concentrated on killing his enemy. His sword came down on the dog-thing's back and cut deep, even as his free hand caught the beast's lower jaw and forced the mouth open against an attempted bite. His hands were living metal and while he felt the teeth that bit down, they caused him no harm. His fingers held the jaw, forced it open, and he grunted and strained as he pulled that jaw lower still. The beast gagged and coughed, and he felt his sword bite deeper still. The thing let out a yowl of pain and Andover would have grinned but the next one bit down on real flesh and broke skin, pulling muscles in his forearm as he tried to block an attack meant for his throat.

The pain was massive, but he had endured worse in the times when the gods made him fight again and again. They had trained him to tolerate pain.

Andover let out a war cry and released his sword, bringing his right fist around and clubbing the hound in the head as hard as he could, hard enough to shatter bone and break the grip the thing had on his arm.

They came in waves, a flood of the savage animals, more than he could readily count, though he did not waste his time trying.

These then were the War-Born recreated as killers, reborn for the sole purpose of fighting and killing.

Andover saw them, knew them and responded in kind. Like them he was made for combat, reborn in the shape his gods had chosen for him. He and all of the Sa'ba Taalor beside him.

Tusk swept forward, a thick sword in one hand and a dagger in the other, carving into the side of one of the beasts. Beside him Stastha fought on, her left arm bloodied, her right hand covered in gore. She was wounded but did not care. No more than Andover cared about his own injury. There would be more before the fighting was over. There was no guarantee that any of them would live, but they were united in their desire to please the gods of war with their offerings, their sacrifices.

The Daxar Taalor would have their bloody offerings and, if they were kind, they would bless their followers. For now, there was only the glory and wonder of combat, the joy of bloodshed. The song of war.

Two more came for him. The first died with its head separated from the rest of its body. The second seized his already bloodied arm in its jaws and tore the wound open even more. Before anything else could happen to him Drask Silver Hand caught the damnable beast with his spear and drove the point through its spine.

The King in Iron was still riding his mount, sweeping through his enemies and cutting them down like a farmer scything wheat. The mount would catch the dog-things in its paws or with its teeth and dismember them if they were too close. Tarag Paedori remained uninjured in his iron armor, his great mount nearly unscathed. But both were soaked in the blood of their enemies.

Not far away Kallir Lundt was ripped from his mount by four of the hounds. Before Andover could consider coming to the man's aid, he was dead. Torn apart by the beasts.

Tarag Paedori roared, and both he and his ride charged into the four beasts, attacking with pure savagery. Kallir had been the right hand of the king, his close friend and companion for many years and he died violently.

Andover felt nothing for the man. He was another Fellein among the Sa'ba Taalor and he died well. What else was there?

Andover kicked one of the hounds, shattering the beast's jaw, and then drove iron fingers into its head. He spun to face the next beast, breathing as steadily as he could as the attacks continued. There were so very many of them. The tide of creatures crushed as best it could, but the Sa'ba Taalor were better organized, even in the chaos. A hundred spears worked together shielding against the attacks, striking, and cutting, stabbing and blocking. The beasts tried to break the line and were repelled.

Further into the mass, the army's archers took their time and fired, raining down death on the enemies of the gods.

Andover's arm ached from his injuries and he prayed to Truska-Pren for the strength to persevere. His faith was rewarded. The pain ebbed and strength filled his limbs. He continued driving into the enemies of the gods, carving through them even as he was attacked again and again.

He was not alone. When he first fought for the gods, he stood against enemies alone and enemies that outnumbered him. He was beaten down again and again, like metal being forged, until he won more battles than he lost, until the lessons of the gods were a part of him, as surely as his hands were a part of him, and the Great Scars marked his face.

He was one with the Sa'ba Taalor. He heard the orders of the kings in his head, the words of the gods, the commands whispered but clearly understood as the battle raged on. He was not alone. He was never alone among the people of the forges. He joined with a dozen others, a hundred others, a thousand as the kings and gods commanded, an endless wave that crushed back against the tides of the enemy, forcing the enemies back, or killing them.

And then the War-Born receded, an ocean at low tide, retreating from the savagery of the Sa'ba Taalor. The ground was littered with the bodies of the wounded, the dead, War-Born and gray skins alike.

Andover eyed the enemy warily, and around him the Sa'ba Taalor did the same. This was not yet a victory, but a slight reprieve.

He was exhausted.

Andover smiled. Yes, this was what he'd needed for years. This was what it meant to be chosen of the gods. He was their champion, selected and forged, made into a warrior despite his humble beginnings.

Tuskandru swept his sword through the air, shaking blood and gore away. Tarag Paedori rode with stiff back, teeth bared past the mask of his iron god, his eyes wild with the need for combat and with the closest thing he had ever shown to grief. But warriors did not mourn. Dying in the service of the gods was the second highest honor they would ever know. Killing in the name of the gods was the only higher privilege.

Drask moved closer to him, his usually calm demeanor replaced by a savage grimace. "They will come again. I can feel it."

Andover nodded but said nothing. There would be more bloodshed soon. It would be glorious. For the moment, however, he and his people prepared themselves mentally for the coming combat.

Whistler

In his dreams he died a hundred times, a thousand, and more, but oh, he killed so many in the process. In his lifetime he had killed a handful of men, all of whom deserved to die. This was different, this was better. His dreams were vivid and brought with them a deep and abiding satisfaction.

Whistler opened his eyes. The sun was up and if he had to guess it was well past the height of the day.

He grinned. He felt well-rested, better than he had felt in a long time, really, and though the voices were quiet he knew they were there. He could feel them, even when he could not hear them.

Whistler closed his eyes and quickly drifted back to sleep.

And in his dreams his great army faced the gray skins again, and he felt the blood of his enemies as they came together again in war.

And it was good.

Swech

She followed more than one god and, though she was Paedle's king, Swech chose to follow Wrommish that day. There was a glory to unarmed combat made more significant because their enemies were unusual. They were not like men, they were beasts, with claws and teeth and a strong physical advantage. Swech had two narrow swords across her back and a short axe on her hip, but she attacked with her bare hands and with her feet.

The heavy leather straps she had tied across her forearms

served well enough as armor against the claws of the monsters. Though she was attacked multiple times the leather held up against the attacks. She had blood drawn, yes, but only minor cuts to go along with the bruises she endured. The same was true of the boots she wore, heavy leather with metal shin guards, that took the brunt of the attacks meant to cripple her or kill her.

And Swech moved into her enemies with the same harsh fury as any of her peers, determined to kill as many of her foes as she could in the names of the gods.

A hound-thing pounced at her, teeth bared, and she side-stepped then caught the thing at the neck, as a mother might catch a cub, and used the weight to throw the beast to the ground. By the time it was shaking off the impact, her heel was caving in two ribs with an audible snapping noise, and the thing was howling in pain.

N'Heelis, the King in Gold and one of her best friends and mentors, struck a killing blow across the forehead of one of the hounds, dropping the beast even as it charged for him. His body seemed to flow like water, but his every strike was like a hammer pounding at untamed metal, forcing it into the shape he desired.

The gods sang to her, cried out their pleasure at every death, demanded more violence, more pain, and she gladly delivered all that she could, long after she should have been exhausted and shaking from her efforts.

The gods rewarded faith in their own ways. She was not tired, not even truly winded despite the nearly endless combat she was involved in. Her mind focused only on the battle. She was aware of her son, Valam, and aware of her people back in the seat of the empire. She had no time for them. She served the gods now, as a weapon and a driving force. The enemies continued to come for her and she continued to defend herself, to strike against them.

Blood flowed from a wound on her right shoulder. Her arm should have been useless, but the blood loss did not stop her, the torn flesh wasn't even a distraction. Adrenaline surged through her body and heightened her alertness, kept her aware of her enemies and where her allies stood around her. Her fingers slashed at the air and blinded one of the things before it could bite down on her side. The thing never even had a chance to yelp in pain before her knee was driving into its throat and destroying its ability to breathe.

There were no battle cries from the follower of Wrommish. There was no time for more than breathing, blocking and striking at the endless tide of enemies. In the distance archers struck telling blows, lancers and spearmen drove wedges through the enemy's ranks and broke the tidal wave of assault into smaller, more manageable groups. Swords and blades defended, attacked, killed and maimed, even as those employing the blades were wounded and killed, or blocked assaults and then struck their own telling blows. She could not remember a time when so many of the Sa'ba Taalor had ever fought together against a common foe, and the song of carnage was a hymn to the gods, a praise of the Daxar Taalor and all their glories.

It was a slow thing, a gradual process, but the children of the forges drove forward and their enemies were pushed back, driven aside and slaughtered. The rough terrain was made rougher still as she and others worked their way across a field strewn with the dead and dying, Sa'ba Taalor and War-Born alike.

Then the call came to her. Nine of the chosen were called together by the gods, because the time had finally come to make their enemies pay for daring to insult the gods.

Seven kings and two others were drawn together by that call.

It was time, at last, to face the Overlords in combat.

Swech did not hesitate. If she knew fear, it was a muted thing easily set aside for the chance to honor the gods, to thank the Daxar Taalor for their infinite blessings and every kindness.

Swech moved forward and stepped beyond the realm of the physical. Drask Silver Hand caught the air before him and ripped a hole in the ether, a great wound that bled stars and screamed a vicious war cry all its own. Andover walked through that wound in the air, and others followed suit, joining him in his quest to find and destroy the enemies of the gods. Tuskandru, Donaie Swarl, Tarag Paedori, Ganem, N'Heelis… all of the kings, Andover Iron Hands, and finally Drask himself moved through the hole in space, and then the wound sealed itself, separated the kings from their followers, pushed the kings into a different realm of reality.

Drove them into the realm of the Overlords, where the creatures held dominion and prepared themselves to war against the gods themselves.

This would not happen. The gods would be honored by their champions or the kings and the chosen would die in the attempt, as the gods decreed.

CHAPTER THIRTEEN

Merros Dulver

When the Empress called, it was best to answer.

Nachia was not in her throne room but in her private chambers, attended by her maid, Gissamoen. She was dressed not in her usual finery, but in riding breeches and boots, with a vest and a blouse. She did not look the part of the Empress, but more the part she preferred, that of Nachia Krous.

"Majesty."

Nachia saw him and nodded, her usual smile not in place. "The sorcerers have offered us knowledge," she told him. "They have found the War-Born in full combat with the Sa'ba Taalor. The passage to Morwhen is a bloody field, with large armies clashing. They fight on the Dark Passage and below it in the badlands alike."

"How is that possible?"

"You ask as if I might have an answer, Merros, but I don't. The wizards use their scrying abilities and see what we cannot."

She hesitated a moment.

"Kanheer has spoken to me again. He says the time for war is here, and that we must ready our forces."

"They are ready, Majesty. I have troops surrounding Canhoon, readied on all sides of Gerheim, moving through Goltha and prepared to go where needed when the time comes."

"That time is now. The question is where to send them. Kanheer says we should be ready but has not answered my question as to where they should go."

It was an effort not to roll his eyes. The Empress of Fellein could talk to gods if she wanted to, but Merros still had trouble with the notion of gods dictating how the world should work. All that he had seen of gods being active was secondhand experience that led to the Sa'ba Taalor attacking Fellein and causing nearly endless mayhem before the war was resolved.

The darkness that struck him was blinding. One moment he was looking at Nachia. The next there was no light, no images at all, only a wall of perpetual night without so much as a star in the skies to light his way.

Merros stood perfectly still and did not let himself panic.

The voice that spoke to him moved through his body, clear and easily heard, but not overwhelming. "It has long been our way to let people make their own choices, Merros Dulver. For a thousand years we have guided through our writings and left the people of Fellein to either listen or move away from us."

"Who is this?" Merros asked, although he knew there could be but one answer.

"I am Kanheer. Consider this and you will know all that I am."

Kanheer, the god of war. The words rang true to him, as simple and elemental as sunlight. Kanheer, the god of war was speaking to him.

"Our children have lost their way. Fellein does not thrive. It does not grow. Fellein is a pool that stagnates, grows sick and slowly dies. That cannot be allowed to happen and yet it does."

"Fellein is the most powerful empire in the world."

"Fellein falls and crumbles, Merros Dulver. You are the leader of an army that is too unwieldy to thrive, ineffective and faltering. Where you should be a sharpened sword you are blunted and useless."

The darkness remained around him, but Merros felt his jaws clench. "What would you have me do then? Send my troops to kill the War-Born?"

"Yes."

"Fight the Sa'ba Taalor?"

"Yes."

"How?"

"With swords and men. With siege engines and weapons. With iron and blood, Merros Dulver, as has always been the way. I am a god of war."

"Yes, but the Sa'ba Taalor have seven gods of war and currently they fight our enemies for us."

The god made no response and Merros added, "I'll let my enemies fight and do battle with the victors if that is your will, but currently I need your advice. Where do you want me to lead the armies of Fellein? Where should we concentrate our might?"

"That is a foolish question. There is one war going on right now. Your armies should advance on that war front and prepare for combat."

The world came back into focus. Merros stared at the ceiling, and between him and that surface, both Nachia and Gissamoen looked down at him with almost comical expressions of concern.

"Merros: please tell me you're alive. I can ill afford to lose any more friends."

"I'm alive, Majesty. What happened?"

"You fell down. One second, we were talking and the next you were on the ground, groaning, your eyes closed tightly. I think you bit your lip; you're bleeding."

He felt the sting of a small wound on his lower lip, and yes, tasted blood.

"Ah. I believe I have been visited by Kanheer. He has spoken to me, Majesty."

"This isn't the way I'm used to doing things." She shook her head. "One thing for them to speak to the Empress but I don't think I like it when gods involve themselves in the business of running the empire by talking to those under my command."

Merros shook his head and then sat up on the floor as both of the women standing above him gave him space to move. Gissamoen frowned at him, concerned. Nachia stayed closer.

"Well, what do you plan to do about it? Ignore the gods?" Merros asked.

"No. But I think we need to have a more formal consultation."

"You have the different churches here in the city. Do you want to meet with their leaders?"

"Don't be foolish. No. I want to confer with the gods. With *all* the gods."

"Well, yes, but how are you going to manage that, Nachia?"

"I'm the Empress. If they want me to run an empire in their names, they'll have to actually speak to me. It seems to work for the gray skins."

Merros sighed and got to his feet. There was a time when he would have been humiliated to fall down before Nachia, but now? No. He was just glad he hadn't been before the entire court when it happened. Nachia would understand.

Nachia was his Empress. She was also a dear friend. One of the few he had left in the world.

"Desh would be having fits." He said the words without thinking.

Nachia nodded her head, but got that lost little girl look on her face for a moment, the one he found both endearing and simultaneously terrifying. It was not an expression one wanted to see on the ruler of the greatest empire in the world.

"Desh would be screaming."

"Or telling you to have a baby."

"Gods, not that again."

"You see? Situation resolved. You can ask the gods for an heir to the throne."

"If I want a baby, I'll make my own, thank you, General."

"I fear you might not know how babies come to be, Majesty." He made the jest and then looked at Nachia, horrified by his own words. There was a time and a place, and this was neither.

Gissamoen let out a shocked gasp. The look of indignation on the woman's face was a sure indication that he had gone too far. Nachia smirked and looked him up and down. "I dare say I have the basic notion down, Merros."

"I can't possibly apologize enough."

"No, you can't. So don't worry about it, but remember your place, or I'll find you a wife to remember it for you."

"I need a wife like you need a husband, which is to say I'm fine without."

"Doubtful. But let us stay on more pressing matters. I don't presume to know better than the leader of my armies."

"Kanheer wants war."

Nachia shook her head. "Well, war is almost inevitable, really. It's just a question of who we will be fighting."

"Alright. How will we meet with the gods?"

"We?" Nachia looked his way.

"I'll not let you do this alone, and Desh is not here. That leaves me and the Sisters."

"No. They're prettier than me. I don't need that much time alone with them. Bad for my confidence."

Merros chuckled. "You've nothing to fear there, Majesty."

She did not respond, but merely shook her head. "I don't think I need to be in a temple for this. I think I'm just going to call on them and see if they answer my summons."

"I wish to be with you when you do."

"Then you will be with me." Nachia shrugged. "I rather like the idea of having a witness for these conversations, especially if I'm going to let gods dictate how the empire should be run."

"So shall we do this?"

"You mean now?"

"Well, why wait?"

Nachia stared at him for a long moment and then very slowly nodded. "Yes, alright. Now is good."

Asher

Daken Hardesty spat and looked at the market grounds. Asher sighed and nodded in silent agreement. The crowds were heavy, and the weather was pleasant, but the air felt wrong and there were few smiling faces to be found.

"All the Pabba fruit a soul could want, but I don't see any of my usual shopkeepers."

"Well, to be fair we are not yet in Canhoon." Hardesty shrugged. He was not a merchant, nor a farmer. He was a guard, here to help protect Asher's supplies and he and his men would do their jobs. And there was something about the atmosphere that clearly worried him.

It wasn't the Sa'ba Taalor: there were none to be seen, though they had heard stories of the gray skins making life difficult for merchants of all types. No, it was simply that this was a new place, literally a town where none had been only a few months before.

The changes in the Wellish Steppes were impossible to ignore. The ground looked wrong, in the best possible way. Though the warmer weather had only just begun, there were already signs that the land was wonderfully fertile. Fresh green shoots were rising from the ground, and already several areas had been marked with short stone walls and wooden fences being built in the distance.

Of course he'd heard rumors about the fresh changes to the Steppes but seeing them was a different thing entirely. A town, no, really a small city, had erupted from the ground as well, and there were tents and different structures rising along the edges of the river on both sides. The area stank of people whereas in the past it had carried the scent of desolation.

This new city was not being planned. It was simply growing from the previously desolate location. People squabbled, haggled, struggled with each other and the City-Guard they could see looked exhausted.

"If this is prosperity, I'd hate to see desperation." Hardesty spit again, his eyes narrowing as he watched the people around him. "Keep your senses about you. There are pickpockets and thieves all around us."

Not far away a man let out a cry and grabbed the arm of a young teen. The youth fought back, struggling to break free, and Daken looked on, his eyes judging the conflict. "Cutpurse just got caught."

The youth swept a small blade through the air and cut open the older man's cheek. The man let go and that quickly the youth was gone, as the victim of the cutpurse tried to staunch the flow of blood.

"Keep your men in formation around us, Daken. I'd not lose my merchandise or my life."

"You won't. Not while I'm here."

The skies above them had been clear a moment before, but as Asher watched, clouds bloomed above them, and the sun was hidden away in a matter of heartbeats. The winds picked up from the west, hard enough to lift his hair and blow it wildly about.

No one thought the event normal. All around him people reacted as if slapped, or threatened. Some let out cries of fear, and others looked about for a way to escape but, of course, it was impossible to flee the skies.

The clouds grew darker still and the pressure in the air made Asher's ears ache. He squinted into the winds and looked around, unsettled.

Daken Hardesty cursed under his breath and grabbed at his sword's hilt as if he might find something to fight. The daylight vanished, and the storms came hard, cold heavy rain falling from the skies at a furious pace. There were three wagons full of Pabba fruit that had enough space to offer shelter, and without hesitation Asher moved to the closest of them and his guards did the same. He and Daken wound up in the same wagon, getting into the shelter before the rain became hail that tapped an energetic tattoo across the hard surfaces above them.

Tataya

It was a gathering of some of the most powerful people in Fellein, arguably some of the most powerful figures in the world, and certainly some of the most arrogant.

Tataya listened on, her mind half numbed by the discussions as Dennal Libraso continued talking about Desh Krohan's many achievements in his life. She admired the words, truly she did, but she also mourned the man who had been her friend, her instructor and her mentor through over a century of learning.

Seshu Reaves, one of the most influential members of the council of Sorcerers – as pretentious a name as Desh had meant it to be when he established the institution, to be sure – sighed mightily and said, "We are all very aware of what Desh Krohan accomplished in his long life. We are also aware of what Jeron managed and what Corin did, despite his attempts to hide some of his most incredible feats. We are all of us aware of what we have lost."

He looked at the rings on his thick fingers. "Let's move on to the matters at hand. We have changes that must be made. We need to move forward, to continue on as the council and to decide what must be accomplished in the near future. The past is just that. The past."

Tataya cleared her throat as Dennal stared goggle eyed at Seshu. Likely extremely offended by his blunt opinion. Seshu was nothing if not an ass. But he was also right. The deaths he'd listed and a few more besides had caused enough of an upheaval in the council and it was time to move forward.

"I agree with Seshu, despite his lack of decent etiquette," Tataya said as calmly as she could, and Pella nodded beside her, offering silent support. Pella, the gods love her, had seldom been one to speak out in public, but she did what she could in her own way.

Goriah was more direct. "We need to vote on who will lead the council now."

Seshu managed to preen and sneer at the same time. "I agree with the Sisters. It is time for definitive leadership."

Dennal sighed. She was a powerful sorcerer, but she was also a touch dramatic. "Must we rush through these decisions?"

"Yes, frankly. There have been decisions made for us, rather than by us, and that must come to an end." Seshu looked pointedly at the Sisters, as if to accuse them of inactivity. Tataya resisted the powerful urge to liquefy his bones. As fun as the notion might have been she didn't have the energy to expend.

Goriah responded. "Indeed, the Empress of Fellein has dictated that we help the armies of the empire and Desh Krohan not only agreed, but put the idea in her head. He wanted us to be significant, not merely onlookers with a reputation. Gods forbid the idea of action instead of studying more manuscripts." Her voice was dry and her expression icy as she stared at the bastard.

Seshu shook his head and managed to put an apologetic

expression on his round face. "I surely meant no insult. I merely feel that we should have a more consultative position within the court of the Empress."

"She has chosen to employ the Sisters as her advisors in the absence of Desh Krohan." Dennal spoke calmly enough. "I hardly think the choice was a mistake, Seshu."

"I never said that it was." He nearly hissed the words. "I'm suggesting that we choose for ourselves who best represents the council to the Empress."

"I invite you to speak to her, by all means, Seshu." Tataya smiled. "I have never felt it my place to correct her majesty in her decisions."

"Is it not your duty to advise her? Then might you not advise her to consider a different path? Might you not advise her to allow us to make our own decisions?"

Goriah chuckled. "Please. Your ambition is showing."

"My ambitions?" Seshu rose from his seat, the robes he wore falling around him like a tent settling after a hard breeze. He was a large man. Not fat, exactly but certainly not thin. His hair was oiled and curled in the same fashions used by the previous emperor, which was not surprising as he'd had political ambitions since the times before the Sa'ba Taalor were ever seen in Fellein. He was nothing if not ambitious and hungry for more power.

"Your ambitions, my friend. We all have them, and you are no exception."

"My ambitions lead only to wanting to make certain the council is well-represented before her majesty. We have been kept from being a true power in Fellein for centuries. No disrespect to Desh Krohan but we should have long since had more influence in the court. We should be among the most significant forces in the empire instead of being little more than a means of faster communication between the various factions of the military."

"What would you have us do, fight the Sa'ba Taalor?"

"If it comes to that, yes. One sorcerer can lay waste to armies if need be."

"And would you be that sorcerer, Seshu? Would you be the one to risk your life against the armies of the Sa'ba Taalor?"

"Well…" He hesitated, thrown by Tataya's question.

Tataya did not relent. "Desh Krohan laid waste to an entire army for her majesty. He destroyed an army of the walking dead and cut a path across the land for miles. He earned his place within the courts of Fellein not with words but with actions. He won his influence and the protection of our council over generations. Your problem is you think a show of force is enough to sway the empire."

"Well, I don't know how else we should make our importance known." Seshu huffed dramatically and Goriah rolled her eyes toward the heavens.

"We have served the empire for generations. The Sisters have served alongside Desh Krohan. Don't feel as if we've somehow forced our will on the Empress, Seshu. We have been serving while you stayed safely in the walls of the Academy and studied the books, taught classes to new mages."

"And you think that's not serving the empire?" Seshu's voice rose to thunderous levels and several of the sorcerers in the chambers flinched. If volume were a sign of power, Seshu would likely have won the day without effort. "Each and every sorcerer serving alongside the armies was trained by me, trained by half a dozen of our esteemed council who have worked just as hard to make certain the empire is safe."

Goriah spoke again. "You can't have it both ways, Seshu. Either we are servants of the empire, or we are slaves to the whims of the Empress. I prefer to think we serve a need and are rewarded for that service."

Pella called out softly, "If not for Desh Krohan's careful actions over the last two hundred years, sorcery would still be outlawed in the empire. He kept us safe, kept our place in the world safe and prevented the execution of our kind."

Seshu shook his head furiously, his eyes bulging. "No one here denies what Desh did, but Desh is dead, and we must move on."

"Enough!" Dennal's voice cracked as she yelled to get the attention of everyone in the chambers. "Enough," she repeated. She had a presence about her when she decided to be forceful, and she meant to have her say just then. "We need to choose a replacement for Desh Krohan? We should try to force our will upon the throne? Who are we to dictate anything at all to the Empress? But if you wish to cast votes and try to decide who should advise the throne then cast your votes now." She looked at Seshu and shook her head. "I for one choose the Sisters. They have experience within the court, and they have sway with the empire. Who votes with me?"

Several voices were raised in agreement. Seshu snorted. "And who would see new blood try to place us in better position within the court?"

Several different voices called out.

The discussions continued and Tataya sighed to herself, uncertain as to how the situation would play out but annoyed by the delays caused by political ambitions.

Nachia Krous

"It's as good a place as any. Besides, I've always wanted to sit in this place and contemplate the sorcery of Desh and his kind." Nachia looked around the small room where Desh Krohan had communed with the Sooth, with its heavy cushions scattered on the floor and its bare walls. There were no seats, no furniture at all, merely the cushions where a person could lean back and relax in peace.

Merros looked around and frowned for a moment before settling himself near the center of the room.

Nachia did the same, draping herself over one of the largest of the cushions and sighing in surprise at how comfortable the thing felt against her. After the throne where she usually perched, a throne she knew for certain Desh Krohan had created to be uncomfortable even as it offered protection to her, almost any surface was a pleasant experience.

"I can see why he spent so much time in here." Merros chuckled. "Seems a good place to take a nap."

"I miss that old fool."

"So do I. Every day, Nachia."

She nodded and blinked back the sudden sting of tears threatening to fall from her eyes. He was an old man who never looked the part. She'd had a deep and abiding affection for him even through a few times when she had tried to seduce him in her youth and been politely rebuffed. Oh, she had never wanted him in that way, not really, but she'd always wanted to see if he could be swayed by the promise of forbidden desires.

No, that was a lie she told herself. There had been a time when she had very much wanted Desh Krohan as a lover. In time she'd gotten past the notion and relied on him instead as a friend and confidant.

"So how do we do this?" Merros' voice broke her away from thoughts of seduction and her foolhardy actions as a younger woman.

"Well, I suppose we just call on them."

"I expect they'll listen to you before they listen to me," he said, a small smile playing on his face as he looked around the unremarkable chamber.

She shook her head, shrugged and said, "I call on you, O Gods of Fellein. You would have me do your bidding? Then come to me and tell us what it is you seek." She felt a fool even speaking the words aloud, but what else could she do?

"What would you have us say?"

The voice threw her. It was Desh Krohan speaking. After a lifetime of hearing the man she recognized the timbre of his speech, the cadence of the words, even before she looked up and saw him. The face was right, but the clothing was wrong. He wore armor and carried a sword at his hip, something she had never once seen him do.

"Desh?" Her voice broke.

"No, child. I am Kanheer. That does not change. But in this place, at this time, I honor the sorcerer's memory." She knew the words were true. It was as she had said before, there was no doubt that she was in the presence of a god. He was not mortal, despite his appearance. He was no more human than a great storm or the stars in the night sky. He was not mortal, despite the image he offered, and there was simply no denying that fact.

She did her best not to cry but it was a challenge. Across from her Merros looked on, his face showing his surprise.

"What would you have us say, Nachia Krous, that you

do not already know? Would you hear us tell you that the Overlords must be destroyed? You already know this. Would you have us remind you that the Sa'ba Taalor are a threat you have not finished dealing with? Would you have us see you through this as well?"

"If you would have us fight gods, where are they? We know nothing of the Overlords but old rumors and older memories written on ancient parchments."

Desh Krohan's voice was stern. "The Overlords were buried alive and left to rot in their tombs. They should have been destroyed long ago."

"By what means?" Merros put in. "The sorcerers did not have the power necessary and if they were not strong enough who was?" He spoke calmly enough but there was a quaver in his voice just the same. He questioned a god.

"It is not the place of the gods to solve the troubles of mortals."

"Then what purpose do gods serve, Kanheer?" Merros shook his head. "You are the god of war? Then help us be at war and crush your enemies." He shrugged and Nachia stared at the man, shocked by his audacity.

Kanheer smiled. "There are those among the gods who would take offense to your tone, Merros Dulver, but you have been my champion for a long time and I know you well enough."

"I have been your champion? How so?"

"You have led the armies in Fellein. They are my chosen armies. If you are not my champion, then who is?"

"Then why have you never spoken to me, or offered me guidance?"

"I sent you the Silent Army in your time of need. What else do you require?"

Merros closed his mouth and frowned.

"The Silent Army is a wonderful force, and they have brought peace to Canhoon and kept that peace, but what of the rest of Fellein? What of Morwhen where even now the armies of our enemies fight against each other?"

Desh... no, she corrected herself, Kanheer... sighed. "You have armies. Use them."

"And fight whom? We wait to see who is victorious."

"To what end?"

"To avoid fighting on two fronts."

Kanheer shook his head. "Liar. You hope to avoid conflict."

"Why is that a bad thing? Why not let our enemies kill each other off and weaken themselves?"

"Because one of them is supposedly your ally right now."

Merros pulled back as if slapped.

"You have allied yourselves with the Sa'ba Taalor, and yet you let them fight alone against a common enemy, Merros Dulver. That is not the way of a warrior, or a soldier. You would honor me? Do what soldiers are supposed to do and fight your common enemy together. There is a war against the Overlords and you do nothing."

Kanheer's voice did not rise in anger, but there was accusation in his tone and no denying the truth of his words. "You have taken sorcerers into your forces. You employ them to speak between great distances, and that is wise, but they could do so much more, including help you move your armies."

Nachia shook her head. "They have said to move our forces would deplete them. They claim that to use that much power would exhaust their ability to help us, because magic takes power they do not have."

Kanheer smiled and shook his head. "You see? And you asked how the gods could help you and you have answered your own question."

"How do you mean?" Merros frowned again.

"You would have power to move your troops? Ask for it and that, the gods can provide."

Tataya

"You're certain about this?" Tataya looked at Merros Dulver and then at the forces amassed before them in the courtyards of the palace. It was not one company of soldiers but a full battalion. Merros himself would be in command.

Merros nodded. "Apparently the gods will provide you with the means to help move us."

Tataya resisted the urge to scratch her head and nodded instead. The very notion of the gods providing anything bordered on the ludicrous. There were those among the sorcerers who were certain that the gods were merely myths, and while Tataya herself had never believed that to be the case, she could understand the argument. Aside from the Silent Army, which had risen only after a very large group of people sacrificed themselves– a gesture that could have arguably provided the necessary power to raise the stone soldiers of the Silent Army without aid from deities – there had been little evidence of the gods coming to the aid of anyone in Fellein for a very long time. Reports of alleged miracles occurred and were studied, but nothing had been verified by the Council for literally hundreds of years.

Tataya looked to her Sisters, who in turn offered non-committal responses.

Goriah said, "We do what we must."

Pella nodded her agreement, and Tataya mirrored her action. "So be it." Pella focused and offered her hand to the other Sisters, and when they were joined together Tataya took the lead. Summoning the power to move a group of that size was going to be…

Easy.

What should have exhausted all three of them instead took remarkably little effort. Tataya concentrated on drawing in the energies to cast a spell of monumental power, fully anticipating failure or the need to call in still more sorcerers, and was rewarded with a flow of dynamic proportions. She had never in her life felt the sort of energies that moved through her body.

The Sisters worked together, as they had so many times over the years, and opened a rift in the air at the far end of the waiting military forces.

Without hesitation Merros Dulver gave the order for his forces to move, to march. They started forward with admirable efficiency. Troops marched, horses moved forward.

Merros looked her way and nodded his thanks, then started forward on his own steed. And then, without truly thinking about her actions Tataya walked along and brought the other two Sisters with her.

The army was going to war, and they would not go alone.

Merros Dulver

He did not know what was involved, not truly. Merros had never trusted magic, never wanted to deal with sorcery, but the transition was amazing. One moment the forces under his command were in the imperial courtyards and the next they marched into a different world.

Morwhen was lost beneath clouds of smoke that were in turn corralled by mountains. The area stank of volcanic activity, but the air was at least breathable. The ground around them was littered with the dead as far as the eyes could see. Bodies had been stacked to either side of the main stretch of road along the area called the Dark Passage, a long path paved in cobblestones, protected by walls that had long since begun to crumble and keeps abandoned years or even decades earlier. Merros had never before been to Morwhen, but it looked much as he'd heard it would.

He called the troops to halt, and they did, and stood at the ready, or as ready as they could be, when they were just as disoriented as he was.

"Tataya, what is this?"

"This is Morwhen," she said. "This is where you told us to send you."

"I did not expect you to come with us, milady."

"Nor did I and yet we are here. We came because you might need us for a quick escape."

The weather was pleasant enough. The air was warm and the ground wet with melted snow and blood alike, but the road itself was in good enough condition.

"Where are the enemy troops?"

"Surely they aren't all dead, General, but there are plenty of dead from both sides here." She looked around, frowning her dark eyes studying the landscape. "I see no activity from either side, but–"

"They are here," interrupted Pella. "There are armies

amassing on both sides of us, miles apart at the moment. Perhaps they have called a truce."

Merros shook his head. "Doubtful. That is not the way of the Sa'ba Taalor."

"We can ask them ourselves. Several of them come now." Pella gestured toward the east, toward Paedle, and indeed a few of the Sa'ba Taalor were riding in on their mounts. They did not carry banners, they did not announce themselves with war cries or horns, they merely rode in hard toward the area, heading for the forces that Merros had amassed.

He shook his head and called for his troops to remain still. Several of the soldiers toward the front of the battalion looked ready to move toward the gray skins, and that would not do.

Merros spurred his horse forward and gestured to four of the closest horsemen to join him. Among those four were two captains he trusted by his side, and the other leaders of the campaign, including Caer Kransten.

"What is this, Merros?"

"Madness, I'm sure."

Caer nodded. "I never thought to see an army moved so easily."

"Nor did I."

The Sa'ba Taalor came closer. Not one of the leaders was recognizable to him… No, he saw the horned helmet of Stastha, second to King Tuskandru, and waited as she and the others approached. There were a dozen of them, and they came forward without hesitation, with no sign of possible fear, which was exactly what he expected from them.

If they made any choice as to who would speak, they

had done so before they got anywhere close to Merros. It was Stastha who talked and Merros found he was not at all surprised.

"Why are you here, General Dulver?" She was direct enough, and her eyes found his and held them. There was a reason she was the second to Tusk and it wasn't simply because she was a competent warrior. She held the man's trust and respect and that was enough for Merros.

"We have come here to help you fight these servants of the Overlords." He gestured to a stack of bodies which looked inhuman. "As I understand it, they'll come back from the dead if they aren't burned."

Stastha nodded. "It takes them time and we are at war. We will get to them if we can." She did the odd hand-waving gesture that marked a shrug among her people.

"Where is your king?"

"Tuskandru and the other kings have left us. They seek a different war on a different front."

"How so?"

"We fight the servants of the Overlords, they seek to fight the Overlords themselves."

"They've found the Overlords? We have been looking but have not yet discovered where these things hide themselves."

"They do not hide." Stastha shook her head. "They are 'between the worlds.'"

"What does that mean?"

"Just that. The Overlords do not live in this world. What we see of them here is shadow and smoke. That is what the gods tell us. For that reason the kings now travel to find them in a place that does not exist here. They have left the world behind and hunt for the Overlords in places where most cannot travel. Though I understand some of your people can."

"I don't understand."

Tataya spoke up. "Some of the Inquisitors learn to move between the worlds. They find… shortcuts to other realms."

Merros stared at her for a long second. "Perhaps we can discuss this later, but I expect there is a reason this has never been revealed?"

"I gave my word when I was told of it." She offered an apologetic smile. "Trade secrets."

Merros nodded.

Stastha said, "In any case, the kings are absent and we fight in their stead."

"Well, if you want us at your side, we are here to join you."

Stastha looked him over as if expecting a punchline to a jest. Finally she nodded. "Your forces would be welcome. The War-Born are many."

He looked away for a moment to focus on Kransten. "You've already had experience. Would you begin disposing of the bodies of the enemy?"

"Yes, at once." With no more said the general wheeled his horse around and rode toward the closest troops, calling to the commanders of two different squadrons for assistance. As the conversation continued, fires were started and the pyres prepared.

"Where are these War-Born now?" Merros asked.

"We don't understand how they do it or why," Stastha explained, "but from time to time they retreat from us and hide. We've tried to follow them, but they are very fast, and we can only capture a few before they are gone."

"So maybe we can work out something better this next time around. There are a lot of troops here to help you. If we can flank them and block their escape, we might tell a different story."

Stastha nodded. "Yes. We should discuss strategies in more depth."

"How long are they gone when they disappear?"

"It is never the same." The speaker was a one-armed man whose name was not known to Merros. The missing arm was fresh, the scar tissue still pink and raw in ways that told him they had sealed the wound with metal only recently. The ability of the gray skins to heal their wounds by calling on their gods was definitely one of the talents Merros envied.

"How many people have you lost?"

Stastha frowned at the question. "We have had many losses, but the enemy suffers more."

"We should prepare ourselves." Tataya spoke loudly enough that Merros and the Sa'ba Taalor could hear her easily. "They are coming soon. I can feel them."

Merros didn't question how she knew. Sorcery was its own thing.

Stastha held up one hand, the others with her did the same, and in the distance Merros heard war horns calling.

"We are prepared now," Stastha said.

"You have time. They are only just awakening." Tataya gestured toward Goriah. "My Sister watches the beasts as they stir."

Merros looked at Goriah, whose eyelids were closed, and her eyes moved behind them as if she might be dreaming.

Sorcery and the Sa'ba Taalor, gods who answered prayers and an army of things that would be arriving soon to try to kill everyone around him. The day was not over, but it was certainly getting challenging.

"Captain Sibaro," he called to one of the soldiers standing nearby. "Call the troops to readiness and ask General Kransten to light several additional blazes. We will have visitors soon and the sun will set soon. I'd like us to be able to see our attackers."

"Aye, ho, sir!" In moments it was just him and the sisters and one nervous looking officer gathered together.

He turned to Stastha. "Let's discuss where to place our troops then, shall we?" They had time yet, for which he was grateful.

The sun had set before the beasts attacked and he was grateful for the fires.

CHAPTER FOURTEEN

Swech

They moved on foot, having left their mounts behind before they began their quest to find the Overlords.

Though she did not understand everything about where they moved or how they traveled, Swech knew that Drask Silver Hand was responsible for allowing them to travel between worlds. He referred to the area they walked through as a "shadow realm", a place that was much like the Blasted Lands, but less turbulent. There were no storms here; instead there was a darkness that fell across the world as if the sun were hidden and the stars could not shine. There was a clear path to walk on, but all around them were great hills and even mountains that seemed carved from darkness. No light shone down upon those areas, but the places where they walked were lit with a silvery light, as if the stars could only shine on the waters of the river that they walked on. The air was neither warm nor cold.

It was a place between possible worlds or, as he had actually explained it, a short cut between those worlds. "Here," he'd explained, "in this place, the Overlords can hide themselves and move without being seen by most. The gods have told me how to be here."

"Why do they hide?" Tarag Paedori's voice was laced with contempt.

Drask looked to the King in Iron. "It is not that they hide. They simply find it easier to be here. The world we live in has put restraints on them. The sorcerers of Fellein could not kill them but managed to imprison them for a long time, and some of those chains are still there. We cannot see them or feel them, but they hold the Overlords back from complete freedom." He shook his head, trying to find the right words. "Here they can move where they will, and find it easier to seek out the gods they wish to kill."

"This is where the gods reside?"

"No. This is where the Overlords hide, but it is a realm closer to that of the gods." He shook his head again. "That is the best way I can explain it. The gods do not answer all of my questions any more than they answer all of yours."

"Do you criticize the gods?" Tusk's voice was not calm as he asked.

"No. I explain my lack of knowledge. I do not criticize the Daxar Taalor any more than I would chastise the stars."

Tusk offered a smile and nodded.

"It is time, I think." Drask looked around and his eyes found Swech. "The gods have gifted me with power. We will all have need of that strength now, if we are to fight these Overlords." He spread his hands in a short wave, a gesture that encompassed all of them. In an instant, vitality moved through Swech and she felt a tingling in her extremities, saw with a new clarity, and felt a greater connection to the Daxar Taalor. Around her the kings and Andover Lashk all stiffened for a moment, most of them looking around with widened eyes.

The world did not look the same, though if pressed she would have had trouble explaining just how it differed from moments before. Everything seemed more… alive, even in this lifeless realm.

Something shifted to the right of them. Whatever it was remained hidden in shadows but slithered between the two closest hills, a patch of darkness in a cluster of shadows.

Drask concentrated and a moment later the dark skies above lit up as he summoned a light as bright as the sun.

Whatever was in that darkness screeched for a moment then thrashed, and then it attacked.

The thing seethed and launched itself from the shadows like a serpent striking.

The Overlord came for them like an avalanche. Swech could not see it clearly, even in the sudden brightness Drask had created. It was a dark blur with too many limbs, a coiled, contorted thing that reached for Drask and struck before he could prepare himself. The blow landed and knocked Drask a dozen feet as the icy cold claws lashed across his chest and the arm he lifted up to defend himself.

Drask rolled, his body hitting the rough pathway and bouncing as if he'd been kicked by a Fellein war horse. Even as he crashed to a halt, he heard the sound of Tuskandru letting out a battle cry.

By the time he was standing, Tuskandru was driving his heavy blade into the side of a shadow, and looked to be drawing blood.

Tarag Paedori was almost as fast despite his heavy armor, and his great sword cut deep into the neck of the thing.

The Overlord did not bleed but it reacted, letting loose a

screech and thrashing across the path through the shadow-cloaked hills. Even with the light around them the thing was lost in darkness, wrapped in shadows like a cloak, and striking at multiple targets at once.

Swech stepped back as a claw came for her and avoided the strike. Andover caught the claw trying for him on one of his iron hands, casting sparks, and then drove his free hand into the side of the thing, fingers stiffened like daggers.

Tuskandru roared a second time and hacked into the shadowy shape once more. In his youth the king had killed a mound crawler by himself and nearly died in the process. It was only one of the tales that made him a legend among his people.

Tusk let out a different noise as the Overlord concentrated on him and retaliated, slashing him across his left side and his back, drawing lines of blood.

Drask moved closer to the creature and hurled his spear, impaling the thing. He pushed with the power he had been given by the gods, sent that energy into the thing through the spear as if casting lightning through a metal post. The spear burned brightly for a moment and then was gone, but the energies continued arcing from his hand into the writhing body of his enemy and the kings stepped back as flesh burned, scales crisped, and whatever bones might exist inside the shadowy form were shattered.

"This is the power I share with you," Drask said. "The power given us by the gods."

The shape seized and spasmed and then became liquid. Dark ichor sloughed away from the dying thing as water runs from melting ice.

"That is an Overlord?" N'Heelis spoke softly.

"Aye," Drask answered. "That is one of our enemies."

"How many are left?"

"I do not know. I sense that they are close, but they are like worms, locked together and twisting in the darkness. I cannot count them or separate them." He shook his head again frowning in concentration. The kings asked no other questions, but instead moved into a semi-circle, eyes searching in all directions. "You can try to sense them too. I see no better than you."

Swech nodded absently. She had already felt the difference that whatever he had done had caused. She did not yet know the extent of the power, but she felt it coursing through her like the thrill she often got when ready to start fighting.

She drew two short blades, little longer than her forearms, and slid them into ready positions. Donaie Swarl settled into a ready stance with her spear, and even N'Heelis, who most often fought without weapons, took a defensive position with a long spear. Lored carried a short bow, one arrow notched and the bow ready. His face was partially hidden in a mask of bronze that, like Drask's hand, was a part of him, a living replacement for damage long repaired by the gods.

"I can smell them." Tusk sniffed the air and scowled. "They stink."

Tarag Paedori shook his head as if trying to rid himself of the buzz of a bothersome insect. The man did not like distractions when he was trying to see what remained hidden from him and Swech understood the notion.

When the Overlords came for them, they came all at one, and they attacked the same way.

CHAPTER FIFTEEN

Whistler

He had not been awake for long, but his body ached and his eyes would not focus. Whistler did not know how long he had slept, but he had soiled himself and the bed in his room.

Someone was pounding at the door. "Pay for the room or I'll break the door down!"

Whistler stood up, staggered as if he'd been drinking, and caught himself on the small table next to the narrow bed where he'd been sleeping. His mouth was pasty and his eyes had a crust around them.

He was not well, and he knew it.

He was also annoyed by the angry hammering at the door, which he had barricaded with a chair, apparently, though he did not remember doing so.

"Be patient!" he growled, and the knocking stopped.

"I feared you dead" came the voice from the other side of the door.

The bag of coins he found tucked into his shirt was not full, but it would be enough. Whistler pushed the chair aside and handed two fat golden coins from the purse to the man outside. He vaguely remembered the fool from when he'd come to the inn.

"That should keep you." His voice sounded wrong to his ears, and his hand seemed made of bone and leather. He did not look right.

"Are you sick? Do you have a plague?" The man's thin face looked at him through the barely opened door and he squinted to try to see better in the nearly complete darkness of the room. There had been lit candles, but they were long since extinguished.

"I have enough coin to pay you. Now go away." Without another word Whistler slammed the door shut and pushed the chair back in front of it.

His head ached as if he'd been drinking, but there were no bottles to show that he'd been imbibing. The chamber pot called, and he used it, blinking irritably at the burning in his eyes.

When the next knock came at the door he scowled and crawled out of the bed where he had just situated himself. "You've been paid! What do you want now?"

He pulled the chair aside again and opened the door to the face of the Inquisitor he had tried to kill.

Darsken Murdro did not introduce himself. Instead he simply swung that walking stick of his and struck Whistler on the temple.

Whistler remembered nothing else for some time.

Darsken Murdro

Darsken caught the emaciated form and frowned. That this was the lad he'd been hunting was evident, but something had happened to him. He looked half-starved and his clothes were soiled. He stank. Still, he was wanted and so Darsken grabbed the thin arm of the boy and hauled him from his room above the Gilded Swan. The innkeeper stood behind him, dancing from foot to foot and looking around as if they were breaking a law. Darsken ignored him.

He was a big, stocky man and the lad seemed to weigh almost nothing. He lifted him easily and marched him through the hallway of the inn, carrying him through the tavern that at this early hour had little business save a few drunkards. They paid as little attention as they could.

A moment later Darsken was in the street with his fugitive and this time he did not wait for the City-Guard but slung the soiled boy over his shoulder and carried him as quickly as he could toward the cells where the Inquisitors kept their prizes. He would interrogate the lad himself as soon as he could, but for now he simply wanted him locked away.

There were other concerns. The Sisters had assured him that the War-Born were being handled, sending the message through one of their subordinates, but the Overlords had not yet been found and they were a continued concern. They hid themselves away and it was a big world with many places to hide.

More importantly, he felt a strange pull from the Shimmer, which was unlike anything he had ever felt before.

The Shimmer was a gift, one that he was always grateful for, but he was not used to feeling it unless he was employing it. The ability to walk the Shimmer was what separated the Louron from all other people. What he experienced now was like a toothache. It did not hurt much, but it was distracting when he could ill afford to be distracted.

Then again, he could seldom afford distractions.

The Inquisitors' Tower loomed large, and he was grateful to remove his burden from his shoulder. By the time he'd reached the doors two of the guards had opened it and awaited him. Both men were known to him, and he smiled gratefully. Dermond, a long-time guard, wrinkled his nose in disgust at the odor but took the unconscious man from him. "Cell number four for this one."

Darsken nodded and rolled his shoulders, trying to restore a bit of blood to aching muscles.

"I will be there soon to question him." Rather than waiting around, he left the burden behind and stalked back out to the Avenue of Heroes before sliding into the Shimmer and moving quickly across a distance that should have taken him days. He did not exactly run, but it was close. The Shimmer was misnamed that day. While it was often true that the passage between worlds was well-lit or merely reflected a distorted view of the world around him – it seemed to depend on the whims of the world, or perhaps the gods, he could not say – the Shimmer was dark now and a cold wind blasted along the way, reeking of ashes and blood. Darsken stopped moving and frowned, trying to understand the drastic change.

A moment after he entered the realm, he saw his sister. Daivem stared around her, frowning with an expression he suspected reflected his own.

"What happened here?" Her voice held an edge of panic.

"I do not know, but I do not like it." He shifted from one foot to the other.

"What has happened to the Shimmer?"

"Something has infected even this sacred place."

"The Overlords." Daivem scowled. "They taint even the skies over Wellish. They destroy everything they touch."

"Do you know this? Or merely suspect it."

"I make guesses."

"We need to find the true cause of this before it worsens." Darsken looked to the skies and saw more darkness and a flaring light in the distance. Something moved close by, but he could not see what that something was.

"Go, Daivem. Find others to help us search for the cause of this. It must be stopped, whatever it takes. The Shimmer is too important to lose." The Shimmer was a living thing and now it felt diseased as if it might well die. The thought filled him with dread.

"Come with me."

"No. I will stay here. I will start seeking answers, but go, get others to join us before it is too late."

"How will I find you?"

"I head toward the only light we can find here in this darkness." He pointed toward the distant brilliance. "Follow me there after you get others. This must be stopped."

Darsken did not wait for her to respond but started moving, fully aware that something moved near him and conscious of the fact that whatever it was, it likely was not friendly.

Daivem left him behind, though he knew she would have preferred to stay. He clutched his walking stick tightly and started moving again, before he could let doubt cripple him.

Asher

The storms abated momentarily and Asher climbed from his wagon and stepped into the chaos left behind by the sudden downpour.

Heavy rains had flooded much of the area, but the waters were not enough to move his wagons or destroy much, merely enough to create a heavy mud and many puddles of deep water. A few tents had fallen in, but most still stood.

The skies were still too dark, but sunlight pushed through the clouds here and there, a reminder that there was something beyond the darkest storms he had seen on this side of Fellein.

Daken Hardesty climbed free of the wagon and shook his head, a dour look on his long face. "There is nothing natural about this." His voice was as gravelly as ever after nearly a day of sporadic silence.

"We've already agreed to that, yes." Asher stared at the horizon where still more dark clouds roiled. "But there is nothing you or I can do about it. We're just here to deliver fruit."

"How far does this go, Asher? Do these storms extend all the way to Canhoon? If so, we might be better off taking the wagons by horse than riding the river." He pointed to the high level of the waters with his chin.

"Aye." He nodded absently. He'd been thinking the exact same thing. He did not want to think about the possible losses on the river. He had lost enough already. "We need to see if there are sorcerers here, someone to help protect the harvest."

"Against the weather?"

"As you said, it's not normal. I know the Empress likes her Pabba fruit. Most of Canhoon does." He sighed. "For which I am grateful."

"I will search out any sorcerers." Hardesty moved and looked back his way. "Watch over your cargo." He was gone a moment later.

Asher moved from wagon to wagon and slowly examined his precious supplies. The guards had stayed with the wagons and only one of them had eaten any of the fruit though he'd have hardly blamed any of them for getting hungry. Most of the crates of fruit were in fine condition.

Daken came back in short order with a young man wearing simple clothes. He had a receding hairline and wide eyes. "Asher, this is Lomar. Lomar, this is my employer, Asher Tarry, who seeks a sorcerer to aid in delivering his goods to Canhoon."

The man bowed his head and then asked, "What sort of assistance do you need?"

"Protection from the storms, for one." He gestured at the sky. "The weather is not normal, and I would see what's left of a full season's crops taken to the capital and sold."

"Easily arranged, but likely unnecessary as the storms are already breaking apart. The weather was caused by, we do not know what, but whatever was causing the disturbance has already departed."

"And may well come back." Asher looked pointedly at the man. "I need my cargo protected."

"As you say." The younger man blushed.

Hardesty looked at the skies and shrugged. "I do not think the storms are getting better." The wind was picking up and flipped his long hair even as he spoke. All around them people started looking for cover.

"Can you stop what is happening, sorcerer?"

"I don't know, but I can try."

Asher nodded and then squinted as a burst of thunder echoed across the area in a long, mournful rumble. "If you can do something there's money for you."

A moment later the clouds grew darker again and the

winds started up in earnest, causing several people to head back into tents. Asher looked to his wagons and frowned.

The balding man reached into a small bag, the sort that might work as a coin purse, and pulled two round, carved stones from its depths. He looked at them for a long moment and frowned, then put them back in the small purse and concentrated.

It took several heartbeats, but the winds calmed down and the clouds scudded apart and began to disperse at an unnatural speed.

Amazing," the man said as he looked around.

"Yes, it is, but why are you surprised by your own sorcery?"

"I am not surprised by the results. I am pleasantly surprised by the ease. Usually, a spell of that complexity would require a great deal of power, the sort I store away. This was different, far easier than it should have been."

Asher frowned.

"It is like outracing a horse, my friend. What I just did should not happen." He knew the man was serious simply by the expression on his face. He was a stranger but the shock on his face was real, as was the underlying sense of wonder.

"What payment do I owe you?"

"None." Lomar shook his head and waved the question away. "None at all, but I must leave you for a while if we are to travel together. I need to prepare and to understand what just happened." He wandered away with shock still etched across his face.

"He looks like a lad after getting his first kiss." Daken offered a rare grin. "Though I've doubts if that particular experience has ever been his."

Asher couldn't hold back a small laugh and a grin.

Merros Dulver

There was a short, blissful break from the War-Born. The damnable things fought savagely and seemed incapable of growing tired, but for a while they stopped attacking and retreated. Wherever it was they planned to go, whatever they intended to do, they came back long before anyone could rest and recover from the combat. Merros knew because his troops were still wandering around in a semi-daze, recovering from the violence that had come for them.

"They're bloody near endless."

He spoke mostly to himself, but Pella answered. "They are under a spell. They've no choice but to attack." Even as she spoke, they saw the hordes coming for them, moving in quickly, and Pella nearly flinched as the howling started.

Merros didn't have to say a word. His troops were reforming, and the Sa'ba Taalor moved into position, forming a living barrier with the Fellein, those forces at the front lowering spears and shields, and a line of archers forming behind them. The beasts might well break through but as before they would suffer dearly for their attacks.

Pella sighed and looked to her sisters, and whatever they communicated it was wordless.

Goriah rose into the air, her cloak whipping and billowing, her hair rising in a wave, and she gestured toward the approaching beasts. The ground before the defending army exploded, thick vines tearing through the soil in a wave that looked like serpents slithering over the field. The vines sprouted thorns as long as daggers and short swords, cutting into flesh, impaling the first of the War-Born. The creatures might have stopped but the crush of bodies from behind them was overwhelming and the heavy barrier of plants thrashed and rustled as the closest dog-things were speared and crushed in the press of bodies.

Pella spoke words that Merros could not understand, that actually hurt to hear, and the area on the far side of the vines burst into flames. It was an explosion of fire, tongues of flame that lunged and lapped hungrily at everything they could find, and the heat was so intense that the creatures scarcely had time to know they were dying before they were dead.

Tataya did not wait for Pella's spell to be finished before she started her own attack. Lightning ripped from a sky that offered no warning and shattered stone, destroyed a part of the Dark Passage, killing the gods alone knew how many of the War-Born, even as the ground beneath them crumbled. Thunder echoed from the nearby mountains and roared across the heavens even as the servants of the Overlords died.

Merros watched it all, stunned by the ferocity of the attacks and, yes, delighted. The enemy of the empire was being destroyed and a hundred paces away an army waited to continue the work that the sorceresses began.

Battered, bloodied creatures writhed still in the burning vines, and beyond them the great bridge that had been the easiest passage into Morwhen crumbled. For all he knew of road construction it would take years to rebuild the stone corridor, but if all went according to plan it wouldn't matter. The War-Born would be destroyed.

Pella attacked again, raining destruction down upon the nearly endless wave of creatures even now pushing to come closer, to hunt and destroy the joined armies.

The Sa'ba Taalor watched on silently, and most of the Fellein did the same. To be sure all of them had experienced the raising of mountains in the war of five years previously, but few had seen such destruction firsthand.

This was close enough to smell, to taste, and it was a terrifying thing up close.

Stones grew from the distant ground. Rocks grew like the vines had previously, spearing through the bodies of still more War-Born, rising toward the heavens in bloodied, jagged fangs. Goriah had changed her method of attack.

In the far distant west, storm clouds grew, and the skies darkened and Merros frowned, because he knew what each of the Sisters had planned, had discussed the entire process with them before the attacks began. He understood that these attacks were beyond rare, only possible because the gods of Fellein granted the power to the sorcerers.

None of them had discussed storm clouds or sudden weather changes of this sort.

This, then, was something else entirely.

Tataya frowned, seeing the same thing, but continued the assault against their enemies. The ground that had only just grown massive stone fangs glowed brightly and burned. The new stone outcroppings turned hot and then molten and sagged back down to the ground, incinerating everything that crossed the area where the War-Born tried to attack. The creatures never had a chance to so much as bark before they were burning and dying.

And then it was over. The attacks ceased.

Merros shook his head. "Too easy. There are more of them, but they wait beyond where we can see."

"Then we will have to see further away, Merros." Tataya rose into the air, lifted as easily as a leaf in a powerful wind, but she did not sail wildly through the air. Instead she soared on those winds, looking down as a hawk might watch the ground below. "There." Her voice was a tiny thing now, distant.

Pella and Goriah rose as well, following whatever communication it was that the three of them used to speak silently to each other. Sorcery. Madness. Even now with the three of them working in collaboration with armies at least partly under his command. Merros did not trust the use of magic, did not like to see it used, even when it was to his advantage.

The sisters rose higher still and then moved to the west, heading toward their enemies the better to see them, he supposed.

And then they were gone.

Stastha rode closer to him, a frown on her face, while all around her the armies waited in ranks still prepared for an attack that was not happening.

"Have they always had this power, your sorcerers?"

Merros studied the woman for a moment and then nodded. "Yes, but they have seldom used it."

"Why?"

"There is a cost. Your gods, could they always move mountains?"

"I expect so."

"And yet they do so rarely."

Stastha considered that and nodded.

"Your sorcerers are as gods then?"

"No. Today they work with the gods of Fellein. They fight for us, to defeat the Overlords and their armies."

"They make us useless, Merros Dulver." She spat the words but with remarkably little venom. "The Sa'ba Taalor follow gods of war, but we do not fight."

"Kanheer is our god of war." He shrugged. "He is the one who told us to do this."

"Does he not want you to fight a war? How is that possible?"

Merros didn't answer right away but listened to the sounds of the Sisters performing their dark miracles further away.

Finally he said, "Maybe Kanheer prepares us for other battles. The gods can see what we cannot, surely."

Stastha said nothing more, but watched on with him as lightning crashed to the ground in the distance and storm clouds grew even further to the west.

Whatever the Sisters did it was likely a powerful display. Whatever came toward them looked equally as menacing.

Whistler

Any student of the arcane could have explained the situation to Whistler, but he likely wouldn't have listened. He was not the sort who wanted debates or lessons he could not learn on the streets of Goltha. He might have been hailed as a king by the voices, but at heart he was a street urchin – and he preferred it that way.

He learned what he thought was necessary and had no particular desire to learn more than that.

He did not quite awaken in his cell, but for a moment he opened rheumy eyes and stared at the ceiling of his prison without truly seeing.

In his mind he fought against armies, he charged toward them again and again, only to be forced back by storms, fire, lightning and worse.

He was in pain, he knew that much, but still he ruled armies. He was a king of sorts, or perhaps merely a general, but he ruled armies and he knew he would prevail.

While he half-slept the War-Born followed his commands, pushed on by the Overlords. They had slept for so many centuries! Some had slept for as long as their true masters, or nearly so, hibernating deep in the ground. Little more than corpses that would not decay, they waited with the patience of the dead for the times when they would be called to fight, to war, to conquer.

Magic has a price and Whistler, whether he understood it or not, was about to pay that price. His sorceries were real, not merely dreams. He commanded a great army to the best of his ability – he did so because the Overlords demanded it of him and they offered him nothing as compensation.

Dazed and bloodied, wounded by the blow Darsken Murdro had delivered to his brow while subduing him, Whistler fell back into unconsciousness as his body paid that price.

He withered in his sleep.

Muscles collapsed and atrophied, devoured by the sorceries he unknowingly committed. He did not eat, did not drink, and could not replenish himself, and so was slowly consumed.

Had anyone come to look in on him, they would have watched as his body shriveled. His limbs pulled in close to his body, his legs bent in on themselves as he slowly assumed a fetal position.

He did not die. The Overlords were not that kind or that forgiving. He collapsed inward, undying, but no longer truly alive as the armies he thought he dreamed of ruling continued their assaults and died for their efforts.

The Daxar Taalor, the gods of the forges, were prepared for war at all times, and they'd chosen and maneuvered their pawns with care and precision. The kings of their people fought the Overlords, but they did so with a strength given them by their gods.

The Overlords were distracted, and so their armies faltered, their general suffered and then their armies died.

All while the Overlords themselves fought a different battle in a different place, with very different consequences.

Whistler dreamed of conquest.

Whistler dreamed his life away one breath at a time.

CHAPTER SIXTEEN

Andover Lashk

The gods wanted the Overlords dead, and he would do all he could to honor that wish.

The kings fought with him, Drask Silver Hand fought with him, and for a time Andover felt very nearly invincible.

The Daxar Taalor had managed what he'd have thought nearly impossible and granted them the strength to fight nightmares.

The Overlords were not human. They were not, near as he could tell, truly anything but nightmares made flesh.

If they had bones, he could not feel them. If they had form, it was a fleeting thing. The creatures seemed made of shadows and water, little more than mud or clay that reshaped itself at a moment's notice. Sometimes they had arms, and other times they were a wave of filth, a sea of pressure trying to crush him and drown him, and not all the weapons in the world would have helped him recover.

The kings were there. At one moment when Andover was certain he would drown, N'Heelis lifted him from the shadowy coils of a form that was crushing the life from him as if he were pulling him from deep waters. Before he could thank the King in Gold, another of the creatures attacked. The things seemed to be everywhere at once.

Andover struck with his iron hands, clawed at the vicious stuff of his enemies and caused wounds of his own. At one point a monstrous head with a mouth large enough to swallow a horse came for him and he caught the jaws in his hands and forced them apart until the bones in that jaw – where no bones had been a moment before – were shattered and the teeth crumbled away before they could strike deep into his flesh. He was bloodied, again, but he was alive, and he felt alive as he seldom did.

The gods of war wanted combat and he gladly obliged. He should have long fallen to exhaustion, but he did not fall, he did not falter. Energy coursed through him, revitalized him when he thought he might have to slow down, and kept the wounds on his body from draining him.

Truly the gods were kind.

Lored grunted and he turned to look at the king as a shadow-form pushed through the king's stomach and sprouted from his back. The King in Bronze died before him, impaled on a nightmare.

Tuskandru hacked down on the thing that killed Lored, carved the shadow in twain, and roared a dozen incoherent words. His actions did not bring the king back. If that was possible only the gods had the ability and though they had brought the king back before that did not happen now.

Swech did something that caused her enemy to shudder and withdraw, the shadows of its body withering like drought-ridden plants. She attacked again and drove the thing back, a retreating wave of darkness on a barely lit field.

The kings attacked, Andover attacked and Drask fought, grunting with effort with each strike he delivered. They fought hard, but did not seem frantic.

"Durhallem!" Tusk cried out his god's name and slashed forward, his odd blade cutting through the plasmic form of his enemy even as the thing flowed like water between his legs and then wrapped his ankles in slithering tentacles. Andover looked away, once again engaged by his own enemy, a thing that rose from the shadows and struck with solid arms. It carried a sword, or formed that very weapon from its own substance. In any event the blade was sharp and screamed across Andover's hand as he blocked and struck back.

They fought but did not get further and that was a problem. One of their number had died, and all of them were wounded, and that too was a problem. The god's gifts helped them, but this was a battle, a war, that had to be won quickly.

Andover drew the axe from his belt and swept it in a short arc as he prepared himself. The blades seemed to work better than his fingers, the sharpened edges cut whereas his fingers struck and caused ripples, not permanent wounds.

Tarag Paedori let out a grunt and was knocked aside by the darkness, swept off his feet. He crashed to the ground and the mass of darkness washed over him, drowning him, perhaps, or suffocating him. Whatever the case the King in Iron was pinned by the damned things and Andover moved forward to see if he could assist.

The question was how he could cut the monstrosity without risking Paedori at the same time.

Drask Silver Hand held up his metallic fist and very suddenly the area was drowning in light from the extremity, even Drask turning his gaze away from the sudden wash of brilliant illumination.

"Enough of this!" he called out and reached down at the same time, the shadow-stuff of the Overlords flinching back from the light. Thick metallic fingers dug into shadows that tried to recede, and he caught hold of Paedori's arm, hauling him forth from the liquid darkness. The King in Iron coughed and spat filth from his mouth through the armored mask he wore, coughing violently.

Andover looked at the faces of his enemy with revulsion. There were multiple faces in the swirl. Eyes formed and dissolved, mouths stretched open in silent screams, what seemed a hundred different shapes half formed and dissolved, were reborn a moment later, again and again, even as the whole mass seemed to flinch way from the light burning across Drask's fist.

Drask cried, "The power of the gods rests inside us all. Let that power scorch your enemies. You all know how to heal with metal, now take with metal instead!"

And it was true. More than once Andover had asked the gods to seal the wounds of fallen warriors, had felt solid metal sag and sizzle like water between his metallic fingers, and watched that falling liquid burn into wounds and seal them, repair the great wounds that should have killed the wounded and instead revitalized.

Andover looked at his own hands and tried to make them glow as well. For a moment there was nothing and then light and heat burst from the iron that shaped his hands, iron gifted him by Truska-Pren when his hands were destroyed years earlier. It was the gift that had sent him to the Sa'ba Taalor in the first place, that started the events that led to him becoming a champion of the gods of the Seven Forges.

One miracle that led to countless others, so surely if Drask could create a miracle of light to fight the enemies of the gods he could do the same.

The world grew brighter, and Andover nodded in grim satisfaction. It seemed impossible that mere light could hurt the Overlords, who were so powerful, who had survived a thousand years of death, but this light was not merely a glow.

It was the power of the gods made manifest.

The gods were kind, and their presence burned his enemies as surely as a torch would burn flesh. He reached for the closest shape crawling from the chaotic mass, and as he touched it, the weird flesh hissed and burned.

"For the gods!"

His fingers reached again and clutched at the vile stuff that seethed and tried to pull away from him, but he would not have it. He would not relent. Both Andover and Drask reached out and burned their enemies, and Swech followed suit, attacking as she had before and corrupting the fluid flesh that had, a moment before, been wrapping around her arms and trying to crush the life from her.

Tuskandru swept his long blade around his head and bellowed his god's name again as the blade began to glow fiercely. It was a different sort of radiance, one that burned with dark smoke even as the blade's keen edge hissed.

Donaie Swarl prayed aloud to Wheklam, watching the example of Drask, and listening to the big man's calm voice. Her prayers were answered, and the spear in her hands burst forth with greater radiance still, different from the others, more turbulent and violent. The light crashed down on her enemy's flesh like a crushing weight.

Tarag Paedori called to Truska-Pren and his heavy armor

burned with a sullen energy, glowing like molten iron, smoldering and sparking even as he rose to his knees in the mire of the Overlords.

The flesh tried to recede, and the Kings followed mercilessly, pushing on, making the most of their new advantage.

Had Andover thought he understood the gifts of the gods? He was wrong. Through the power they had given, finally, there was an advantage against the Overlords; the undying creatures felt a new weakness, and even as he pressed forward and cut with his axe, blocked with his free hand, the power of the gods continued to wound and burn his enemies.

Ganem and N'Heelis shimmered. They did not glow in the same way as the others, but that they were touched by the gods was obvious. Ganem's eyes burned and his strikes made the darkness scream with a hundred agonized voices. N'Heelis *flowed* into his enemies, struck again and again delivering damage with each strike, even when he blocked blows meant to incapacitate or kill him his enemies seemed to rot at his touch.

There was no time for celebration, only for slaughter. It was time to kill, to destroy the Overlords in the names of the Daxar Taalor.

Darsken Murdro

The Inquisitor expected to die. He had wandered deeper into the tainted, violated Shimmer and felt the things that crept closer to him as he sought the light source in the distance. They did not strike, despite his fears, but the shapes continued stalking him and then – as the lights in the distance grew suddenly brighter and revealed the horrors around him – the shapes moved away, surged across the warped, ruined landscape of the Shimmer. They slithered toward the distant lights amid hisses and half-heard cries of outrage.

The Shimmer was attacked and all he could do was follow after what he believed must surely be the source of the damage.

All his life the Shimmer had been a place of peace, an odd reflection of the world he was born in, that offered pathways to other places both in his birth world and beyond. Though he had seldom explored those other worlds, others, like his sister Daivem, had traveled to different realms, to places where the very rules of existence defied what they knew of reality. She had told him of visiting worlds far removed from theirs, even places where the gods threatened to end the world because they were not offered proper sacrifices, and where the servants of the gods could not be destroyed, and other realms where magic was as common as rain.

The Shimmer had never changed in all that time, but now it seemed diseased by darkness, and he felt he had no choice but to follow that light and know what waited at its source.

And after what seemed a night worth of walking, he found the source of that incredible illumination.

The Sa'ba Taalor were fighting with the darkness. Some of them he recognized. He had seen Swech, and he knew Andover of the Iron Hands, but the others were not familiar to him. Whatever the case, whoever they were, their attacks shattered the darkness that corrupted the Shimmer. Around them the endless black pools of flesh seethed and struggled and were driven back by the lights that burned in their hands, bodies and weapons.

He had never understood the notion of gods, not truly. He knew they existed, and he supposed that the Shimmer might be seen as a god by some – certainly it offered the miraculous – but, as the Sa'ba Taalor called out, he wondered if they called to their gods and, if so, did their gods respond? This seemed nearly like sorcery but none he was familiar with.

Something hissed behind him and Darsken turned in time to see one of the shadowy forms coming from the darkness, a silhouette lost in shadows.

He struck without thinking, brought his walking stick down across the shape, and was knocked aside as if he were a child.

Darsken staggered backward and the thing pushed past him, unconcerned with his existence.

Worst mistake it could have made. When he struck again it was with malicious intent, and he struck to cause as much harm as possible. It was a vile thing, alien and diseased and he had no doubt at all that the thing and its ilk were the cause of the illness permeating the Shimmer.

He struck with his walking stick and summoned his limited magic. Necromancy, the ability to control the dead. The ability to feed from death.

Darsken did not understand what he did, not really. If he had, he would have reconsidered his actions. What he did not comprehend was simply that the Overlords were the progenitors of necromancy, the very first creatures to study the dead and their secrets.

He was fortunate. The thing did not know what he could

do until it was too late. His attack ripped at the lifeforce of the Overlord, clawed a great wound through the thing and tore it open.

The creature turned to lash out, but by then Darsken pulled the power from it into himself, into his walking stick, and he was invigorated. Though it tried to attack, the damage was too great. Even as it reared around and came for him the shadowy shape collapsed on itself and fell to ruin.

Darsken looked down at the formless mass and drew upon it again, not to steal more of its power, but to steal the thoughts the creature might have, to understand what it was he dealt with.

He was punished for that, perhaps. The thoughts that filled him were of death, of dying, of pain and loss and anger that burned across his mind; not thoughts he was unfamiliar with but simultaneously seen through a lens that distorted the thoughts and concepts.

It was a vile creature, and his mind recoiled.

Darsken staggered back, his brain seeming to burn with darkness, to seethe, lost in shadows and whispered voices.

He collapsed to his knees and grunted.

The pain was not overwhelming, but it was sudden and drove him to close his eyes against the ache in his skull.

Not far away the Sa'ba Taalor fought on, and Darsken did his best to stand again, made weak for the moment, made sick by the unexpected thoughts and images that assailed him past closed eyes,

The darkness around him screamed, and he joined in the chorus.

Nachia Krous

It hardly mattered that she was the Empress of Fellein. That was what Nachia decided as she sat in her throne room and looked around at the strangers around her. Her closest confidant was dead. Her closest living friend fought on in an effort to save her empire from multiple enemies.

Her cousin Mallifex Krous stood nearby, but he was not someone she really knew well, king of Morwhen or no. Her brother, Brolley was present but remained preoccupied with Lanaie, the nominal queen of a land that no longer mattered. Roathes was rebuilding slowly, true, but the small kingdom was centered between two of the Seven Forges, and little could happen there that wasn't a sign of danger. Tuskandru and the followers of Durhallem were possibly the most warlike of all the Sa'ba Taalor, and most agreed that if there was going to be a kingdom attacked by the gray skins, it was likely Roathes.

Mal stared at his half hand and sighed again. The wound had been healed as best it could be and the risk of infection was gone. According to a few sources among the Council of Sorcerers, something had happened that might change that. Sorcery was now, somehow, easier to use. It did not tax the wizards as it had before.

Mal was waiting for one of the wizards to see if they could do anything to mend his ruined hand. He would pay well if they could.

"Whatever they want to do, they should be swift about it." Nachia repeated what she had said to her cousin previously. "The gods have granted power to all of the sorcerers, apparently, but who can say if it will last?"

Ovish spoke softly, but his voice carried. The man was

dressed in clean clothes, but they were old and well worn. He was a beggar, after all, a follower of the god of beggars. It would not do to be dressed too well. Ahdra stood next to him, a virtual opposite of the older man. Where he was heavy and limped, she was slight and glided; he wore old clothes and she dressed in finery. She was the very epitome of what most men wanted in a mate, and Ovish was the exact sort of man most women failed to notice. That they were apparently close friends always rather boggled the Empress.

Ovish said, "The gods seldom grant favors only to take them away, Majesty."

Ahdra added, "The blessings of the gods are many."

Nachia replied, "I don't make assumptions regarding the gods, but I am grateful for their favors."

Ahdra smiled. Ovish bowed as if a compliment had been cast his way.

Merros would have snorted and possibly made a comment but at this point the Empress was grateful for any help and that the gods had changed the rules was a given.

The Sa'ba Taalor said nothing, but they were close enough to hear every word being spoken. Merros' son looked her way as she smiled at him. He smiled back, but it was a tentative expression he wore, as if uncertain how he should, or if the very act of smiling was punishable. Perhaps it was. She knew so little about the ways of the gray skins when it came to raising children.

Ovish did not speak again, but he looked around the throne room as if expecting something more. Nachia offered nothing. She had long since grown tired of the religious factions. She did not forbid them, or demand they be removed from her presence, but sometimes she still wanted to.

The world was changing, and she did not always approve. The last meeting of the unified churches had drawn over a thousand people and the attention of a full twenty of the Silent Army.

A thousand followers.

"How may I help you today, Ovish?" She relented, if only to hear what the man wanted to then dismiss him if possible.

"We are here to serve, Majesty."

"I have listened to the gods themselves, Ovish. How would you serve me?"

"The faithful offer prayers to protect the empire, Majesty. There will be a ceremony five nights hence in the Garden of Remembrance and we hoped we could inspire you to join us."

It was Brolley who stepped in to answer for her this time, and Nachia clenched her jaw but let him speak.

"The Empress is flattered, of course, but there is a war going on."

"And I will attend the ceremony, with gratitude for all that the gods do and the people of Fellein as well." She smiled and looked at Ovish, then Ahdra and only when both had smiled their surprised smiles did she look to her brother. "The very gods of Fellein have blessed us, how can I do less than offer my thanks?"

Ahdra nodded and smiled. "The ceremonies begin when the sun sets, Majesty. Thank you, we are honored by your presence."

"I am grateful for all that you offer, Ahdra. I am honored by the gods of Fellein." She looked toward Jo'Hedee of the Sa'ba Taalor. "Perhaps our guests will join us in this ceremony?"

Jo'Hedee tilted her head for a moment and then faced the Empress, raised her open arms toward the ceiling, showing that she had no weapons, and bowed formally. A heartbeat later the rest of the gray skins joined her, and so did Valam.

"We serve, Empress, as commanded by the Daxar Taalor."

Rather than speak, Nachia bowed her head for a moment and smiled.

She was done being dictated to. Brolley did not answer for her, and she would remind him of that fact properly when they were alone. For now she had made a statement and pleased the religious factions and, hopefully, the gods with her responses.

Valam stepped closer to her and offered another tentative smile. It was her turn to smile back. She considered the boy. Had Desh Krohan had his way, she would be with child even now, and she felt an odd stirring of guilt at that thought. These were, indeed, trying times, and as he had said more than once, damn him, he would not be around forever to support her.

The First Advisor might well have advised against backing the churches. But what else could she do? She had to acknowledge the gods in her own way, and she had to do so publicly, and this seemed like as good time as any.

Merros would likely disapprove, and she knew Desh would have argued against it, but she was the Empress, and in a very real sense she had to serve the gods and people of Fellein to the best of her abilities.

Mal stepped closer to her and leaned in carefully. "Would you like an escort for the festivities, Majesty?" He looked her way without locking eyes. He seldom met her gaze for long.

"I would be pleased to have you by my side, King Mallifex."

"Your will be done." He did not bow to her, but only because she'd asked him not to. He was her cousin and, more importantly, he needed to show strength right now as his kingdom was threatened by the war and had suffered enough. Once again Desh Krohan might have disagreed with her, but he was not there to help, and she was not in the mood to be questioned about her decisions.

Nachia frowned and lowered her head for a moment as the thought that he would never offer advice to her again made her eyes sting.

And, damn her foolish emotions, she considered his previous words and wondered if she should seek a mate to sire an heir. Her time in the world might be shorter than she wanted to think about. After all, even seeming immortals were dying these days.

She knew that her empire was strong, but still it needed tending to.

That was her duty. Her responsibility.

CHAPTER SEVENTEEN

Merros Dulver

The war ended quickly.

The Sisters continued their attacks against the War-Born, but that was not what caused the cessation of the enemy's attacks.

While three of the most powerful sorcerers in the world destroyed the armies of the enemy, they had continued on, savage and brutal and hungry, until they suddenly stopped. As one, the great horde of the War-Born came to a halt, and the nightmarish beasts that managed to slip past the attacks of the Sisters, that had come to slaughter as many of his troops and the Sa'ba Taalor as they possibly could, simply fell over and died.

They did not sleep. They did not rest. They did not become living statues.

No, they died.

Rather than wait for his order, or for any orders of their own that he could hear, the Sa'ba Taalor responded quickly and followed the earlier example of the Fellein Empire, dragging the bodies of the dead things together and starting massive funeral pyres.

Merros had his own troops join them, even as Tataya approached him. He had no idea where she had come from. One moment she was far to his east and the next she was merely a dozen paces away and coming closer.

She looked invigorated, and as surprised as he was.

"They are dead, Merros. All of them as far as we can tell."

"The War-Born? All of them?"

"To the last, that we can sense."

He dared a smile at the thought. His troops had barely been touched.

"If that is true, then I have you and your Sisters to thank, milady."

"You already know my response." She smiled. It was a beautiful expression on a face that he had always found beautiful.

"Then I suppose we should all thank the gods this day."

"The war may not be over, I fear. We cannot find the Overlords. They are lost to us, and I fear they've gone into hiding again."

"If they are hiding then they are not attacking us. That's something, I suppose."

Tataya swept her hair back from her ear and frowned briefly in concentration. "True, but that they can hide so well is unsettling at best."

"They do not hide." It was Stastha who spoke and both he and Tataya were surprised to see the woman standing so close to them. She had managed to approach without either of them seeing her though she did not seem to move with any particular caution; he wondered if she was stealthy enough to accomplish that feat or if he were simply too tired to notice her approach. The latter seemed more likely.

Though he admired Stastha for her combat skills she was seldom subtle in her approach.

Tuskandru's second spoke softly. "They are… elsewhere. Tusk and the other kings of my people fight the Overlords even now. They fight and they are winning."

"Indeed? How are they managing this?"

"Your gods have helped us on this front, have made it possible for your sorceries to work, yes?" She looked at Tataya as she spoke, and the Sister nodded her answer.

Stastha looked from the sorcerer to Merros. "Our gods have offered similar power to the kings. They have not won yet, but they are winning. There have been losses, great losses, but they are winning."

"'Great losses?'" The words sank his heart.

"One of the kings is dead and another is dying." Stastha watched his face and said no more.

"Which kings have fallen?"

"Lored, the King in Bronze was killed. Tarag Paedori and N'Heelis have suffered severe injuries and may not survive." He hated himself a bit for the relief he felt that Swech was still alive. He did not want to think of her. He did not want to care.

"Can we offer them help?"

Stastha shook her head. "They fight for the honor of the gods, and they fight with the chosen champion of the Daxar Taalor and one of their greatest warriors. None may aid them in this battle."

What could he possibly say to that? When the Sa'ba Taalor invoked the gods, it was the end of any discussion, just that simple.

Tataya nodded and said nothing about the situation. Instead, she replied, "The gods are wise."

He resisted the urge to say anything about the gods. They were trying to end a war, not start another.

Stastha looked from one of them to the other and said, "I shall let you know how this progresses." Merros thanked her and Tataya did as well, and a moment later the woman was gone, leaving general and sorcerer to stare at each other.

There was a moment when he was filled with doubt and hoped that they did not learn of the Overlords' defeat with the sound of war horns from the Sa'ba Taalor.

Drask Silver Hand

How long had he fought? He no longer knew. Time usually came to mean little in the middle of battle and, in this place, night and day were the same. Usually when they killed their enemies there were corpses to see. Here the dead melted away instead of falling down and dying.

Drask could no longer think clearly. Every time one of the Overlords died, a scream echoed through his mind and left him feeling deafened.

He could not hear his own thoughts. The cries of the dead and dying were too many.

Ganem added his own scream of pain as something dark cut through his arm and peeled flesh from bone with ease. The King in Silver said nothing, but pulled back what was left of his left arm and shifted his spear to a one-handed grip before striking back. The thing that had wounded him shrieked and died and deafened him again with its death throes.

Andover Lashk struck another creature and Swech joined him in the killing blow and then, suddenly, there was true silence.

Drask looked around, shifted warily from place to place, seeking any more targets for his wrath but there was nothing. The battlefield lay emptied of enemies, and he had no idea how to feel about that.

"Is this victory then, Ydramil?"

"OUR ENEMIES ARE SLAIN."

Drask looked from one king to the next and then nodded slowly. He reached for Ganem and tried to heal the man's wounds but the power the gods had granted him was either exhausted or had been taken from him.

"I am sorry, my king." He shook his head.

Ganem stared at him as if he were mad. Instead of answering Drask, he lowered his head and beseeched the god of reflection. "Great Ydramil, I have served as your king and have honored you with blood and death. I would ask you to help me at this time, to make me complete once more."

For a moment there was nothing, and then Ganem bit back a scream and held his left arm away from his body. The glow that had ignited his spear's head disappeared, and Ganem shivered as his arm burned with brilliant luminescence. Blood flowed freely from his wounded arm and a moment later that blood was replaced with a flow of burning metal. Droplets of fire dripped from his arm and quickly congealed into tears of solidified silver.

Drask lowered his head in shame. Had he thought to emulate the gods? To fix the wound of a King with the power he had been given by the Daxar Taalor? Had he, even for a moment, dared think himself the equal of the gods?

Ganem shuddered as burning metal wrapped itself around his wound and then screamed as the metal cooled and continued to warp and bend itself into a new shape. The great wound that should have left him crippled or possibly dead was gone, replaced by a forearm and hand crafted from silver and fused to flesh in a miracle very similar to the gift Drask had been given years before.

Not far away, half lost in the darkness, the light that had guided them weakened. N'Heelis curled in on himself and shivered violently. His chest glowed and burned, and the heavy wound at the back of his head hissed as his hair burned away. Gold crawled across his flesh in several places, ranging from his skull to his jaw to several spots along his stomach and legs where he had been torn open by the Overlords.

Closer to him, the King in Iron did not move. He had failed in the combat and now he remined still, and if he breathed, the evidence was hidden by his heavy armor.

Tuskandru was beside the man and pulled the helmet from his face. The dead king's eyes stared at nothing, but his corpse wore the remnants of a smile.

Tarag Paedori was dead, lost in service to Truska-Pren. There was no sorrow to be found within Drask. The man died for his gods, and there was no higher honor in the world.

Swech looked like she wanted to help N'Heelis, but she kept her place as the King in Gold slowly rose to regain his footing.

"It is time to go home, before we are lost here forever."

Andover spoke softly, but everyone present nodded, and Tusk lifted the body of Tarag Paedori, straining under the weight of a man almost his size who wore heavy iron armor.

Drask took the task of lifting Lored on himself. The King in Bronze was dead. Two kings destroyed in service to the gods. All blooded as few had been wounded before.

A great slash ran across Andover's back, from left to right, a deep serpentine slash that was already healed but had not been there before the combat began.

King Swech did not speak. Tuskandru spoke softly, though if he spoke to himself or to his god Drask could not say.

N'Heelis spoke softly too, offering his thanks to Ganem for allowing him to live, for replacing his ruined arm. He did not look toward Drask and Drask could not blame him. Shame burned through him at the thought that he had assumed too much, but Ydramil spoke to him and said, "FOR FIVE YEARS YOU CARRIED THE BURDEN OF THE POWER WE OFFERED YOU. IN THAT TIME YOU DID NOT WANDER WHERE WE DID NOT SEND YOU. YOU SERVED US EVEN WHEN YOU FELT THAT TO DO SO WAS A BETRAYAL. YOU WERE TESTED BY THE GODS, DRASK, AND YOU DID NOT FAIL US. THERE IS NO SHAME IN YOUR ACTIONS."

He did not weep with relief at the words, but he wanted to. Oh, how he wanted to.

Truly the gods were merciful.

Andover sighed and moved forward. The air before him tore itself open, and Andover walked through the trend in the darkness. One by one the Kings followed him and when only Drask was left, he followed suit, walking away from the place between the worlds, close to where the gods resided.

Whistler

Whistler's body burned. When the Overlords were finished with him there was little left but a few large pieces of bone, which were ground down like meal and scattered across the docks along with the other bodies that were not claimed and never identified.

For one brief moment he had been all that he ever hoped for, had been as powerful as any king, and had inspired fear in thousands of hearts, no matter how unwittingly.

If anything can be said about the situation, it is simply this: Whistler slept through all the best parts, and he would have found that notion hilarious had it happened to anyone else.

Asher

Canhoon was as wonderful as he remembered, filled with amazing sights and enough people to leave Asher very nearly speechless. In the Garden of Remembrance there were too many people for him to count, gathered in prayers and songs the likes of which he had seldom heard before. He knew Plith, the god of the harvest, as his family had for as long as anyone could remember. Tyrea was often the preferred god, but he did not argue with followers of Tyrea – instead he simply accepted worship of both gods. He did not see any signs that Plith was worshipped here, but he offered prayer and thanks just the same, his purses now full and heavy with the monies he had earned selling his crops in the markets of Canhoon and Goltha alike.

The journey should have taken weeks but instead took hours. He paid a good price in gold and did so gladly. There were no other farmers who had delivered Pabba fruit to the area and those who bought from him paid dearly for his harvest.

He had survived the harvests. He had survived the sales. The struggle for the next crop had already begun but the gods were kind, and Morwhen was once more held by the empire – and, even as he considered that fact, the King of

Morwhen walked beside the Empress within sight of him. All around them people celebrated and made their thanks and offerings to the gods, sang in celebration of the gods, especially Kanheer, who had allowed them to win the war against his enemies, if the stories were true.

All he knew for certain was that the wizard who'd helped him continued to cast his sorceries easily and he was grateful for that even more than for the gold he'd been paid.

One of the most beautiful women he'd ever seen walked past him, moved with several men and women in the robe of a priestess, and stopped long enough to smile at him. Her light blue eye regarded him warmly.

"I heard you singing to Plith."

Asher blushed and nodded, uncertain how to speak to a woman of such grace and beauty. "He has always been important to my family."

"Are you staying here in town for long?" Her eyes moved over him, saw the way he was dressed, and knew him for a stranger in an instant. Truly he dressed the part of a traveler, his heavy cloak far too warm for the event, his boots well-worn but too comfortable to consider replacing.

"I will remain here for at least a week." He smiled. "It is a long trip back to Morwhen." The others with her nodded their approval, as if he had passed a test he did not know he was taking.

"We would like you to join us, if you can, and tell us more of Plith."

A heavyset man dressed in ceremonial robes and wearing a boar's head crowned with antlers nodded solemnly. "I have long followed Tyrea, always will, but I would know more of your harvest god. We all would, if you could offer us proper insight."

Asher looked around, wondering if there was a joke at his expense. In all his life no one had ever cared what gods he worshipped unless they wanted to mock him for his old ways.

"I would be pleased to join you."

The woman smiled again and put a delicate hand on his arm, her fingers gently squeezing at his bicep and sending a shiver of warmth through him. Truly it had been a long time since he had been close enough to a woman to touch, and in Morwhen few women would offer so intimate a gesture. He was wise enough to understand that the people of Canhoon lived in closer proximity and that the gesture was innocent, but he was still affected by it.

"Thank you. Your name is Asher, yes?"

"It is." He looked around, wondering who might have offered his name to the woman.

"Daken Hardesty speaks highly of you." She offered the words and one more smile. "We would like the both of you to join us."

"I cannot speak for Daken, but I will join you gladly."

Another man, older and heavier with a sad smile and kind eyes said, "We can promise you nothing but many questions and good wine."

"That's enough for me."

The man nodded and pointed to the garden wall where a moving stone statue watched over them. He had heard of the Silent Army but never believed he would see one of the eternal guardians. "Meet us just there when the ceremonies are done. We will not be much longer. We must offer a blessing to the Empress and then we will join you."

Asher smiled nervously and bobbed his head.

A moment later the gathering was moving away, but the woman, the beauty who offered so warm a smile, looked at him one last time before they vanished into the crowd and out of his sight.

Asher stared after them for a long, lingering moment and then offered his thanks to Plith again, uncertain what else to do except enjoy the moment.

King Swech

Swech went with the other followers of Paedle and watched the celebration of the gods of Fellein. People moved in currents: some stood still while others shuffled around them across the paved walkways and the grassy areas between, shuffled round the different bushes that decorated the area, and leaned against the pedestals of statues designed to honor the dead. Flowers bloomed even in the darkness, but the scents of those blossoms were lost beneath a crush of sweating bodies, incense and several small fires where merchants offered roasted meat or baked treats.

Ten feet away from her, Merros watched as well, though at least half the time his eyes were on her.

"You're ready to head home?" He looked from her to Valam and then back again. Valam stared at all of the people around him and absorbed every detail of their ways. Even after weeks in the city, the world of the Fellein was new to him.

"Yes. It is time. I have a kingdom that must be repaired. The war was worse for Paedle than for the others."

"I'm glad you're well, Swech."

"I am pleased we saw each other." She watched a gathering of youths dancing and laughing and wondered how her gods would have reacted to the same sort of celebration. Not well, she expected. They had little need of joy and laughter.

"I wish you well, King Swech, and your son. I wish him well also,"

"You are pleased you met him?"

"I am pleased and honored. He is a fine young warrior. I watched him practice several times." The notion brought a smile to her face, and she nodded and found herself looking away. She did not know if she would see him again. That notion bothered her, but not like it once had. She had too many responsibilities and her world was still changing all the time.

And there was Valam to consider. He was her son, her responsibility for as long as she was alive. She had spoken to Tuskandru about him, and the man was delighted to hear she had a child. He had also offered to meet with the boy and teach him the ways of Durhallem personally. That was an honor she could not resist.

Swech watched the celebrations and pondered them carefully. The Fellein had their strengths, she supposed. But mostly they seemed surprisingly weak. Their greatest advantage was simply numbers. All the armies of the Sa'ba Taalor were less than half the armies of Fellein, but they lacked the skills to withstand her people.

Merros was looking at her expectantly and she thought back on what he must have been saying as she considered her son.

"I will miss you, Merros."

"And I'll miss you, Swech. I hope our people exist in peace with each other. I would like to see you and Valam again."

"If the gods are kind, we will." She imitated the waves

of the ocean with her hand and forearm, a gesture that always brought a smile to Merros' face for reasons she did not understand. "The gods are mostly kind."

Merros smiled and nodded and for one moment his fingers found her hand and squeezed in a way that was both foreign to her and oddly comforting at the same time.

"Be well, King Swech Durwrae Tothis, until we see each other again." His smile was sad and wistful and sweet. A moment later he was walking away. He did not look back.

Nachia Krous

"You're serious, aren't you?" Merros Dulver stared into her eyes, his smile lopsided and his eyes mirroring the confusion he so obviously felt at her words.

"Of course I am." She leaned back on the bed and her fingers ran gently over the sweat that fell across his shoulder, his chest and then down to his ribs. He was panting softly, and she rather liked the sound he made.

"I don't know how to answer that, Maj… Nachia."

"Say 'Yes, Nachia. I would gladly be your husband and consort.'"

"There are rules against commoners marrying into royalty, Nachia."

She'd expected that one. "I will make you a king."

"Of what?"

"The Wellish Steppes would make a lovely replacement for Tyrne. New Tyrne, like New Trecharch, only with less trees and more farmlands."

He chucked and rolled his eyes toward the ceiling for a moment. "I expect most of the kingdoms would have fits."

"Most of the kingdoms would be excited, and the people would have celebrations across all Fellein. To have their greatest living hero honored with his own kingdom? I'm surprised Desh never thought of this."

"Desh had other things on his mind."

"Yes, like having me sire a child and get married, which is what I am proposing, though not in that order, of course."

"You're actually serious." He shook his head.

"Now you risk offending me. Do you find me that hideous a possibility?"

"What?" He laughed at her. "By the gods, no. You're a beauty as I've said before, and as I hopefully have just demonstrated. Twice."

She chuckled and leaned forward until her lips grazed his chin and then his neck. Her teeth playfully scraped along his nape and Merros shivered and gasped lightly.

"So, marry me. We can arrange all of the formal announcements without much difficulty, and get on with the idea of living in comfort. I can have all the damnable suitors sent home and, you know, actually be with one of the few people in this world that I actually enjoy speaking to."

"Nachia."

"Say yes, or I'll tell the entire court you took advantage of me and have you flailed to death." Her words were an obvious jest, and Merros smiled.

"What sane man would say no to that sort of offer?"

"Most of them."

"Do you have any idea how boring I am, Nachia? I also expect I snore."

"You make up for it by being funny and intelligent." She paused a second and then added, "You also agree with me most times, and that helps."

"If you are serious, then yes. I think I'd have to marry you. I was already trying to figure out what we were going to do about this." He gestured to the bed they were in.

"I have maids. They'll clean up the mess." She chuckled and looked at his face, his eyes. "You were honestly worried about what happens next?"

"I'm not notorious for my romantic encounters."

"And yet I seem to know about them all."

"You're one of my best friends. Also, you're nosy."

"Never speak to me that way in public, Merros, or we go back to my previous threat to have you flogged."

"You realize this could be a double wedding right?"

"Beg your pardon?

"Apparently Brolley has decided to marry Lanaie. He's building up the nerve to tell you."

Nachia sighed and shook her head. "That was inevitable. I've been waiting to hear from him on that front for well over two years."

"What makes you say that?"

"He has always had a weakness for a pretty face and doubly so for a woman with large breasts, and, well, look at her."

"I can't. I'm engaged to the Empress, and she's a jealous sort."

She placed her hand on his shoulder for a moment and then leaned back to study him again. He was a handsome enough sort and, truly, very nearly the only person she could tolerate for long spans of time. He was also her closest friend, and the closest thing she had to a sane solution to several problems.

"Do you think you can work with this arrangement, Merros?"

"Do I think I can marry a beautiful woman and be with one of the best people I've ever known? Possibly. Just possibly."

Before she could say anything in response, he leaned forward and kissed her softly on the mouth and then with more force, slowly urging a response from her.

Her hands moved to explore him, and he returned the favor, and for a while she forgot about the empire and trying to keep peace in trying times.

She focused on happy things for a change and enjoyed the moment.

Darsken Murdro

The Shimmer was once again what it was supposed to be, both light and darkness in a world that was not quite the reality he knew but close enough to feel familiar.

Darsken Murdro stepped from the Shimmer into the early morning light of Canhoon and stared across the docks and out at Lake Gerheim. The sun reflected from calm waters and the waves rolled gently in to vanish beneath the piers and the docks. The boats were already heading out, seeking fish, or moving to the distant side of the lake to ferry people across from Goltha.

The world was still alive.

For the moment at least, there was peace around him, and Darsken smiled.

In his head a dozen voices whispered endlessly, speaking softly to him and uttering promises.

He had never experienced voices like that before, but he found them oddly comforting.

The Overlords were dead. They'd been slaughtered by the Sa'ba Taalor and their gods, driven into dust and lost for all time.

Somewhere nearby, Daivem was likely looking for him. His sister was persistent and protective, and he loved that about her.

The Overlords were dead. The world was at peace, at last.

In the shadowed recesses of his mind the Overlords talked to each other and considered their deaths and the fact that they were fortunate enough to find a necromancer in their most desperate time of need.

He was not an experienced necromancer, but in time he would learn, as they learned.

This time, necromancy would be a subtle art. Jeron had seemed a wise choice when they awoke from their long slumber, but they knew better now. They understood that this was not the time for displays of power or for arrogance. Darsken Murdro understood the need for subtlety as few Inquisitors ever had. He was a strong man, but he did not flaunt his strength unless it served a purpose.

Darsken said nothing for the moment, but moved to one of the heavy dock supports and leaned against it, letting his body relax, his gaze soften as he considered the world around him.

The early morning world was peaceful.

He would change that soon enough.

For now he was patient. He had all the time he would need, and the dead were nothing if not patient.

AR
ANGRY
ROBOT

TRISTAN PALMGREN
Quietus
TRISTAN PALMGREN
Author of QUIETUS
Terminus

THE TIDES OF WAR
JAMES A. MOORE
THE LAST SACRIFICE
THE TIDES OF WAR
JAMES A. MOORE
FALLEN GODS
THE TIDES OF WAR
JAMES A. MOORE
GATES OF THE DEAD

LAUREN C. TEFFEAU
CONNECT • ENCRYPT • CONSPIRE
IMPLANTED
SEAN GRIGSBY
FORGOTTEN
LIGHT
SMOKE EATERS
AMANDA BRIDGEMAN
THE SUBJUGATE
CRIME IS OVER

Silent Hall
N.S. Dolkart
Among the Fallen
N.S. Dolkart
The Gods are drawing battle lines
A Breach in the Heavens
N.S. Dolkart
The end is nigh

The Bullet-Catcher's Daughter
Rod Duncan
Unseemly Science
Rod Duncan
"Elizabeth Barnabus will entice readers from the first page"
The Custodian of Marvels
Rod Duncan
Paige Orwin
The Interminables
Moonshine
Jasmine Gower
"Rare and precious... compelling and true."
An Oath of Dogs
Wendy N Wagner

We are Angry Robot

angryrobotbooks.com